Bloodlust: Vampire on the Titanic
Patrick Prior

First published by Malachite Quills 2012.

2nd Edition Strumpet Books 2019.
Strumpet Books

"If ever there was in the world a warranted and proven history, it is that of vampires: nothing is lacking, official reports, testimonials of persons of standings, of surgeons, of clergymen, of judges, the judicial evidence is all-embracing."
Jean Jacques Rousseau-Philosopher

***

"…upon her neck and breast was blood, and upon her throat were the marks of teeth having opened the vein; to this the men pointed, crying, simultaneously struck with horror, 'A Vampyre! A Vampyre!"
Dr John Polidori 'The Vampyre'

***

"The grave's a fine and private place,
But none, I think, do there embrace"
Andrew Marvell, Poet

Chapter 1

He followed her into the thickening snowfall. The ship wallowed and pitched and rolled as it made its way through the clubbing waves. He was oblivious to everything but the maddening sensuality of the woman who stood a few yards away at the ship's rail, staring out into the channel.

The steward knew he shouldn't be thinking such a thing, wanting to do such a thing. His job might be lost, he would betray his wife and family, yet all he could think about, all he knew, was that he wanted this woman more than anything on earth. To kiss her sinful mouth he would give everything he owned. To slide his arm around her waist and pull her close, to let his hands drift over her wonderful breasts he would sell his very soul.

In the darkness he could see the lights of another ferry as it beat its way in the opposite direction towards Calais. The snow, which had been flickering fitfully on the winter air all day, had now started to come down in heavy, spiteful flakes.

He wiped at his eyes as a flurry of cold whiteness clung to his lashes. For an instant his heart lurched. She was gone! He scanned the rail section frantically. Oh God, no! But there she was. She had moved further into the shadows. Her dark dress making her almost invisible. Only a faint outline created by the yellow light seeping from a porthole showed she was still there.

He moved to within a couple of feet of her, the sound of his steps obscured partly by the throb of the ship's engine and partly by the thin carpet of snow already coating the deck. Her bat-black hair was piled on top of her head in thick luxuriant coils. Her slim shoulders, tight waist and round hips were all accentuated by the elegant and stylish dress. He wondered if she was cold. No coat on a night like this?

At that moment she turned towards him. The man was transfixed by the devastating beauty of the woman who faced him. A face, pale and flawless; dark, compelling eyes; a mouth, crimson with want. Those lips still had the faint smile he had seen in the dining room. It was a smile amused; a smile promising; a smile pitiless. Now that smile was for him. Just for him. He knew it. He tried to say something. Tried to build in an escape clause in case she found his presence unwelcome. Some nonsense about perhaps madam would like a blanket came into his head.

But no excuse was needed. As those lustrous eyes grew large in his vision he trembled. Somewhere in the back of his mind a stab of unease rose and sank. Was it only the snow that made him shiver?

Her arms opened wide then closed around him. Her mouth was on his. Nuzzling. Licking. Her lips parted slightly and her tongue darted against his briefly. Amid the kisses he thought for a moment his senses caught the faint aroma of damp earth, but he was lost in the overwhelming sexuality of the woman. His erection was unbearable. Rigid and demanding. He pushed himself against her hard.

Her lips teased down his cheeks and across his neck. He closed his eyes and gave himself up to her. As her lips reached the sensitive skin just below his ear he felt the first stirrings of an orgasm. Now as he felt her teeth nibble gently at the flesh he knew that his climax would not wait much longer. Frantically he slid his hands over her full firm breasts. As he squeezed and caressed her he felt the nip of her teeth but he was too lost in the eroticism of the moment to feel the pain fully. Until it was too late. Until steel fingers clamped around the back of his neck and held him helpless. Her grip was so paralyzing that the messages carried down the spinal cord to his limbs were lost in a welter of crushed bone and tissue. The paralysis was so complete he could not even cry out. Her canines sank smoothly into his skin and found the hot blood pumping through his jugular.

From the bar the sound of laughter and a burst of song drifted through the night air. But the man was far away from it all. His eyes closed as his life slipped away in a dream of the sweetest terror.

Chapter 2

Adultery surrounded her like a halo. He knew the signs. He had followed too many men and women who had betrayed others to mistake the aura. Davis could see it, the barely suppressed sexual excitement that coiled within her like a spring.

Harry Davis stepped into the shadows as the woman crossed the road, drawing her coat collar up against the wind. The snow was now falling in unrelenting sheets. Davis slipped slightly as he stood on a patch of slush created by a scattering of salt flung in front a butcher's shop. As he adjusted his balance, a bolt of pain shot through his ankle.

Christ! For a moment he thought that this work was not for him anymore. A detective for the Pinkerton Agency needed mobility, and he did not feel very mobile.

With an instinct honed by following countless suspects he turned away and looked in the shop window as the woman suddenly stopped and looked around. Perhaps some atavistic sense had told her of his presence, but Davis knew it was probably just the exaggerated caution of the guilty.

She turned off Camden High Street and walked past a row of small mean houses, their familiar yellow London brick dappled with snow. Here it was more difficult to follow her. There were no crowds to hide behind, no shop doorways to duck into. He stood at the top of the darkened street and let her get further ahead, but he muttered a curse as she vanished, turning a corner.

Davis hurried down the street and reached the junction, peering cautiously around the edge of the brickwork. Christ! She was only ten yards ahead, stopping in front of a house. Again she glanced around before patting her hair and walking up the short path to the front door.

The detective heard the *rap rap rap* of the door knocker. It spoke of anticipation. The door opened and around the edge of the corner he saw the arms of an unseen man reach out and pull her inside.

The fence in the back garden was low and broken. For this Harry was profoundly grateful. He knew anything that required athleticism at this stage might be beyond him. The house was at end of the row, so the fence was set in a little alleyway. This made what he had to do easier.

Straddling the barrier he eased himself into the small garden. A faint light coming from a room on the ground floor at the back of the house spread across the falling snow, giving it a phosphorescent golden tinge. His boots made soft scrunching sounds as he stepped carefully through the undulating whiteness. There was no telling what traps lay under the snow.

The window had heavy lace curtains. Through these he could see opaque figures moving to and fro. Stepping to one side of the window he crept up and peered in.

They were both naked. The woman was on the floor, her legs spread wide as the man drove into her. A look of ecstasy suffused her pretty face. So now he was sure. Davis turned away from the sight. He had seen this so many times. Seen the stunned look on so many faces when he had confirmed a spouses betrayal.

As his wife made love to another man only a few feet away Harry Davis sank to his knees in the snow and was sick.

Chapter 3

'Tonight we will talk with those no longer of the earthly world.'

There were ten of them sitting around the large circular table. The room was opulent. Heavy velvet drapes; lush carpets; embossed wallpaper. Gilt and polished expensive furniture was placed tastefully around.

The medium was a small, unremarkable looking woman, with a surprisingly common London accent considering her surroundings and the class of those who sat at the table.

George Bowers hated these sessions. Hated the mediums, or 'spiritualists' as they liked to call themselves. He thought them nothing but spiritual vampires who preyed on the sad and desperate grief of those who sought their help.

'I would now like us all to join hands.'

The medium's nasal voice was annoying him more by the second. He took Lilian's hand and was rewarded with a faint smile, but only on her lips. The sadness that had lain in her eyes for more than two years still remained. On his other side, a rather overweight man grabbed his fingers. George winced as he felt the man's hot sweaty palm.

The tide of spiritualism which had engulfed Victorian society was still going strong even in 1912. Originally begun in America, where the Fox sisters of New York became a sensation when it seemed they could contact the dead, the movement had reached almost epidemic proportions.

Despite fakery being exposed again and again, people still sought comfort in trying to reach their loved ones on the other side.

'Now, as the lights lower I want us all to form a circle of welcome for those who have passed over.'

Passed over! Bowers wanted shout. Dead, you fraud, you mean dead! But to do so would have destroyed the glimmer of hope in his wife's eyes. So he sat in silence.

The room was lit by the subtle placing of lamps. The shades were of muted red, green and blue, creating a rather theatrical, but nevertheless effective, feeling of other-worldliness. Bowers mentally tipped his hat to the designer.

A thin, wraithlike man appeared at the corner of his vision, almost as if he had come out the walls. Silently he began to glide from lamp to lamp turning down the wicks and gradually bringing the room into darkness.

As the lights dimmed Lilian squeezed his hand slightly. He returned the gesture and gave her a half smile. Even in the gloom, even in her sadness, she was beautiful. Her lustrous copper hair caught the dying rays of light. Her face, pale, but lovely. The wonderful figure hidden by the dark and shapeless dress had almost become a widow's weeds.

Across the table, in the half light, he could see the burly figure of Sir Arthur Conan Doyle, creator of Sherlock Holmes. Conan Doyle was known as a keen follower of the spiritualist path. He saw Doyle give his wife, Jean, a smile of reassurance. George marveled. The man who had brought to life a hero who lived by logic alone and here, listening to this mumbo-jumbo.

The lights continued to dim and silence fell on the room. Only the metronomic tick of the large grandfather clock in the corner could be heard as the medium sat with her eyes closed, taking in deeper breaths as if willing herself into a trance.

She gasped a little, her tiny cry causing those around her to look expectantly. Bowers saw the elegant woman sitting next to the medium grasp the hand of her companion a little more tightly. A small wiry man, with greying spiky hair and wispy beard, ignored all that was going on around him and stared fixedly at the table.

George knew the elegant woman was Lily Langtry, the legendary 'Jersey Lily'. She, like Conan Doyle, was deeply interested in spiritualism. Bowers thought that even at almost sixty the actress was still beautiful, the famous red hair and porcelain complexion remained perfect. A woman who had been mistress to a prince. So celebrated had she been as the loveliest woman in the world that a town in Texas had been named Langtry when the infamous hanging judge, Roy Bean, been had become besotted by her.

By now the only light came from a dim blood-red glow thrown out by the large ornate lamp which dangled over the table three feet above their heads. The feeble luminosity barely broke the inky blackness. The disembodied voice of the medium, lower and huskier, came at them out the gloom.

'I must insist ladies and gentlemen that at no time must the ring of hands be broken, or must I be touched while I am in communication with those beyond the veil'

Beyond the veil! Another euphemism for death. It was all Bowers could do not to stand up and shout that all this was a macabre farce. These were intelligent people, educated people yet here they all were sitting listening to this common little trickster leading them by the nose, and charging them for the privilege!

Suddenly a deep low moaning was heard from the medium. The noise continued unbroken for more than two minutes. Bower found himself wondering when she took a breath. She must have lungs like a pair of bellows.

It was then he felt the table move gently. At first he thought someone had merely knocked it with their leg, but the movement became more pronounced. He heard a gasp from someone in the darkness. Lilian again squeezed his hand gently. The table slowly lifted into the air a few inches and then sank down into place. Then it began to move violently up and down and from side to side. The movements became erratic. The heavy legs of the table bumped and slammed up and down on the floor. He heard a woman sob with fear. It was Lilian. He was about to stand up and take her out when the table suddenly was still. There was silence for a few seconds.

'Those who love you want to speak.'

The medium's voice had lost its everyday tone. When she spoke it was with a sonorous drawn-out timbre, almost masculine.

'Those in this world still feel love for you. Come forward and give them comfort.'

There was stillness. No one stirred. Despite his scepticism Bowers shivered slightly. Even to a cynic that atmospheric darkness was un-nerving. It was then he heard it. The faint, almost inaudible cry of a child floated on the air.

'There is a little one. A little one seeking her mother.'

Lilian's grip became tighter and he winced as her thin, delicate fingers squeezed his tightly.

The child's crying become louder. Then he heard a voice

'Mother? Mother? Where are you mother? I'm cold, mother. Can I have my blue coat, mother, I'm cold?'

'Jenny? Jenny, is that you?'

Bowers hardly recognized the voice as his wife's. A loving desperation raised her normally mellifluous tone to something approaching a shriek. She half rose.

'Stay still. Don't break the circle or contact will be lost.'

The medium's voice, sharp and angry, caused Lilian to slowly sit down. Bowers wanted more than anything to be away from there. Away from that claustrophobic room with its talk of death. He heard Lilian sobbing quietly and he was about to whisper that perhaps they should go *when he saw something emerge from the darkness.*

Transfixed by a luminescent shape which began to form in the far corner of the room, George Bowers felt a chill of fear sweeping over him. There was something. Something taking a vaguely human form. A child! A little girl!

He almost cried out in pain as Lilian gripped his hand so tightly that his ring bit deep into the flesh. There was no doubt about it. The ghostly shape was that of a little girl.

Lilian moaned and again half rose.

'Jenny? Jenny, is that you, Jenny?'

The apparition, its face still obscured, lifted its arms towards her.

'Mother, can I have my blue coat? I'm very cold, mother.'

As the figure said these words, it stepped nearer and Bowers felt a wave of love and terror sweep over him as *he saw the face of his dead daughter.*

Chapter 4

CUTTING FROM 'THE TIMES'

BODY FOUND ON BEACH AT RAMSGATE

The body of a man was found on the beach at Ramsgate yesterday. It is believed he may have fallen from a channel ferry…

The earth of home surrounded her like a womb. Deep, deep down in the loving embrace of the tomb Mina Harker waited for the velvet comfort of night.

The journey had been long, the dangers great. She had crossed sea and land. Now she lay in the vampire sub-world between death and life, waiting. Waiting for the unearthly metabolism of the revenant to wake her and begin the hunt. As it had the night before, as it would till the end of time.

Hair, sable, tumbled across the satin of the coffin. Her lips glowed with a deep rubescence. She had fed and now lay sated. The terrifying beauty she possessed brought victims willingly to her mouth.

In the fading light of day, only a few yards from where she lay, hurrying humanity went about the business of life. Laughter, crying, shouting, loving, hating, all the thoughts and emotions and hopes and fears that went into being mortal carried on around her. But Mina lay still. With the dying of the light her time would come.

He slid his hand onto her unresisting breast. Through the silk sheaf of her nightdress he could feel the full warm ripeness. The quickening in his loins began, and he moved closer to her, pushing his hardening cock against her hip. He leaned over and kissed her gently on the mouth. As his excitement grew he squeezed her breast more urgently, his fingers seeking the nipple through the delicate material. Bowers mouth pressed harder on hers, his hands working slowly down from her breast to the flat, smooth expanse of belly. He tentatively pushed the tip of his tongue into her mouth and at the same time trailed his fingers lower. But even through his growing sexual arousal, he became aware of her utter passivity. She lay there cold and unresponsive, eyes closed, ready to *submit* to his love-making rather than take part.

He tried to press on, tried to think only of his own needs, but suddenly, all desire died in him. With a sigh of frustration he slipped away, leaving a space between. It had been more than a year since they had made love.

Wordlessly Lilian turned on her side and lay with her back to him. He despised himself for trying to have sex with her after such a shattering experience, but it had been so long and his need was very great. Not only physically, but emotionally. Bowers felt the gulf was widening and that soon there would be nothing left of what they once had.

In the gloom of the bedroom the man stared sightlessly at the ceiling. The silhouette of the window frame thrown over his head by the streetlamps was given a strange distorted geometry by the low angle of the light source. The snow lying outside reflected off the sky and imbued the room with a translucent sort of half-light.

It had been like this for two years. Since Jenny had…Even now he couldn't bring himself to think about it. He and Lilian had watched by the bed day and night as the Diphtheria slowly took their daughter. Watched as she fought for breath, watched as the fever grew and raged and ravaged her little body. Watched as the light went out in her eyes. She died a day before her sixth birthday.

Somewhere outside, Bowers heard men talking. They were too far away to hear what they were saying, but then they both burst into laughter. The first laughter to be heard in his house for such a long time.

It was shortly afterwards that Lilian had become obsessed with the idea that she could contact Jenny. Mediums and spiritualists were the talk of society. Tales of objects flying through the air, voices calling from beyond, spirit photographs, all fuelled Lilian's desperate hopes.

George Bowers was an intelligent man and in his heart knew that all this was ridiculous. Lilian, too, was bright and astute, but her needs overcame any rationality. He knew that the harm done by not letting her hold onto this hope would be far greater than denying her. He hoped that by colluding with her the obsession would eventually burn itself out.

They had traipsed from séance to séance. Most were embarrassing. Po-faced men and women speaking in silly voices, giving out information that was so general it could have applied to half the population. Some were sincere in their beliefs and efforts, some were such obvious charlatans that he wanted to laugh aloud when he saw them.

The séance of a few hours ago had been a terrible and traumatic fiasco. Lilian had set such store in the reputation of the medium. Even the intelligentsia like Conan Doyle were there in the belief that here was a woman of genuine psychic gifts.

George felt a wave of desolation and shame sweep over him as he remembered the shambles, remembered Lilian's heartbreaking sobs. He, too, had wanted the figure to be his daughter. For a moment he truly *believed* the spectral figure had been his daughter. The scene was played out again his mind's eye. The ghostly apparition calling to his wife; Lilian standing up; breaking the circle; crying out Jenny's name.

It was then the quiet, wiry little man opposite had stood up and shone a 'bullseye,' a policeman's lamp, full onto the spectre. There was a scream from medium and she leapt up and tried to grab the lamp. But the damage was done. The 'spectre' was merely a girl draped in muslin. Hidden lighting had made her appear to be luminescent.

Conan Doyle had reached up and turned the large lamp on and the whole sad fraud was revealed. The young woman in the muslin cloak fled from the room. The medium screamed a stream of filthy obscenities at the man with the bullseye. The meeting broke up in disorder.

Afterwards, as they collected their coats, the spiky little man revealed that he was from the SPR, the Society for Psychical Research, an organization set up in the late 1880's to examine psychic phenomena from a scientific standpoint. When Bowers asked him how they could know about Jenny's blue coat, he explained that such sophisticated fraudsters did research on those coming to the séance. They would fit together fragments of information, speak to servants and gradually build up a range of facts they could use.

On the way home, Lilian had become even more withdrawn. She was existing in a place where he couldn't reach her any more. The vibrant young beauty he had met and courted and married was now only an automaton going through the motions of living.

      Despair washed over George Bowers. What was to become of them? Outside and far away came another peal of laughter. He closed his eyes and tried not to cry.

Chapter 5
Extract of Post-Mortem Report by Dr Reynold Richards Police Surgeon.
Dover Dist.

The body is that of a male, thirty six years old. Well nourished. The deceased was found on the beach at Ramsgate, and it has since been ascertained that he was a steward on the ferry crossing between Calais and Dover.

Although the victim had been in the water some forty eight hours death was not by drowning (there was no water in the lungs) or exposure to the cold. Massive damage to vertebrae of the upper spine, consistent with crushing or pounding, resulted in injuries which would most certainly have led to death, but for the fact that the body seemed almost entirely devoid of blood. With no external injuries visible, apart from two small wounds to the neck, it is at this point impossible to say the source of this blood loss…

The house had brooded by the river for almost a hundred and fifty years. Through the dark eyes of its windows it had seen émigré French aristocrats land by the wharves, glad to be out the shadow of Madame Guillotine. It had seen a nation amazed and astounded at the antics of a mad Hanoverian king and an army jaunty and bright and brave march to the Crimea before shattered bodies and minds and coffins returned. Originally built by tobacco money gleaned from the rich fields of Virginia the house had lain empty for decades, *but now there was a presence in it once more.*

Mina Harker stared out at the snow falling. Her obsidian eyes took in the tumbling, ramshackle buildings which seemed to totter towards the Thames. Limehouse, named after the lime kilns that had been there from the 14th century, was a melting pot of cultures, poverty and vice deep in London's east end. Bounded by Commercial Road to the north, Wapping to the west and the Isle of Dogs to the east, the area was a lost land.

The river was its life-blood. From all corners of the earth goods and people moved to and fro in an endless, restless parade. For the vampire it was a rich and anonymous feeding ground. Death here was a constant companion; death by the knife; death by disease;

death by want; death by heartbreak. Here life rich, red and vibrant was to be found in a ceaseless stream. Those she took would not be missed.

She turned and made her way across the room towards an open door which led to the wine-cellar. Even in the simple act of walking the awesome perfection of the vampire as an organism showed. An effortless gliding. Muscles, stronger than that of any human on earth, propelled her with an unthinking gracefulness.

Mina, like all revenants, was indifferent to her own perfection. Indifferent to her own supernatural loveliness. As a mortal she was pretty, but with her change to that of the undead this became a dark, compelling beauty which transfixed all who saw her. Her body ,too, had in the act of transformation, burgeoned into a feline voluptuousness; breasts, heavy and firm; waist slim; hips rounded; all aspects of her earthly form became accentuated.

She knew the weakness of mortals. Sex. The primal drive. So, like any good predator, she used this. Countless had fallen, lured on by the irresistible sexual attraction of the vampire.

The room she stood in was of dazzling splendour. Priceless Turkish carpets and rugs were spread across the floor Drapes of the heaviest and finest velvet hung around the windows in resplendent shades of deep crimson and midnight blue. The furniture was antique, the centre-piece being a large Louis XVl dining table which dominated the room. Reflected in the amber glow of the table's polished surface was a huge chandelier, its myriad glass pieces sending out a constant stream of ever-changing spectrums.

Mina was oblivious to the sumptuousness of her surroundings. As a vampire the appreciation of aesthetic beauty had been lost when she was transformed. She could not see colours in anything but the weakest of sepia tints. Music was merely noise. All the things that made the human heart rise were lost to Mina Harker.

She closed the door of the wine-cellar and then with an effortless movement slid a large bookcase across the entrance effectively hiding the existence of the doorway. The bookcase was several feet high and crammed with more than five hundred heavy volumes. The weight was phenomenal yet the muscles which moved it had the strength of twenty.

With the bookcase in place, there was no indication there was a doorway behind. Mina's resting place lay deep under the house. The wine-cellar was dank and dark, submerged in eternal blackness. A perfect place for the vampire to sleep.

Mina had returned to England because it held one basic necessity-the soil on which she had to rest. Every Nosferatu had to lie in their native earth. When she had fled England to escape the pursuit of Harker and Seward almost twenty years before, she had taken with her several boxes of earth, just as her master, Dracula, had done when he left Transylvania and came to England.

But this was an Achilles heel, the Achilles heel which had allowed Van Helsing, Seward and Harker to trace him and eventually destroy him.

Mina was aware of this. Using all her vampire cunning she had tried to ensure her resting places were always sacrosanct. Unfortunately a combination of ill-luck and carelessness had almost destroyed her. A barge carrying most of her home earth sank in a storm on the Danube. This left her dangerously short. Hubris in northern Germany, almost led to her downfall. She had grown contemptuous of humanity and her blood-taking became brazen, barely hiding her attacks. A priest, who was learned in the old ways, had come to where she lay. Only by chance did she escape with the last remnants of her resting soil.

It was then she decided to return to England. Like her master, Dracula, before her, she had immense single-minded cunning. By letter and telegram she had contacted several solicitors. By using different legal representatives she ensured that no single firm knew all her business and would start to see any pattern.

It was by these means she had purchased the house by the river, one of many resting places. The age of the house, its high surrounding walls and obscure location all made it the perfect lair. The furnishings and décor had also been done by proxy. Those involved were only too eager to serve the mysterious Mrs Murray who seemed to have limitless wealth.

Within her sanctuary below the ground, piled carelessly around her coffin, were riches beyond the dreams of avarice. For the vampire collected these spoils as a child would pebbles from the beach. She had taken jewels taken from the necks of her victims, lifted gold and silver as she left the bedrooms of the dead.

In Vienna Mina had walked into a jeweller's shop just before it closed. The owner was alone and mesmerised by the hypnotic beauty of the female vampire. There, amid the sparkle and glitter of precious things, his life was drained away. After feeding Mina left with a collection of priceless gems. These she had thrown indifferently alongside the other precious things she had gathered.

The accumulation of riches meant nothing to the vampire, but it was essential to helping her function in the mortal world. Money would buy a place of safety. Money would buy services she herself, trapped during daylight hours, could not carry out.

The opulence of the finished house was merely a stage prop. A theatrical conceit by which she could give the illusion of normality. A woman seen coming and going from a derelict building might arouse suspicion, but not an elegant lady coming from a grand property.

Blood and sleep were her prime needs. However Mina Harker also needed to learn, to accumulate knowledge, to mix with humanity, assimilate all she could. But deep in her vampire brain there was also a different need; a need for others. Even if was only those she preyed upon. It was a subliminal longing no vampire consciously knew they had. A sorrow for the loss of their humanity.

And so she resolved to mix with the fashionable society of Edwardian London. With her money entry would be easy. With her beauty all would want her.

Throwing a heavy dark cloak, trimmed with ermine, around her shoulders she prepared to step into the darkness. She didn't need the cloak. The vampire was impervious to heat and cold alike. But without some sort of protection against the snow she would stand out. Mina's greatest safety lay in humanity being unaware.

The heavy snowflakes danced and swirled and settled about her as she stepped outside and closed the heavy front doors. Mina looked about, her senses heightened to a point where she could detect a mouse moving through the grass a hundred yards away. Nothing was amiss.

The thirst was upon her, raging and growing. She hadn't fed for three nights. From further up-river came the melancholy sonorous boom of a ship's horn.

Pushing aside the heavy wrought iron gate which fronted the property she slipped into the twirling whiteness and began the hunt.

The hurt had passed. The anger had passed. The sorrow had passed and now all Harry Davis was left with was a profound emptiness. Alone in the house he thought again of the betrayal. The woman he'd thought was his, the woman to whom he'd given all he had to give, had…

He tried to drive the image from his mind. The bodies, naked and locked in lust. The look of sexual ecstasy on her face, a look that had long gone from their own love-making.

When she had got home that night her belongings were outside in the snow. He had sat in the living room, the heavy curtains drawn, and listened as she pounded on the door. He listened as she shouted to be let in, her calls gradually changing from that of the puzzled innocent to that of the contrite wife. She had begged and pleaded, wept and prayed. Her cries grew shrill and then angry and finally her mocking, jeering shouts had derided him as a man. Had told him her lover was only doing for her what he couldn't.

After what seemed like hours she had given up. He had sat in the chair all night. Thinking of his first wife, Jesse. How he missed her. Consumption, had robbed them of a life together.

Davis rose and went over to the large bureau in the living room. He winced as his weak ankle, once shattered by a bullet, took his weight. A permanent reminder of the Boer War when he had volunteered to fight under a hot African sun. Two sides fighting for a country that didn't belong to either of them.

In the bureau drawer was a framed photograph of him and Jesse on their wedding day, both looking impossibly young and solemn. She had teased him about the moustache he had grown. Always younger looking than his years Davis thought that a police sergeant should look more mature.

He had met Mary about five years after his return from South Africa. He had resumed his place as a Detective Inspector in the Metropolitan police. Living alone had wearied him. She had been bright and lively and pretty, a waitress at the tea-room he used when he couldn't face an empty house after coming off duty.

She had flirted with him and he had merely enjoyed her vivacity and boldness which animated her face and made her even prettier. She was more than twenty years younger than him, barely more than a girl. But she was coquettish and knowing beyond her years. He was lonely, she was vibrant and good-looking and sexually attractive. They were married less than a year after she'd served him his first tea and cake.

Revitalized by a young wife Harry enjoyed life again an began to socialize. Theatres, music-halls, parties. With a good-looking, lively woman on his arm Davis was the envy of his colleagues. Sex, too, after so long was thrilling. Mary had a supple and shapely body and she knew how to use it in bed. Their love-making left him happy and exhausted. But even then the first stirrings of unease came to the marriage bed.

For a start his new wife was so knowing in the arts of sexual intercourse. She had told him shortly before the wedding she was a virgin, but when they shared the marital bed for the first time Harry couldn't help the feeling that there was something false in her response. Almost as if she was playing what was expected of a virgin wife too well. Ashamed of his doubts he mentally chided himself for such a traitorous thought about his new wife.

However it gradually dawned that Mary was too well versed in the arts of sexual love. It was her who was adventurous, who showed him things he had never done with any other woman. In bed she was bold, but he was also aware she was bold with other men. The flirtatiousness which was at first endearing became a source of anger and embarrassment. At functions, even with his colleagues, his pretty young wife would smile a shade too long into another man's face, would leave her hand a shade too long on another man's arm, would stare a shade too long at some man across the room.

He'd told himself it was only the vivacity of a young woman, chided himself for being staid and set in his ways, but he knew in his heart it went beyond high spirits.

He thought perhaps the problem would settle down when he took early retirement from the Metropolitan Police. His hope was that working for the European branch of the Pinkerton Detective Agency would give their lives an impetus, a chance to start over.

Despite his initial optimism his marriage continued to ebb away. Mary would go out and not return till late. Tales of distant elderly aunts were so transparent that if it had not ripped at his heart every time she came out with a story he would have laughed.

Deep down he knew what was happening, could have exposed her lies with little effort, but the fact was *he was afraid to confront her.* For confronting her might mean he would not only have to face the truth, but take its consequences. He still wanted her to be his wife, still loved her; not in the way he'd loved Jesse, but nevertheless she held a place in his heart.

Harry let things drift and she became bolder, sometimes barely bothering to concoct a story to cover her absence. Once he had almost forced the situation when he had waited at the end of their street one night and saw her come out of a carriage. A man's hands stroked her hair as the door closed. Rage and sadness rose within him but still he kept silent.

It was only when she had broached going away for an overnight visit to some cousin whom she had never ever mentioned before that he knew the marriage was over. His pride would not let him play the cuckold in such a blatant manner. Things could only be allowed to go so far and no further. It was after this he had followed her to that house in Camden Town and watched as another man took her on the carpet.

Harry gently put the wedding picture of him and Jesse back in the drawer. He turned wearily and made his way to the door. Suddenly he stopped. On the sofa, partially hidden by a cushion, was a stocking. He lifted it up. A last remnant of her presence in his house, in his life. Harry lifted the stocking to his cheek and held it there gently for a moment. He then dropped it into the fading embers of the coal fire. The dying fire leapt into life for a brief moment. And then the stocking was ashes.

Stepping into the hall Davis closed the living room door and then began a plodding climb up the stairs to his empty bed.

Chen Lee was ruined. Dishonoured. He would be known as a thief and his family would share his shame. He made his way through the shouting, yelling crowd of gamblers. At the far end of the smoky room a group of Fan Tan players watched with greedy eyes as a basin was lifted revealing the Haricot Beans below. Each man counted the number of beans feverishly. One of the group an elderly man, with skin like lined, decaying parchment gave a squeal of joy as he saw his guess was correct. He pulled his winnings across the board.

Chen felt a pang of angry envy sweep over him as the old man swept his winnings into his lap with palsied hands.

Why this old man and not me? I need it. I need to win more than he does.

The thoughts whirled and raced through his head, wild, ludicrous schemes for getting money. If he could just get a little more he was *sure* he could win.

In one corner he heard the caller at Pak-a-Pu call off the random numbers from a sheet of paper. Men, slack-jawed with avarice waited, hoping they would be the first to have the four winning numbers.

Quieter and more intense were the quartet of players who moved the tiles around the Mah-jong board, trying to gather the combination which would win the game.

The low lighting caught the swirl of winding, crawling tobacco smoke as it curled itself around the lamps.

A guard at the door of the gambling den stared hard at Chen Lee as he moved towards the exit. Perhaps his ruin was written in his face.

Stepping outside he heard the bolt slam as the door was closed firmly behind him. The din and frantic venality of the gambling room ceased. Replaced by the austere silence of a Chinese grocer shop. An old man was behind the counter, his shrunken form so desiccated that he appeared to be a figure made of dry sticks. The old man didn't raise his head as Lee made his way along the shop. Trance-like Chen took in the shelves of dried sharks fin…pickled eggs, aged for decades, dried fish and duck. The smells of a culture older than the ages.

His eyes watered as the chill wind rushed into his face and the snow drummed against his eyelashes. Brushing them away he began to walk along Narrow Street, which lived up to its name. The mean thoroughfare was one of the arteries connecting Limehouse to the river.

Chen bent low against the driving white squall, shivering as the vindictive wind found its way through his thin tunic. As he passed under the bridge recently built across Narrow Street to carry coal to Stepney Power Station, the snow was thwarted for a brief moment before returning with even more venom.

Light and noise spilled from the Three Foxes pub as he made his way along the pavement, hugging closely to the wall in an attempt to gather meagre shelter from the blizzard.

Suddenly a group of sailors burst through the pub doors. Their angry drunken voices, in different accents and different languages scored the air. Limehouse as a port was a cacophony of races. Scandanavians, Lascars, Africans, Dutch and a dozen other nationalities thronged the streets and pubs in an international orgy of drinking and whoring.

Chen Lee slipped past the group. Even in the darkness his eyes were caught by the brightly coloured turban and white tunic of one of the sailors. He pressed on. His friend Yei, who lived at Limehouse Causeway, was his only hope.

Lee had done a terrible thing. He had taken the money from the shop where he worked and gambled it away. His habit had become all-embracing. He was incapable of passing a game of chance. Loses had mounted but he was convinced that his luck was about to change. When he was left to cash up and close the shop the temptation had been irresistible. He had taken the money, convinced he would be putting it back in an hour or two and at the same time making himself a rich man. But now his heart beat wildly with a mixture of fear and desolation.

With unseeing eyes he stumbled on through the snow. At the gate of the Regent's Canal Company he stopped for a moment. The cold was intense. He could feel his body temperature drop. Frantically he crossed his arms and rubbed furiously, trying to speed up his circulation. A policeman on his beat strolled past on the other side of the road and looked at him with a mild curiosity. Chen moved on.

He had just reached the entrance to the oddly named Shoulder of Mutton Alley when a dark figure materialized from the entrance. Chen caught a blurred glimpse of a white face and vermillion mouth open wide *and then the pain of something sharp and terrible at his neck.*

Chapter 6

Mourning became her. The black evening dress, slightly décolletage so that the modest cleavage hinted at the splendid bosom beneath, made her look breath-taking. Bowers held out his arm to her as they entered the hallway. The house was a pleasure-dome. Luxury pervaded every corner. The high ceiling was a copy of the Sistine Chapel.

A line of chandeliers caught the rich colours of the walls and highlighted the glints of gold gilt around the panelling. The place was draped in the murmuring, well-modulated voices of the upper classes at play.

Bowers looked at Lilian and gave her an encouraging smile. She wanly returned the gesture. He knew just what a sacrifice it had been for her to come to this ball. It was only because it was important that he attend, important to his career, that he had managed to persuade her.

The house was in the inner circle of grandiose dwellings by Regent's Park. Large stately homes, with fluted columns which reminded Bowers of the ante-bellum mansions he had seen when visiting the southern states of America.

Music could be heard playing faintly in the main ballroom. He recognized the tune as something from Gilbert and Sullivan. A servile butler took his coat and he helped Lilian with her cloak. As her shoulders were revealed, once again George Bowers marveled at his wife's beauty.

Their hosts, Rodney Heskwith and his wife, Veronica, greeted them warmly. Heskwith, a tall figure, looking rather ill-at-ease in his evening wear, immediately took Bowers by the elbow and began to talk about the real purpose he had been invited for that evening. Business. Heskwith was involved in raising capital investment and George Bowers was a man supreme in his field.

In the refined hubbub, underscored by the music, Bowers asked Lilian if she would excuse him for a moment. She nodded her acquiescence, relieved to be free of making chit-chat. Veronica, sensing her detachment from the scene, made a few awkward socially expected remarks. They fell on the air. The hostess could see that Lilian Bowers was there only in body. So it was with some relief that another pair of guests arrived giving her the opportunity to escape.

Lilian wandered through the crowd like a ghost. In it but not part of it. Her looks brought many admiring glances but she was oblivious. Even if she had seen them they would have meant nothing. Her emptiness was all-consuming. It was then she saw her. Surrounded by a crowd. A woman of unearthly beauty. She heard someone call her Mrs Murray.

Men were gathered around, each vying, jostling, pushing for her attention. She seemed to be listening but the slight smile suggested that she viewed their attentions in the indulgent way an adult might treat the capering of child.

It was then the beautiful woman turned and stared straight at Lilian. As their eyes locked Lilian Bowers felt a thrill run through her, a thrill which was a mixture of fear and sexual longing.

'Bless me father for I have sinned. It three weeks since my last confession…'

In the claustrophobic confines of the confession box the priest bent his head as if in contemplation. The line of penitents had been long that evening. Sins venial and sins mortal had drifted through the grill of his dark little cell.

All the petty insults to God were revealed. Stealing, swearing, missing mass, sins of omission, sins of impurity, sins of deception. All came and all were absolved. Confession was a cleansing. A new start. Each and every confessor left with a soul shining and pure and ready to be stained again.

With a start he realized the woman through the grill had stopped talking and was waiting. He mumbled the words of absolution and then gave a penance of five Our Fathers and five Hail Marys. He almost fancied he could hear the relief in the woman's voice as she thanked him. He was known for giving light penance. He expected that was why his confessional was always the most popular.

As the confession box door opened and the woman left, a whiff of incense stirred by the moving air eddied around. He rubbed his hands over his eyes. He felt weary. His duties had begun with seven o'clock mass that morning and now it was almost nine in the evening.

He heard the door swing open and someone enter. He waited patiently. There were a few seconds of silence. It was something he understood. Sometimes those in need of absolution found it hard to speak. He cleared his throat and spoke quietly.

'Is there something you'd like to say?'

The silence hung on the air for another couple of seconds.

'Actually, Father, I was wondering if you fancied getting really drunk?'

She stood looking in the dressing room mirror. The image which stared back was of a lovely woman with copper hair, wearing a black evening dress. But Lilian wasn't aware of her own reflection. Her mind was full of the mysterious woman whom she had glimpsed only for a few seconds but who had haunted her thoughts since. Lilian had learned from others that Mrs Murray was a widow of fabulous wealth recently returned from living abroad.

London's rakes and fortune hunters had gathered like jackals but it seemed she was unattainable. She arrived alone and she left alone. Lilian would have liked to have met her but she slipped away. No one had seen her go.

Since the tragedy of a lost child Lilian's feelings had been cauterized. Now, in the space of a few moments her whole equilibrium was disturbed. She had never thought of another woman in that way. On the journey home she had told herself that it was an aberration, a maverick response to the overwhelming beauty of the dark woman. Everyone at the ball seemed besotted. She saw them all look, men and women, with the same hunger.

That hunger had been aroused in Lilian Bowers. Always a passionate woman the sex drive so long repressed after Jenny's death had seem to come back in a flood. The longing deep within her was growing.

George entered, taking off his cuff-links. He had noticed the change in Lilian when he returned from talking business. She was still quiet but her eyes had regained a little of the vitality he had thought long gone. She had even attempted a smile or two.

'It wasn't too bad tonight, was it, Lilian?'

'Would you mind unfastening my dress?'

Something in the way she asked caused him to pause. Her voice had lowered, was huskier It was a tone that suggested intimacy. He walked over and began slowly to unbutton her dress. As each button popped more of her creamy back and shoulders were revealed. Bowers found his fingers shaking a little as he reached the bottom fastening.

The dress dropped to the floor. Lilian stood there, staring into the glass. She was wearing a set of whalebone stays and a pair of French silk knickers. Black silk stockings reached the middle of her thighs, held up by red garters.

George swallowed. God she was lovely and so desirable. He felt himself begin to grow hard.

'The hooks on the stays, undo them.'

Her demeanor hadn't altered. She still looked straight ahead. Their eyes met in the mirror. George saw a man of middle height with brown hair and a hearty sort of handsomeness. She was as tall as him. Magnificent as her breasts spilled over the unforgiving edge of the stays, her tight waist accentuated by the cruel pinch of the frame.

'I said undo them will you, George?'

He had been in a trance. He muttered an apology. She smiled in a way that was almost coquettish.

His finger trembled even more as he worked his way down the hooks and eyes of the stays. Lilian's body emerged from the constricting material. The white, smooth expanse of her figure hardly needed to be shaped artificially.

Bowers fumbled badly at the last hook and eye, tugging ineffectually several times. She laughed softly.

'If it won't unfasten, break it.'

He leaned forward and kissed her lightly on the shoulder before taking the two sides of the stays and tearing them apart. The undergarment fell away revealing Lilian bare to the waist, her breasts full and ripe. For a few seconds the man and woman both stared at each other's reaction in the mirror. Lilian reached behind, took his hands and placed them on her bust.

As if a dam had burst all Bower's frustrations flooded out. He kissed her neck frantically and at the same time squeezed and fondled her bosom, rolling and teasing her nipples between finger and thumb.

Lilian let her head fall back against his shoulder. Her eyes closed in pleasure. His hands slid down from her breasts, down her flat belly and down inside her knickers. She gave a gasp of ecstasy as he eased her open with two fingers of one hand while with the other he found her clit. As he played with the nub her hips rose to meet his finger, pushing herself against it. He could feel her wetness grow. His cock, hard and frantic, pushed against her bottom.

'Now. Take me from behind. Now!'

He slid his hands up from inside her knickers and began to ease them off her hips.

'Tear them off. *Tear them off.*'

Her voice was heavy with lust, heavy with need. Bowers, in turn, grasped the sides of the delicate knickers and tore down. The ruined silk floated to the floor.

She grasped the back of the chair with both hands and bent over, raising her bottom high in the air. Naked, but for the black stockings, garters and ankle-high boots.

George pulled open his fly, sending several buttons cascading across the floor. He freed his cock, grown massive with need of her, and slid it deep inside.

Both gave a collective gasp of pleasure as he eased himself fully into her. His balls touching her warm, shapely behind. He began to move in and out of her, gently at first but then with greater force. She moved to meet each thrust. Driving her bottom backwards so that she was taking his full length.

George felt his climax approach. He had never had sex like this before. Lilian was strange…wonderful…wanton. Her mouth hung half open, her eyes glazed over with lust. The eroticism of the act was raised to new heights by the fact they both watched in the mirror. Saw the primitive, sensual, *dirty* pleasure on each others faces. His thrusts became shorter, more frenzied as his climax approached. His eyes closed and with a final spasmodic thrust he pumped his seed deep into her. Lilian climaxed at the same moment. She closed her eyes as the orgasm began. And as pleasure flooded her body the face that she imagined was Mrs Murray's.

The pub was rowdy. Beery bonhomie and tobacco smoke filled the air. Shouts and laughs, a snatch of drunken song. A potman carrying a tower of glasses piled so high they swayed and reeled weaved between the tables. He was given a cheer as for a moment the whole crystal edifice looked like tumbling before he made a dexterous adjustment and saved a disaster.

At one end was the saloon bar. This section was meant for the slightly more refined drinker, but was in fact merely an extension of the main bar except for a large wooden partition. This partition had a frosted glass panel set in the top half, giving at least the impression of seclusion, if not the actuality.

Davis arrived at the table after fighting his way through the crowd at the bar. He put down a couple of large brandies.

'It would have been easier to go to bloody France and collect the stuff myself. Place is packed.'

The priest smiled and raised his glass.

'Thanks, Harry.'

Davis raised his glass and returned the salute.

'So, Jack, how are things in the God business?'

Father Jack Seward smiled. It was good to be spoken to as a friend and not God's representative on earth. Jack Seward had come to religion through a baptism of fire. He had rejected science as the only world view when faced with irrefutable proof that the supernatural existed, that Evil existed as an entity.

Nearly twenty years ago he had been a doctor, specializing in the treatment of madness. But he had become embroiled in the mission to destroy the arch-vampire, Dracula.

Dracula had made Lucy Westenra, the woman Seward loved, one of the undead. With the help of Jonathan Harker, Quincy Adams and Professor Van Helsing, they had ended Dracula' evil reign. But Mina, Jonathan's wife, was also infected. And when she again reverted to a vampiric state they were forced to hunt her through the streets of London. He had seen Mina destroyed, enveloped in an explosion in the train tunnels deep under the city.

But the price he paid was the loss of his own wife, Ellen. She, too, had been tainted with the vampire strain and was only freed by a stake driven through her heart.

The evil had been ended, but the final reckoning was terrible. Van Helsing dead, Ellen dead, Mina vaporized. In a final apocalyptic battle Davis's friend and colleague, Sergeant McNeil had also been killed. So much death.

It was after this that Jack Seward turned his back on science. Sought to help mankind through spiritual means. His faith was strong. Sometimes he would be faced with the contradictions of religious belief and empiric proof, but his past always acted as a lodestone, always gave him the resolve that his choice of the spiritual path was the right one.

He only met Harry occasionally. Both gone on to other lives. But both with a bond that could never be broken, a bond forged in risking their immortal souls.

'So, there's no possibility of your getting back together?'

Harry shook his head. Seward could see the devastation in his friend. Davis had always looked younger than his age, but now his face seemed to sag, seemed to have grown immeasurably older. Always square and upright his whole frame was somehow loosened, diminished.

'Glad you came to see me, Harry. Sorry it had to be for something like this. Cheers.'

He lifted the glass to his lips in salute. Davis returned the gesture, forcing a wan smile to his face.

'So, what are you going to do?'

'What is there to do, Jack? Go on living, I suppose.'

'Of course I shouldn't be asking you this but will you go for a divorce?'

Harry shrugged. 'Who knows? Not sure it matters.'

Seward felt there must be something he could say, some words to ease the pain, but knew anything he said would appear trite and clichéd in the face of the man's grief. They both sat in silence for a few moments, each nursing his drink, each lost in his thoughts. Finally Seward spoke.

'Seen anything of Jonathan?'

'Not for a while. You?'

'Not for more than a year.'

In the twenty years since they had banded together to hunt down his wife, Mina, Jonathan Harker, once a bright and ambitious solicitor, had fallen further than any of them. A mental lassitude and depression had fallen on him. The career once so promising had started to slide. Jobs in law offices came and went, but each one a little bit lower down the pecking order. Large and respected law practices gradually gave way to smaller, dingier places. Shabby practice took the place of proper law. Jonathan's drift into oblivion was inexorable.

Of course Seward and Davis had tried to help. Gave him encouragement; at one point Seward gave him a home. Davis had used his contacts with solicitors, engendered by his work as a policeman, to get Jonathan positions which he promptly lost. They realized a man can only be saved if he wants to be saved. Gradually contact was lost. Meetings became less frequent. Jonathan Harker was a lost soul.

'Last time I heard he was working as a clerk for some solicitor in south London somewhere.'

Seward shook his head. 'A clerk? My God, Jonathan's a solicitor, a bloody good solicitor. You know that, Harry.'

'He was.' Davis's laconic reply said everything. Seward drained his glass.

'Another?'

'Why not?'

Seward stood up. He automatically checked that his jacket was still buttoned to the top, making sure his priest's collar couldn't be seen. He made his way through the jostling crowd towards the bar.

Harry sat quietly. Deep in thought. Without even being conscious of it he had dipped his finger into the little pools of spilled drink on the table and began doodling. And he was unaware that over and over again he was drawing heart shapes.

Chapter 7

CUTTING FROM THE 'EAST LONDON ADVERTISER':

MAN FOUND IN LIMEHOUSE 'TORN TO PIECES'

An Asiatic man was found dead in Leg of Mutton Alley, Limehouse, early Friday morning. The victim had severe lacerations to the throat and neck, believed to have been the work of a wild animal. Police have warned the public to be on their guard...

Bowers smiled as he looked out of the omnibus window as it made its way past Charring Cross station. Around him the packed and surging thoroughfare reflected two eras overlapping. Horses and carts clip-clopped alongside the rattling, trundling motor cars. The nineteenth century of Victoria was gradually being superseded by horseless carriages and flying machines.

But at moment the symbolic difference of the changing age was lost on him. The smile was that of a man whose life had suddenly become better.

Since returning from the ball at Regent's Park the night before, Lilian's sudden sexual burgeoning made George feel that there was hope once more. Her rekindled sexual urge had driven them to make love twice more that night.

When he'd left her that morning she was still not the vivacious women he wooed and married, but at least he'd seen evidence that her nature was reasserting itself. He felt a pleasant twinge in his groin as he remembered what they'd done, what *she* had done to him. Even when they were at their happiest and Lilian at her most sexually demanding she had never been so voracious, so inventive.

He looked up ahead and saw they were passing St Paul's Cathedral, Wren's triumphant symbol of the capital's phoenix-like rise from the ashes of the great fire. The City of London, and his office was just ahead. He reluctantly let go of the impure thoughts, as his catholic grandmother used called them. But as they reached the sobering grandeur of the Bank of England, and as he prepared to disembark he allowed himself the brief indulgence of thinking what he and Lilian could do when he got home.

"My Dear Mrs Murray…"

Lilian screwed up the letter and threw it into the small wicker basket by the writing desk. There it joined four other crumpled attempts. A flush of annoyance swept over her. Lilian was not familiar with vacillation. Normally a strong, decisive woman it was alien to be faltering over something as simple as a letter.

But she knew that this was beyond mere letter writing. This was something disturbing. She was contacting a woman she had only seen for a few seconds yet couldn't get out of her mind.

Mina's face haunted her thoughts. Not just during the sexual climaxes of the night before but almost continuously. Even now a picture of that red mouth and those compelling eyes formed in her mind. For the first time since the tragedy of her child's death Lilian Bowers was engaging with life. But at what level? She was deeply shaken by the association she made between sexual pleasure and the mysterious woman.

She got up and walked to the window. Outside the snow had stopped, but a layer almost a foot deep had turned the scene into a Christmas card. People, swathed in winter clothing, lifted their feet high in an exaggeratedly comic manner as they tromped through the white blanket. A carter walked slowly along the road holding his horse's bridle, making sure the animal didn't lose its footing on the treacherous under-surface. Some children came into view, throwing snowballs. One of the missiles whistled past the carter's head and she smiled as she saw him silently mouth a stream of abuse at the youngsters who ran on, laughing.

She returned the writing table and lifted the pen.

"My Dear Mrs Murray..."

Chapter 8

Melancholy had hung on him like a cloak for so long that when they came for him he felt nothing. No fear. No curiosity. No resistance.

The jolting vehicle rattled over the cobbles as they made their way northwards out of the city. The mass of factories and shops and houses and pubs gradually made way for suburban villas dotted among green swards.

The two men sitting opposite said something, firstly to him, but when he did not answer, to each other. Their words came from afar and he did not care enough to decode them and make a response. Again one of the men spoke to him, but he merely turned and stared sightlessly out of the window. The men shrugged.

After a while he shut his eyes. Lassitude lulled him into a state of semi-sleep. Not a sleep that refreshed, not a sleep of healthy tiredness, but the numbing doze of a soul in desolation.

When he opened his eyes it was dark outside. The coach had stopped. One of the men leaned past him and flicked open the door. Faces, indistinct in the gloom, looked in. Hands and arms reached for him. He was pulled out and ushered firmly into the building. In the panelled entrance a severe-looking woman and a man, dressed in a frock coat, stared at him. They asked him questions but he kept his gaze fixed on the tiled floor.

Voices echoed down the long corridors. Shouting. Laughing. Screaming. Then he was in a cramped room. The door closed. He was utterly indifferent to his surroundings. He lay down on the small iron bedstead and stared unblinkingly at the walls. Somewhere someone screamed again.

Chapter 9

My Dear Mrs Bowers,

Thank you for your letter. I ,too, remember you at the ball and was disappointed we did not get a chance to speak. I sensed there were things to be said between us. I know of your sadness .I have faced such things also. I make no claims but I have certain gifts which I have used to help those like yourself caught between the living and the dead.

It would give me great pleasure to welcome you as a guest to my home. I am most readily available in the evening.

Yours,
Mina Murray.

Mina sealed the envelope and wrote in the same bold hand Lilian's name and address. She looked again at the correspondence she had found on the floor beneath the letter box when she had emerged from her sleep. She remembered Lilian Bowers and seen in her eyes the sadness of those who have been touched by death.

The letter had been overtly a light, social communication. The type of thing that women of Lilian Bowers class wrote half a dozen times a day with an effortless touch. Mina's vampire sense told her that beneath the text was the cry of a woman lost.

Such a woman, on the cusp of life and that which lay beyond, was perhaps the companion she was looking for. Mina was incapable of love or affection, was incapable of having any feelings for another creature, but even a vampire needs its own kind.

Dracula chose her and Lucy. He also had his brides in the castle in Transylvania. Companions in the darkness. The vampire mainly killed. Drained a victim till their hearts no longer beat. But sometimes they created a new *nosferatu*. One of their own kind. A hideous parody of human procreation.

She picked up the envelope addressed to Lilian Bowers, turned it over and wrote her own address on the back.

Mina was ready to share the darkness.

Chapter 10

Lilian's fingers trembled as she fastened the earring. She stopped for a moment and took a deep breath. This was ridiculous. She was behaving like a love-struck young girl. *Love-struck?* She wondered why that particular simile had come to mind. Driving the thought away she concentrated on fixing the earring in place.

Finally the task was complete. She stepped back and surveyed herself in the ornate, full-length mirror which stood in the corner of the bedroom. Her discerning gaze swept down the image before her. The copper hair was piled high and elegantly up, with subtle touch of make-up enhancing the beautiful face. The new dark green satin dress swept off her shoulders and clung to her slim waist and softly curving hips.

She made a cursory attempt at adjusting the bust line of the dress, wondering if it was just a little too low, showing a hint more of the swell of her breasts than was absolutely *de rigueur*.

Another flutter of butterflies in her stomach told her that this was not just another of the endless rounds of social calls that made up the life of the Edwardian lady. All day her nervousness had been more akin to the feelings she had experienced when George first began to woo her.

All the signs of…Once again the phrase '*love-struck*' crossed her mind. Her strong personality reasserted itself and Lilian Bowers, on the surface, took command of her emotions. But there was no denying that the letter she had received three days ago had unsettled her being. Mina Murray's invitation had filled her every waking thought from the moment it had arrived.

Her new-found sexual appetite was driven to even greater heights by the delicious anticipation of meeting this woman. George had discovered his wife had not only become a sexual being once more, but a sexual being of unbridled passion, leaving him happily exhausted. Despite the frantic excitement of their love-making always in her mind's eye Lilian held the image of Mina Murray's red mouth.

Finally she was satisfied with her appearance. Draping her coat about her shoulders she made her way downstairs.

'Mrs Bowers, you look lovely.'

'Thank you, Agnes.'

The maid stared in awe. Agnes, eighteen and still bedazzled by the life-style of her elegant mistress, had never seen a woman look so beautiful. A beauty from a storybook. From the wan and lifeless woman she had known since taking up her situation, she now saw Lilian in all her glory. Glowing with life, sublimely pretty.

'The cab's waiting, Mrs Bowers.'

Lilian gave Agnes a warm smile. 'Thank you, Agnes.'

The girl opened the front door and Lilian stepped out and was at once enveloped in the winter chill. The snow had stopped but the air was nipped with frost and the constant wind made her shiver as she stepped gingerly through the mounds of snow, interspersed with ice.

The driver held open the door.

'Limehouse, please. Here's the address.'

Lilian held out a piece of paper with the address given in Mina's invitation. The driver took the paper and touched his hat, mumbling an indistinct phrase she took as a thank you.

She settled into the seat. The cabman asked her if she would prefer the window shades drawn against the frigid breeze. She thanked him and the interior of the cab darkened as the blinds cut out the light from the house. Lilian felt the cab sink and lurch as the driver climbed aboard. She heard him make a *click click* noise with his tongue, geeing the horse into motion. As the cab rocked gently into life Lilian snuggled into the corner and wished the miles away.

They were in the dark, somewhere…everywhere. He looked around. A scurrying. A whisper. A malevolent snicker danced on the air. He wanted to run. Wanted to get away from them and yet more than anything he wanted them to find him. Wanted to feel their kisses, their touches. Wanted to sink deep into the decadent embrace. Wanted to pull those maddening heartless bodies close to his. And as they knelt around him the scent of the scent of the earth and blood filled his nostrils.

Jumping up he ran to the door and pulled frantically at the handle. But it refused to open. In a silent frenzy he turned the handle relentlessly, pulling at the same time. Finally exhausted he sank down on the floor. A feeling of hopelessness replaced the brief energy of his panic. He was sealed in the darkness…

'Death isn't as terrible as you might think.'

They sat alone by the fire In the bickering light thrown out by the flames Lilian looked into the dark eyes of Mina Harker. From somewhere outside came the muffled commingled sounds of talk and music. To Lilian the outer world seem so very far away and sitting in the firelight she felt at peace.

When she arrived she was at first surprised that Mina Murray lived alone, without servants. But here in the warm intimacy of the room she was glad. She took another sip of wine and tried hard not to stare at the overwhelming beauty before her.

'Death is a freeing. I know of your loss. I can see it. I can feel it.'

The vampire's voice floated through the air. Calming, soothing, comforting.

'I miss her so.' Lilian's voice trembled. But she wanted to speak more. Wanted to tell this woman everything. 'I want her to know that. I want her to know.'

'I understand Your longing sits on you like a shroud.'

As she spoke Mina softly stroked Lilian's face. Her fingers felt cool, sensuous.

'I have a gift. I can bring you comfort if you wish.'

Lilian's eyes were locked on hers.

'Close your eyes and hold the dark.'

Lilian closed her eyes. Mina's voice washed softly over her.

'Now open your eyes. See her. See her now.'

Lilian slowly opened her eyes. There, shimmering on the air was Jenny. Smiling, happy, golden.

'Jenny?'

So real was the image that she stretched out her arms as if to hold the little girl.

'Death has blessed her. Decay can no longer affect her. Never to grow old, never to feel pain or unhappiness. Your child is beyond all that the world can inflict.'

Lilian's voice broke and she cried out.

'Jenny, come to mummy, Jenny.'

Mina' voice, soothing and mellifluous came as if from afar.

'She waits for you, Lilian. Waits in another place. Let her rest until you meet again.'

The smiling figure of the little girl faded on the air.

Tears streamed down Lilian's face. A great peace was upon her and her body was flooded with a sense of well-being. She looked gratefully at Mina.

'Thank you. Thank you.'

Mina smiled a wonderful smile. Lilian was captivated by that smile. She stared until that scarlet mouth filled her vision.

The vampire reached up and gently stroked her face again. The touch of her fingers felt wonderful, made her tremble. She was captivated by lips that were sensual; crimson; inviting. Suddenly Lilian knew that more than anything else in the world she wanted to kiss that mouth.

Leaning forward Lilian placed the softest of kisses on Mina's lips. The vampire's hand slipped around the back of Lilian's neck and pulled her mouth hard against hers. The mortal woman made a tiny mew of pleasure and responded, pushing her half open lips against Mina's. Tongue sought tongue. As Lilian grew more excited she was aware that beneath the sweetness of Mina's kiss ran an under taste of something…unclean.

As her excitement grew she took Mina's hand. Cold. So cold. Slowly she placed it on her breast. A thrill of pleasure ran through her body. She felt a growing arousal. Felt her nipples grow erect. Mina moved closer. Her eyes held Lilian's. Dominating. Promising.

She felt the revenant's hand slid down the front of her dress and gently caress the ample bosom below. Teasing, calculating fingers sought her nipple and gently played with the hard pink bud.

A rush of sexual pleasure swamped Lilian and she leant back against the settee, taking the submissive role as Mina's fondled her breast with greater urgency.

The vampire's hunger was upon her. The scent of the woman and the need for the hot rich blood which surged through her veins drove Mina into a frenzy of need. But she would not kill without thought like she had done in Shoulder of Mutton Alley, where her kill was merely to slake her thirst, and the anger of hunger made her savage.

The beautiful victim was destined to be her companion and so she would induct her into the realm of the undead in the way that her master, Dracula, had done. An unholy seduction which would gradually prepare her for crossing over.

Mina kissed down Lilian's face and neck, each touch heightening the sensual thrill which ran through her yielding body. With eyes closed Lilian gave herself to the overwhelming sexual power of the vampire.

Lilian felt her dress being drawn down off her shoulders. Felt the stroke of cool air as more of her breasts were exposed. The red basque she wore lifted her bust high, creating two perfect white mounds. Mina kisses continued down her neck. Lilian gave another little cry of pleasure as she experienced the cold lips on her bosom and the gentle nibbling of teeth.

Mina felt the hot rush of blood under the skin and could hold back her need no longer. Opening her mouth wide she bared the penetrating fangs and sank them deep into the warm yielding globe.

Lilian gave a little yelp of pain as the canines plunged deep into her breast. The subtle aura of sensual domination created by the vampire was disturbed. The pain almost broke the spell, but even if she had been fully aware there was nothing she could do. She was Mina's. The power and dominance of the vampire was complete.

There in the firelight Lilian lay still and the only sound was that of the vampire suckling at her breast.

Chapter 11

The woman rushed towards him, her face contorted with anger. Davis stepped back as the placard she carried narrowly missed his cheek. She moved on, oblivious. The Strand was crowded as the army of determined women of all ages, but by their dress almost exclusively middle-class.

He stopped to watch as the Suffragette army, chanting and shouting their demands, brought traffic to a standstill. Horns tooted and abuse poured down on them not only from the men held up by the procession but men on the pavements. Some of the jeering was good-natured, some patronizing, but some filled with intense hatred.

THE WSPU DEMAND VOTES FOR WOMEN. The placards and banners all proclaimed the same message. Harry, like every other man in the country, knew that the WPSU, 'Women's Social and Political Union' was the driving force, the militant branch of the Suffragette movement. In their midst he could see Mrs Pankhurst, the leader of the Union. She was a striking figure, with an attractive face, neat form and dark hair. Not the Medusa created by the mainly Tory press who sought to ridicule and demonize her at every turn.

Several objects were thrown from the crowd and the policemen lining the route seemed to have little inclination to stop those who jostled and pushed and kicked out at the women as they marched past. Davis shook his head as a gob of spit hit a young woman on the cheek. Without breaking stride or looking anywhere but straight ahead, she wiped the spittle from her face and marched on.

Harry had a profound admiration for these women. They fought the state and all its machinery for their right to vote. Prison; force feeding; beatings by the police during their demonstrations.

'Need a bloody good hiding that's what most of them need.'

Davis turned towards the man who spoke. A clerk by his dress. He looked him up and down. The insufferable primness and self-appointed righteousness of the weedy man was overwhelming. Harry fought down the impulse to punch him straight in the smug face. Any of these women, he thought, are worth ten of this fucker. Looking the man up and down again in a blatant show of disgust Davis shouldered his way through the crowd.

On the door was the picture of a huge eye and underneath was the maxim, 'WE NEVER SLEEP.' Harry pushed the door open and stepped inside. A bell jangled over his head. Alice, the lady secretary, looked up and seeing that it was him and not a client smiled and called out a breezy 'good morning' before resuming her work.

Harry walked across to his desk. The office was empty, most of the investigators were out in jobs at this time. He sighed with relief as he sank into the chair, taking the weight off his weak ankle.

Dotted around the walls of the office were the photographs and descriptions of the various tricksters and embezzlers and bigamists and dozens of other flee-ers of justice.

Pinkerton's Detective Agency, founded in the nineteenth century by a Scot, Allan Pinkerton, in America, had flourished and grown to be the most famous detective agency in the world. Pinkerton's had resources which rivalled those of governments. In fact during the American Civil War Pinkerton men worked in close collaboration with the official secret service.

Davis rubbed his face rapidly across his face and tried to excise the lassitude that had gripped him since he had exposed his wife's infidelity. After his talk with Seward he had sat in the house for three days, drinking whisky and looking at the picture of Jesse, his first wife. Eventually he took off his wedding band and threw it into the dustbin. Going to a drawer he took out the ring he'd worn on the day Jesse and he were married. He'd kept it carefully hidden in a piece of tissue paper at the back of a drawer from the day she'd died.

He had walked to the cemetery in Leyton. The snow had made it difficult to locate her grave even though he had visited it so many times over the years. The white blanket altered landscape and the wind had whipped the snow in drifts obliterating the tombstone. He had carefully swept the stone clear and then took out the golden band, unwrapped it from the tissue and placed it again on his finger. As the snow swirled around his face he renewed his wedding vow to his dead wife. He told Jesse he missed her so much and that there would never be another woman but her, until they met again.

He was suddenly aware that the secretary was walking towards him. An unbidden tear had trickled down his cheek. Putting on a show of blowing his nose into his handkerchief he muttered something about a cold and then tried to look in a business-like manner at the files on his desk.

'Mr Terry said he'd like you to get onto the top file first thing.'

Davis summoned up a smile.

'Right, Alice.'

'You alright, Harry?'

The secretary's thin, pinched severe look often gave her a rather forbidding appearance but Davis knew she was in fact a very kind woman.

'I'm fine.'

He picked up the file and began to undo the red ribbon. As Alice walked away he called out.

'By the way, you know I'm in court later? The grocer case.' He was referring to a case he had investigated recently when a very respectable shop manager was found to have been taking money from the till of the grocer's shop he had worked in since a boy. Apparently the family had gotten into financial difficulties and the man had taken a few pounds to tide them over. It was a classic case of a single slip from grace. The money involved was less than twenty pounds and the man was distraught. Relatives had offered to pay it back but the shop owner was determined to prosecute despite Harry's advice to the contrary.

'Didn't you know? Of course you wouldn't,' Alice said. 'Apparently the poor man hanged himself yesterday morning.'

Davis felt a wave of despair sweep over him. Poor bastard! A life gone for twenty lousy pounds! And he had caught him. For a moment he thought he was going to be sick. He took a couple of deep breaths and the feeling of nausea passed. Is this what he had come to? Helping drive a man to his death. An impulse to get up and walk away almost overcame him. Never hunting or prying or spying on another human being again. But then practicality kicked in. What else would a crippled ex-policeman do? What else in the world was there for him?

Picking up the file he opened it, hoping it would something that would take his mind off the events of the last few days. He sighed as he realized the assignment was to follow a man whose wife suspected him of adultery.

Chapter 12

She wondered what Dr Crippen, the murderer, was doing at her dinner party. She turned to George.

'Do you think it's alright for him to be here?' she whispered. 'Oh, yes, the poor man may have killed his wife but he is a doctor.'

She looked over at the inoffensive-looking little man. She was sure he'd been hanged. Standing by the fireplace, King George V was reading extracts from the The Times Obituary column aloud to several ladies who were bare from the waist down.

'I think it would really be hospitable if you took off your dress now, dear.'

She looked at George who grinned benignly.

'My dress?'

'Oh, yes, it's all the rage.'

'Well if you think so. I wouldn't want people to think I'm rude.'

She slipped her dress off. She was naked beneath. At once a ripple of applause ran round the room. She smiled graciously at the compliment. Winston Churchill, wearing his familiar silk hat and coat with a fur collar, stopped chatting to Little Titch, the music hall star, to say how lovely her breasts were. Titch, only four foot tall, was wearing comic shoes more than two foot long and constantly leant forward until he was almost parallel with the ground before straightening up again. Every time he did this Churchill roared with laughter.

She passed on, still smiling and thanking every new compliment. Outside the window a brass band played 'Hands, Knees and Boomps-a-Daisy'

'I do think there should be more attention paid to bats and rats.'

'Bats and rats?' she asked the man with albino eyes who cupped her breasts in his hands as he spoke.

'I really don't know, my husband usually deals with those matters.'

She moved on through the crowd. They really were very pleasant people. She stopped several times to have her bosom fondled before George held up a glass and indicated she should join him.

'A toast.'
'A toast?'
'To bats and rats.'
'Of course.'

She raised her glass as George made the toast. 'To bats and rats.'

The company repeated the toast and she raised the glass to her lips. The wine was red and sweet and thick. Very thick. With a coppery, salty under-taste.

'I'm not sure this wine is very nice, George.'

'Of course it is. Drink. You wouldn't want out guests to think you're rude now, would you, dear?'

'No, of course not.'

She began to drink. The taste grew stronger. Red gobbets began to fill her mouth. She started to gag and the wine spilled down her shoulders and breasts. George smiled at her encouragingly. She felt sick. Across the table the others watched her with fixed, rictus grins..

Dr Crippen raised his glass and then she saw a woman was sitting by his side. His wife, Belle. But there was something not quite right about Mrs Crippen. Her face was twitching. Moving. Maggots writhed and turned and in the space beneath there was the gleam of skull and bone. Lilian tried to scream but George pushed the glass against her lips and her mouth filled with thick, turgid blood.

Lilian sat up kicking and gasping. Frantically she drew in a series of short jerky breaths, trying to fill her lungs, trying to escape the choking sensation. Gradually the panicky inhalations gave way to a steadier and more normal breathing rhythm. Such a terrible dream.

Weak, so weak. Her senses swam for a moment and the vertigo induced a feeling of sickness. She closed her eyes and kept very still. Finally the spinning stopped and she opened her eyes carefully. She was on the floor in front of a settee. Dazedly she tried to remember where in the house she had such an item of furniture. Tassels. Yellow tassels all along the apron of the settee. She reached out to touch them but her dazed state threw out her spatial judgement and she found herself grasping at air, her fingers feebly falling several inches short of the material.

She looked slowly around her and began to realize that she was not at home. But where? Narrowing her eyes in concentration she struggled to get her bearings. Another wave of nausea crept over her and she gagged as if to be sick. Taking another couple of deep breaths the feeling passed. Fragments of memory began to coalesce. Mina! She was in Mina Murray's house!

The events of the night were lost. She remembered drinking… The image of Jenny. Jenny? Then…Then…That was all she could remember.

'Mina? Mina? Mrs Murray?'

Her voice was thin and weak, and faded on the air. She looked around but the unmistakable aura that an empty house carries told her she was alone.

With an effort of will she pulled herself onto a kneeling position and rested her elbows on the edge of the settee, waiting for the dizziness to subside. Every movement seemed to take such effort and her breath became laboured even after this simple move.

Lilian Bowers was a strong woman both in mind and body and this unfamiliar helplessness frightened her. Steeling herself for another effort she pushed herself into a standing position and waited for a few seconds until the trembling in her legs ceased. Tentatively putting on foot in front of another, and holding out her arms for balance as a tightrope-walker might use a pole, she shuffled across the room and looked down a small flight of stairs which she presumed led to the kitchen.

'Mina? Mrs Murray?'

In the enclosed space created by the stairwell her voice sounded stronger. Encouraged by this she called down again but more in hope than belief. Instinctively she knew there was no other living soul in that house.

Turning away she rested her arm on the ornamental wood pillar situated at the bottom of the balustrade. She looked up but the effort caused her to feel giddy once more. She discarded the idea of climbing the stairs.

Shaking her head in an effort to clear the dullness of mind she felt she edged slowly over to the where her cloak was draped over the back of a gilt chair. The few steps took such a toll of her that she sank down in the seat and rested for a few moments before painfully standing and draping the garment around her.

The material's heavy. familiar texture reassured her and slowly and with the fixed deliberate concentration of a child who had just learned to tie its shoe laces, she managed to fasten the cloak about her neck.

By the door there was a small *escritoire* and she opened the desk drawer with the thought of leaving a note for Mina. In the drawer were several sheets of writing paper, the same type of paper she had received when Mina had invited her to visit. An elegant gold fountain pen rolled across the paper when she pulled the drawer open. Lilian reached for the pen but the trembling in her fingers and the utter lack of energy turned the idea of writing into a task beyond her.

She pushed the drawer closed. Moving slowly to the entrance she managed to turn the heavy handle and with a last look around stepped into the snow, closing the solid door behind her.

As the last echoes of the closing door shivered on the air; behind the bookcase; behind the wall; below the ground, Mina slept. There in the stygian blackness she lay replete. A half-smile played across the mouth stained with the blood.

Chapter 13

The night had stretched out endlessly in a series of ever more terrifying imaginary scenarios for George Bowers. When he'd arrived home that evening and found that Lilian had gone out he'd been disappointed. Their new found sexual passion had made the return journey at the end of each day one of delicious anticipation. Asking Agnes where she had gone the girl could only say she'd went out to visit a friend. Who the friend was, or where she lived was more than the maid knew.

At first Bowers felt nothing more than a mild irritation at her absence but as the hours passed this had grown to concern and finally frantic worry. He had paced the house, alternating between planning how he would tell her off for worrying him like this and moments of panic as he imagined a series of terrible possibilities involving carriage accidents which grew more spectacular as time passed.

He had phoned several of their acquaintances, hiding his concern under a smoke-screen of banter. But she wasn't with any of their closest friends. Several interrogations of Agnes, each one more aggressive until the girl was on the verge of tears, elucidated no more information. Bowers eventually had to apologize to her.

Just before dawn he had lain down and dozed fitfully, waking in fits and starts as his fears sliced through his sleep. Now he stood looking at his gaunt, unshaven face in the mirror. Worry had etched creases and shadows onto his normally smooth complexion. He turned on the tap and bending low dashed handfuls of cold water onto his face. Taking the towel he dried himself and prepared to go to the police. It was at this moment he heard the front doorbell jangle. Dear God, make it be her. Make her be safe!

He was halfway across the room when he heard Agnes call his name frantically. Rushing along the landing he reached the top of the stairs and saw the girl standing by the open front door, half supporting an unconscious Lilian.

Running down the stairs he crossed the hall in a couple of strides and caught Lilian up in his arms. He carried her into the drawing room. Agnes followed close behind. Bowers laid her gently on the sofa.

'She's so cold, sir, so cold. Like ice.'

George turned to the girl. 'Get blankets and tell Cook to bring some tea, no, hot soup.'

The girl turned and ran from the room. Bowers looked down at his wife. She looked ghastly. White. Bloodless lips.

'It's alright, Lilian, everything's alright now.'

He lifted her hand and was frightened by the icy feel. My God, she was almost frozen. He rubbed her fingers, trying to inject warmth then went to the phone. As he tersely asked to be connected to their doctor his eyes never left Lilian. She was like a picture he had seen in a storybook when a child. The Snow Queen.

In a few sentences he told the doctor of the urgency and then replaced the phone. Just then Agnes entered carrying three or four heavy woollen blankets. He grabbed them and began to pack them around his wife. He turned to the maid, who stood staring wide-eyed at the recumbent Lilian, and told her to tell Cook to hurry up with the soup, and then get more coal to build up the fire.

Wordlessly Agnes hurried away. Bowers touched Lilian's earlobes, rubbing them, trying to ensure there was no possibility of frostbite. She responded to the friction, moaning softly. George felt a sense of relief. She was at least still in the land of the living.

'It's alright, dear, it's alright. You're home. We'll take care of you.'

He gently kissed her on the forehead and her eyes flickered partially open. When she spoke her voice was weak and cracked and he was only able to make out one word.

'Mina.'

The doctor shook his head. 'I've never seen anything like it, Mr Bowers. She was as near frozen as it's possible to be and still live. How she made her way back home is a mystery.'

Both men looked down at the unconscious figure of Lilian, now in bed, huddled beneath a pile of extra coverings. Her face was still deathly white but the faintest of pink tinged her cheeks showing that her temperature was rising. Under the bedclothes a small legion of ceramic hot water bottles helped in the process.

George felt drained. The fears and terrors of the night hours, coupled with the condition of his wife had robbed him of all vitality. He gently brushed a stray hair from her forehead.

'Apart from the hyperthermia, is there anything else wrong with her, doctor?'

'It's difficult to be sure because her frozen condition could mask any other problems at this time, but I'd say your wife could also be suffering from anaemia.'

Bowers turned sharply to the doctor.

'Anaemia? But Lilian's always been healthy.'

'Maybe, and as I say the cold makes diagnosis more difficult, but the lack of colour in the lips suggests it as a possibility.'

'So what do we do now?

'Keep her warm. Plenty of hot drinks. When she can eat give her lots of red meat, liver, stuff like that. And I'll write a prescription for some iron tablets.'

The doctor wrapped a long scarf about his neck, lifted his bag and said goodbye, waving away the man's thanks. As he reached the door the physician turned.

'Oh, by the way, it's nothing serious, but I did notice your wife has a couple of small wounds.'

'Wounds?'

'Yes, two little puncture marks on her breast.'

Chapter 14

The mist from the river sent its tendrils drifting gently across Limehouse. The miasma slithered along Three Colts Lane and coiled about St Anne's Church

Wind, all the way from the Siberian steppes, swept like a razor through Limehouse Causeway, through Pennyfields, swirled around the Confucian temple, found its way along Willow Road, rattling the windows of the Sacred Heart Infants School as it passed.

Men and women huddled close to the protection of the coffee stalls on West India Dock Road, frozen fingers grasping gratefully at the huge mugs of mahogany brown tea which poured in an endless stream from the massive cast iron kettles. The lucky ones wolfed down thick-bodied sandwiches in which the bacon still sizzled, or bit into great fat snarling sausages fresh from the pan.

The chug of an engine heralded the passing of the river police, known locally as 'Water Rats.' Three officers, frosted with ice and a sprinkling of fine snow, stood as still as sugared statues in the boat, hovering near the little engine in the centre of the craft.

Along the dockside were moored a couple of Scandinavian three-masted barges. Now sitting high in the water they had discharged their cargoes of timber from the Swedish pine forests and were silent and still and white, like ghostly galleons.

Lining the banks of the jet-black river were paper-mills and coal barges and rope works and saw mills, all in bondage to the needs of the Thames.

Vicky Nolan and Molly Summerson were inured to the sights and sounds of Limehouse. Both raised in Stepney, the place was merely their place of work.

Vicky, the taller and darker of the two, had been a prostitute for three years. Still only nineteen the harshness of the life had begun to tell. Thin to the point of emaciation she had almost completely lost the last semblance of youthful prettiness. She now had the hard, merciless, distrustful look of the experienced streetwalker.

Stockier, and at two years younger, Molly, had still had the freshness which attracted men. With a full figure, generous hips and ample breasts, she had no difficulty in finding clients among the sailors who thronged the streets. Truth be told she knew that it was her appearance mostly that caused the mariners in groups of twos and threes to pick them up for business. Vicky, it seemed, was brought along as ballast for the sailor not quick enough to fasten onto Molly.

She felt this again as she and her friend hurried along the whitened pavements of the Causeway. She glanced surreptitiously at the bedraggled figure at her side. A couple of times she thought they had found some business only to be rejected as they got closer. Molly, had almost decided that after tonight she would work alone.

Both the women were cold and hungry. The windows of Scudder's Confectioners Shop shone brightly in the night air. In unison they both stopped and looked in at the myriad of coloured sweets piled high on stepped shelves. Sherbet and toffees, liquorice sticks and chocolate soldiers and dozens of other names and shapes that for a few moments took them to a place of innocence.

Molly could see a little girl of about ten pointing to sweets under the glass case of the counter. Her father smiled indulgently and nodded. To Molly the man looked like the dad she'd often imagined but had never met.

They moved on, lowering their heads against the gusts of slicing wind. Both women wanted to find shelter but without money to pay for their lodgings the streets were their only alternative.

They had just reached Gill Street and the Spread Eagle pub when the sailor came out, calling back into the bar in a drunken, jocular voice. He laughed at the indistinct reply and then turned away. As he buttoned up his coat he spied the two women.

'Good evening, ladies.' His voice had a Nordic lilt. He was tall. Molly took in the broad, open pleasant face and fair hair, jutting out from beneath his cap. The blue eyes were slightly glazed with drink but he stood steadily enough.

Both women immediately slipped on professional smiles.

'Hello, mate. You look as if you've had a nice time.'

Molly stood looking archly up at him, pressing close and opening her shawl to show a hint of cleavage.

'Would you like a bit of company?'

The sailor smiled a slow smile as his drink befuddled brain translated the foreign language.

'How much? For a suck?'

Vicky put her hand on her chin pensively as if considering a suitable price.

'Well, let's see. For a good-looking bloke like you, ten shillings.'

The sailor narrowed his eyes and then turned to Molly.

'Same price for you?' Molly nodded. The mariner tilted his head towards the younger girl. 'Her.'

Vicky's smile turned off immediately. She scowled and half turned.

'Suit yourself.'

Molly shrugged as if to indicate it was only the luck of the draw, but inwardly she was triumphant. The sailor's decision only confirmed the conclusion she had already come to, that Vicky was a liability. This would definitely be their last night of working together.

The trio walked away from the pub looking a suitable venue to consummate the arrangement. Molly knew of a stable yard a few yards down where she had done business before. They reached the narrow alley which led to the stable. Molly turned to Vicky.

'You want to wait here, Vicks, or see if you can find a bit of business further down?'

Vicky looked along the empty howling street and shrugged resignedly.

'Might as well wait for you here.'

'Suit yourself.'

The younger girl could hardly contain her smirk of satisfaction. Both women knew the balance of power had shifted irredeemably. The sailor grunted impatiently and tugged at Molly's arm.

'You're bloody keen aincha, love?' She laughed and they both disappeared into the alleyway.

Almost immediately the smell of hay and horse manure enveloped them. The sailor sniffed in disgust. Molly patted him on the arm reassuringly.

'Don't worry, love, I'll soon make you forget a little bit of horseshit.'

The end of the alley was almost in complete darkness. The sailor stretched his arms out ahead of him, uncertain. Molly, took his upper bicep and guided him towards a rickety wooden gate set into the wall of the alley. She reached between the spars and slid up a crude latch. The door swung open, creaking on its hinges. They stepped inside.

On the pavement Vicky, cold and angry, stamped her feet in a desperate attempt to keep them warm. A group of drunken dockers came tumbling out of the Spread Eagle. Notoriously rough, the east end dockers were not the type of business Vicky was looking for. She sank back into the shadows of the alley and watched as they shouted and bawled at each other in heavy, coarse voices. She was relieved when they started walking in the opposite direction from where she stood. A vicious slap of wind caused her to shiver and she wondered if Molly would pay for both their digs that night.

The horses moved and neighed quietly in the warmth of the stable. The two mares, used to draw coal carts, reacted to the presence of the man and woman. The sailor tried to kiss Molly and at the same time squeeze her breasts.
'You want to do that, love, it's extra. Ten bob for a suck that's what we agreed. You want to pay a little more for a little more?'
The sailor closed his eyes and rested the back of his head against the wall. Molly, with an impersonal efficiency, knelt down in front of him and undid his trousers. She took his cock out and as it was still flaccid began to massage it gently, at the same time cupping his balls in her left hand and playing with them teasingly. At first there was no response.
'Reckon you've had a little too much to drink, mate.'
The sailor remained with his eyes closed and she resumed her ministrations until he began to grow harder. His penis was big, very big and she wondered if it would fit in her mouth. When he was almost fully erect she began to smother the tip with quick, tiny kisses. The man groaned with rising ecstasy. Molly stuck out a small pink tongue and slowly and lasciviously licked the head of his cock.
Sure that he was now fully hard she leant forward, slipped her lips over the enlarged glans and began to suck gently at first and then with greater vigour.
So intent on the act were they that neither of them heard the horses begin to whinny and snicker and clop restlessly. The sound of

the beasts grew more uneasy, more fearful. Snorting, one of the horses began to kick at the back wall of the stable.

Molly was vaguely aware of the growing noise but she wanted to finish and get her money. Wanted to find a nice warm bed and climb in and forget men.

He was almost at climax and his taste grew stronger in her mouth. The man muttered an indistinct phrase in a language she didn't understand, but she knew what he meant. She had heard the same thing from so many men, from so many countries. She closed her eyes and prepared for him coming.

Neither of them saw the shadow which fell across them.

Bowers watched his wife anxiously as she tossed and turned and muttered. In the twelve hours or so since she'd arrived back at the house she'd been in this state of sustained restlessness.

He was no longer afraid that her internal body temperature had fallen too low to sustain life. The room was sweltering. The fire was banked high, the curtains were drawn, and several oil stoves dotted about had created a sub-tropical atmosphere.

This effort had been rewarded with a deepening pink colour spreading across Lilian's cheeks. Her hands, like blocks of ice when she was first put to bed, were now warmer and tinged with a healthy flow of circulation.

He again tried to spoon-feed her some clear broth. After trying to get her to swallow some of the thick vegetable soup Cook had prepared he was now attempting to get her to take something lighter and more digestible.

As the spoon touched her lips and the first drops of liquid trickled across her tongue Lilian grimaced, twisting from side to side and causing him to drip broth down the edge of her cheek. He put down the bowl and dabbed the spillage away.

He was deeply worried that she had not yet awakened. Had not yet eaten or drunk anything since she had fallen in the door. Another call to the doctor had resulted in him being told that rest at this stage was more important and that her body would tell her when it was good and ready. Bowers found this rather simple advice deeply unsatisfying. He thought a doctor should be more ready to leap into the fray with all the miracles of science behind him. Let her rest and be patient didn't seem helpful.

He felt sick of heart. He loved his wife very much and seeing her lying there, so fragile, so ill, filled him with a feeling of helplessness. He leaned forward and tenderly stroked her brow. Lilian's eyes flickered almost open and then closed. Her lips moved and she seemed to be attempting to say something. George leaned closer.

'It's alright, Lilian, it's alright. I'm here. You're safe.'

She muttered something indistinct. He moved closer, putting his ear almost against her lips.

'What did you say, darling?'

Her words came out in the softest of breaths.

'For the blood is the life.'

'For Christ's sake!'

Vicky spat the words angrily into the frozen air. She stomped up and down furiously as the cold worked its way up from her feet and into her legs. She had been waiting almost half an hour at the entrance to the alley. A suck should have taken ten minutes at the most. In fact Molly was fond of telling her she could make most men come in less than five.

What the hell was she doing in there? Going on fucking honeymoon? With a show of resolve she started to walk away. I'm not hanging about here all bloody night! She only walked a few yards before she stopped, racked with uncertainty. What it the bloke's cut up rough.? The beating of prostitutes was common. Men who didn't want to pay afterwards, or men who couldn't perform at the vital moment, or even men who harboured a deep-seated hatred/fear of women. Vicky herself had been battered a few times, at one point barely escaping with her life.

She turned and walked back to the entrance of the alley, her concern for her friend overlaid by the knowledge that she had no money and without Molly no place to sleep that night.

It was the first fluttering of light snow that decided her. She would go and see what was happening. Pulling her shawl even more tightly around her in an attempt to keep out the probing chill she walked down alley. Even though it was in almost complete darkness Vicky knew the way. She, like the other street women, had used the stable many times before.

The familiar outline of the stable door showed faintly in the meagre light which found its way down the alley from the street. The door was lying half open. Vicky stepped forward gingerly. She called out. 'Molly? You in there? You alright?' The silence was broken by the low, distressed snickering and whinnying of the horses.

Calling out once more Vicky stepped up to the door and eased it further back. The creak of the rusting hinges caused the neighing of the horses to rise to a new frightened pitch. Vicky felt an atavistic surge of fear race through her and for a moment the mad desire to run from the place almost overcame her. But the harshness of the life she led had made her able to face many things which repelled or scared her.

Moving fully into the stable she called again. What if that cow's gone out the other end of the ally with the money? She noticed there was a smell under the familiar stench of manure and rotten straw. A coppery, warm smell. At that moment she stood on something soft. For a moment she almost fainted, thinking she'd stood on a rat. But whatever it was lay inert. She peered down, straining to see. It looked like a glove. Bending forward she touched it. It was warm. She drew her fingers back and then with her eyes adjusted to the gloom she saw what was on the earthen floor.

Her screams seemed to go on forever.

Chapter 15

Her body raged. The natural defences fought against the biological insult brought about the vampire's attack. Massive loss of blood coupled with the beginnings of contamination caused her system to veer wildly and feverishly in an attempt to repair the damage.

Rapid eye movement behind closed lids showed she was in a state of high dreaming. Images of blood and lust swirled through her unconscious mind, creating a disturbing hybrid of fear and sexual excitement.

The heat in the bedroom was stifling and sweat plastered her hair against her forehead. The clamminess of her skin moulded the nightdress to her body. And always the dreams returned to the same image. A red mouth fastening on a white breast. The sound of sucking and the feeling of sexual ecstasy. Even unconscious her body reacted. Her hips raised and lowered as if in the throes of intercourse.

It was the chiming of the clock that brought Lilian back to consciousness. The sonorous striking cut through the deep layers of sleep and her eyes flickered open. For a moment she didn't know where she was. Her addled senses struggled to make sense of her surroundings. With difficulty she drew her arms out from under the heavy pile of blankets and wiped the perspiration from her eyes and face.

The weight of her coverings was oppressive and despite her weakness she managed to push most of the top layer onto the floor. She sighed with relief as a waft of slightly cooler air rippled over her. Lilian lay still for a few moments and then with a series of little struggling movements managed to sit on the edge of the bed. She was light-headed and a spell of dizziness caused her to feel faintly sick. After sitting still for a little while this feeling passed and she slid off the bed and stood up.

Her legs felt weak and rubbery and she half-leant back to support herself on the headboard. So weak. So tired. Gathering herself she stood up and by an effort of will tottered with trembling legs over to the window. She drew back the curtains and at once made a little moue of annoyance as the light, coupled with snow glare, lanced her eyes. She shielded her face until eventually she could look, with some discomfort, at the scene below. London was still in the thrall of the blizzard and a heavy fall during the night had buried the streets so laboriously cleared the day before.

A knock on the door was followed by Agnes entering. She carried a tray. Her eyes widened in amazement when she saw Lilian by the window.

'Mrs Bowers! You're awake! Here, you shouldn't be walking about like that.'

The girl put the tray down on a chair by the door and scurried over to where Lilian stood.

'Now, you come on back to bed, Mrs Bowers. You'll make yourself ill again.'

On the slow trip across the room Lilian learned her husband had gone to work but had left strict instructions that he should be sent for immediately if his wife worsened. He had also arranged for the doctor to call later that day.

Lilian sat upright on the bed, her back supported by a bank of pillows. She had steadfastly refused to lie under the stifling pile of coverings again. Agnes fetched the tray, containing a bowl of broth and some dry toast and sat on the edge of the bed. She took out a little napkin and fixed it around her mistress's neck. As the girl leant across her Lilian could smell the fresh skin, could smell the scent of carbolic soap. For an instant she felt an impulse to softly lick the girl's smooth vital neck that lay so close to her lips.

As Agnes sat back Lilian felt a wave of shame sweep through her. How could she have thought such a thing? And yet the idea thrilled her. Agnes, unaware, lifted a spoonful of broth and tried to feed Lilian who dutifully opened her mouth.

As soon as she tasted the broth Lilian gagged. The little that had gone into her mouth was spat back into the spoon, some spattering her nightdress. Agnes tutted and wiped the mess away with a napkin from the tray. The girl's tone was tender. She asked Lilian if maybe she could manage a little dry toast. Lilian refused, even though she now felt hungry. Instinctively she knew she could not eat anything yet.

Agnes wiped the woman's face and hands with a flannel and then plumped up the pillows to make her more comfortable. As she did so she again leant over her again. For an instant an image filled Lilian's mind.

She was kissing and biting every inch of the girl's naked body.

Chapter 16

CUTTING FROM THE 'EAST LONDON ADVERTISER':

DOUBLE MURDER HORROR IN LIMEHOUSE

The bodies of a man and woman were found in the early hours of Wednesday morning. Judging by the savage nature of the attack, it is thought the dead couple were the victims of a homicidal maniac…

<u>Extracts of Post-Mortem Reports by Dr Gerald Mansfield Melvin Police Surgeon (Limehouse Dist)</u>

The man is approximately 30-35 years of age. He appears to be well-nourished and there are no obvious signs of ill-health previous to his death. The body was found face down. The victim had obviously recently indulged in sexual activity.

Death was as a result of two wounds, resembling animal bites, to the deep tissue of the neck. His exsanguine condition could be explained by massive loss from the wounds, although there was little or no blood in the vicinity of the corpse….

The body is that of a young woman, approximately 16-20 years old. She was found lying on her left side. Semen in and around her mouth point to sexual activity immediate to her demise. Death was as a result of two small, but deep wounds to the neck, resulting in fatal blood loss. The damage pattern suggests an animal attack rather than they were caused by a knife or any other weapon.

The exsanguine condition of the corpse matches that of the male victim, and the same lack of blood in the vicinity is puzzling…

George Bowers sat on the edge of the bed and held his wife's hand. Relief, mixed with gratitude, filled him as he saw her face had regained its natural colour. The hand he held was warm and glowed with the pulse of life. He smiled and squeezed her fingers gently. Lilian tiredly returned the smile.

She lay back against a hill of snowy white pillows, her copper hair spread out like a sunburst around her head. Despite the fact that she was obviously exhausted her eyes shone with an unnatural brilliance. Bowers had noticed them as soon as he had entered the room. She had wonderful eyes anyway, but now they had grown *compelling.* That was the word that had sprung to mind when he noticed how lustrous her eyes were. They were eyes that caught and drew and held the gaze.

He lifted one of her hands to his lips and kissed the back gently.

'Would you like something to eat? You really should.'

Lilian shook her head, the voice still weak, but more growing in strength as the hours passed.

'No, no thank you, George.'

She reached up and stroked his face. Her touch sent a tingle across his skin and he felt ashamed that so tender a gesture at once caused stirrings in his loins. Since he had entered the room his wife had exuded an overwhelming sensuality. It took all his mental strength to concentrate on her in a tender sense and not in a sexual one.

But her whole image was that of the ultimate male sexual fantasy. Her hair, shone with a deep burnished lustre, her eyes, mysterious, compelling, challenging, her mouth had become fuller. The lips, redder. Even the modest nightdress seemed to cling to her provocatively. The neck, slightly open, showing a hint of tempting cleavage. Ironically her narrow escape from death had left her even more desirable.

With an effort he drew his eyes from her breasts and taking hold of her hand again spoke quietly to her.

'Do you still have no idea what happened, Lilian?'

She furrowed her brow in concentration for a few seconds and then shook her head.

'I remember the snow…and music…'

'Music? What music?'

Again Lilian shook her head. 'I don't know.' She closed her eyes for a moment and then opening them said, 'Eyes, red eyes. And a stinging…' Her voice died away as if the effort of speaking had drained what little energy she had. George patted her hand gently. 'All right, plenty of time. The main thing is to rest and get well.'

He stood up and moving across kissed her tenderly on the mouth. Her lips felt soft and parted slightly with the pressure of his. Again he felt his manhood stir and it was with some difficulty he fought the desire to push his tongue into her mouth and cup his hands around her full breasts.

Stepping back Bowers put on an air of heartiness. 'Well, in a day or two we'll have you ready for anything, dear.' He picked up his jacket and put it on. He had a business meeting at Greenwich that day. He would have cancelled it if it hadn't been so important. There was a lot of money at stake and a lot of people depending on him. He shook his head apologetically.

'I'm really sorry about having to go to this bloody meeting, Lilian. If I could get out of it…well you know I would.'

Lilian waved away his apologies. 'Of course you've got to go, George. I'm fine. Agnes is here.' George clasped his hands together as if giving a pledge. 'After this I'll be here all day till you get better I promise.'

At the door of the bedroom he looked back and blew a kiss. The door closed and Lilian lay alone. She closed her eyes and an image of a mouth dripping blood across a breast flashed across her mind. She whimpered and opened her eyes again. She was afraid to sleep, in sleep came the dreams of blood and sex.

She shivered despite the warmth of the room. With George gone she felt more afraid, felt a desolation of spirit.

Thick snowflakes danced past the windows as the afternoon began to deepen. She wished she had asked George to draw the blinds before he went.

The light, it hurt her eyes.

Chapter 17

They took him to places that echoed madness.

Noise beat at his head like a club.

The door opened and grave men, with grave voices conferred in low tones and looked towards him. With owl-wise expressions they studied papers and muttered and mumbled.

One of them came to him and said something. He may have understood but he was beyond the effort of translating it.

Even when they all gathered round with the full power of their combined owl-wise expressions and raised his eyelids and felt his wrist and listened to his chest his utter indifference was overwhelming.

They gave him something to drink and he drank it. Then he slept.

Like he was dead…

Chapter 18

Only light from the street lamps broke the gloom. This oblong of illumination, set against the wall opposite the window, was dappled by the dancing outlines of snowflakes. Lilian stared at the ever-changing patterns. A moving, fascinating shadow show.

She had lain awake for many hours staring at the animated wall. She had no idea of the time but she knew it was late. She felt alone and afraid and wished George would return soon.

She needed him to be there. She needed someone to be there to watch over her so that when she slept and the dreams of blood and sex woke her she would feel safe.

Her eyes burned with fatigue and she closed them for a moment.

Mina Murray's eyes. Her red mouth on her breast!

Lilian snapped awake. She trembled. A flicker of memory. In Mina's house. There was talk of Jenny. A pain in her bosom and then such ecstasy.

Lilian, with shaking hands, gently opened the top of her nightdress and slipped her hand down onto her left breast. She winced in pain as she felt the tender, inflamed flesh. Her finger played around the area and found what seemed to be two small indentations. Even pressed gingerly these sent a stab of pain through her. Dear God, what's happening? What's happening?

Lilian wanted to rise, to call out, to have light and sound and people fill the room. But even in such a state her innate strength of character and pride would not allow her to such a public display of weakness.

She closed her eyes again. Sheer exhaustion overcame her resistance. And when rest came it was at last dreamless.

It was the chill of the air on her uncovered shoulders which brought her back to consciousness. She shivered and turned towards the window. *It was wide open!*

For a few seconds she was unable to comprehend what had happened. The lace curtains billowed and swayed as the icy breeze swirled around the room, carrying small flurries of snow across the carpet. Had someone come in and opened the window? Cold. It was so cold. She saw her breath on the air.

Lilian tried to sit up and felt a wave of nausea sweep over her. She fell back and closed her eyes for a few seconds. When she opened them *Mina stood over her!*

Lilian stared up at the terrible beauty of the vampire. A mixture of terror and adoration filled her. Mina wore a long black cloak over a low-cut gown of the same colour. Her scarlet lips parted slightly and she ran her tongue lightly over them.

'Mina?' Lilian's voice was plaintive, like that of a child meeting a parent both worshipped and feared. Without a word Mina sat on the edge of the bed. She gently stroked Lilian's forehead and then teased her long cool fingers down the woman's face. As the vampire's fingers brushed her lips Lilian licked them with darting animal-like motions.

Mina smiled and held the woman in the psychic trance woven by all vampires. To dominate the will of mortals, coupled with an irresistible sexual allure, gave the revenants eager victims.

The vampire leant low over the human and kissed her on the mouth. Lilian moaned with a rising sexual excitement. But the unbearable eroticism of the kiss could still not disguise the faint under-taste of the grave.

Mina pulled top of the nightdress down, exposing her victim's breasts. She could hear the throb of life in every vein. She bent nearer and kissed the warm, firm flesh. Her tongue found the erect pink nipple and she teased and sucked at it until it was hard and erect. The surging rise of hunger rose to a madness in her brain. Her razor teeth brushed the marks of her previous feeding, causing Lilian to moan.

The vampire was now beyond all but her own needs. She widened her mouth, sank her fangs deeply into the yielding tissue and began to feed.

Two wagons were slewed across the road as the cursing carters struggled to unhitch their horses in the steadily falling snow. In the middle of Baker Street traffic piled up in an impatient stream of tooting and hooting behind a harassed Peugeot driver whose elegant car, with its long body and canopy hood, had skidded into the side of an oncoming tram. George could see the unfortunate motorist alternate between shouting at the tram driver and shaking his fist at those behind who demanded he get his car out of the way.

Bowers sighed. The journey back from his meeting at Greenwich had been a nightmare. The severity of the weather had caused chaos. Trains ran late and the streets became almost impassable. It was nearly one in the morning and now his taxi had ground to a halt amid the carnage.

He decided to walk and shoving a few coins into the taxi driver's hand he stepped into the blizzard. The severity of the cold blast took his breath away. Pulling up his coat collar he strode as fast as he could through deep drifts.

West London ceased to be a familiar place and he peered constantly to take sight of recognizable landmarks. At times he almost fell over as the snow disguised the edges of pavements and the dips of gutters.

At last he reached Kensington High Street and clumped his way to his front door. His hands were so cold he could hardly grip his keys properly. It was only with a great effort he at last managed to open the door.

He stepped quickly inside, closing the door quietly so as not to disturb the rest of the household. The dark hallway, although not particularly warm, felt like a tropical zone after the biting wind and snow.

George was hungry and he thought for a moment of going to the kitchen and making a sandwich before going upstairs. But the thought of scrabbling around in a darkened pantry trying to find things put him off. Besides, he was anxious to make sure Lilian was alright.

As he opened the bedroom door a thrill of horror overwhelmed him. His wife lay sprawled across the bed, her head and shoulders clear of the mattress, her hair trailing almost to the floor. The image took a moment to register. Bowers was transfixed. The sight of her bare breasts and throat covered with rivulets of blood, the marble skin. The curtains blowing and fluttering, the wind riffling the pages of a book on the bedside table.

His trance lasted only an instant before he rushed across the room and lifted her back into bed. She felt so cold. So cold. He called her name several times but she remained insensible.

Bowers pulled her nightdress closed and then covered her with blankets. He rushed to the door and called loudly for the servants before hurrying back to his wife's side. Lilian was icily still.

Only the wheeze as she gasped for breath indicated life. He rubbed at her arms and shoulders and whispered frantic endearments, promises that she'd be fine.

A noise behind him announced the arrival of a wide-eyed Agnes, who wore an ordinary street coat over her nightwear. Bowers called urgently. 'Get hot water bottles, then make up the fire.' The girl turned to leave and then he called her back. 'Agnes, for God's sake shut that damned window.'

As the girl crossed to follow his orders the cook arrived at the door. She gave a little gasp of surprise when she saw the scene. George spoke more calmly. 'Mrs Bowers has had some sort of accident. I'm going to phone the doctor. Cook, I want to stay here, don't leave her for an instant. An instant. You understand?'

The woman nodded, still unable to take her eyes off Lilian's bloodstained form. Bowers had to call again sharply, telling her to sit by the bed. The cook reluctantly came forward and joined him. He patted her on the shoulder in reassurance and then raced downstairs to phone.

Left alone the cook glanced around the room nervously. She could not shake off a feeling of dread. There was something in the room which affected her at an atavistic level. A natural antenna which all humans once had but was now buried beneath layers of civilization, was telling her she was in the presence of evil.

Lilian moaned softly and turned, pushing down the bedclothes as if they were constricting her breathing. The cook stood uncertainly for a moment, unwilling to approach the sleeping figure. Finally her fears were overcome by her need to guard the woman's welfare as best she could. She took the edge of the bedclothes and began to pull them up over Lilian. As she did so the top of the nightdress had fallen open again and she could see the source of the blood. Above two similar, but partly healed wounds were twin punctures. It was from these the thick dry threads of blood ran.

Raised a catholic the cook had not practised her religion for many years, yet as she saw the wounds she instinctively made the sign of the cross.

Chapter 19

They stared at the immenseness. As high as they could look and as long as they could see. Across the steel, workers swarmed like drones. Inside, opulence beyond dreams was being formed out of the chaos. The ship rose like a supreme gesture to humanity's mastery of the earth.

The two men saw again and wondered at what stood before. Never had the world seen such a ship, majestic in its power, awesome in its scale. One of the men let his gaze once more run along her lines. He shook his head and spoke in a manner that was almost a prayer.

'God himself couldn't sink this ship.'

Chapter 20

The doctor pulled on his coat, lifted his bag and stepped outside. The heavy door closed behind him, leaving a haggard and distraught Bowers alone in the hallway.

A massive blood loss! The words echoed in his mind. No explanation. Fresh wounds in her breast had bled a little but the doctor had ruled out them being the source. He'd told Bowers that losing that amount through the wounds would have resulted in the sheets and bed being saturated.

The physician's professional mask of imperturbability had slipped when he arrived and saw the terrible deterioration in his patient in the space of a few hours. The streaks of blood had been sponged from Lilian's face and body but her condition was still shocking. She struggled for breath and she veered between shivering with cold chills and tearing away the bedclothes as she began to burn up.

George, almost beside himself with anguish, had questioned the servants closely. None of them could throw any light on how such a thing could have happened. All doors were locked and the window was twenty feet high. Logic told Bowers that only someone in the house could have entered the room and opened the window, but who? He trusted the household implicitly and it was obvious by their own shocked reaction that the condition of his wife had been as much a horrifying surprise to them as it was to him.

Since Lilian's illness had so dramatically worsened there had been a muted atmosphere in the house. The inhabitants had walked softly, spoken in whispers. All the day to day tasks had been performed almost as reverential rituals. Pots were gingerly placed back on racks, cutlery was slipped carefully back into trays, crockery was set silently. It was almost as if all vitality had been drained from the house, and in its place a feeling a dread.

Bowers stood at the door, lost in a vortex of despair. So much, so soon. Only a week or so ago it seemed as if his wife was at last beginning to emerge from the purgatory of their child's death. Life had started happen. And now this!

He was so dazed by the enormity of his grief that Agnes's presence didn't register until she touched him gently on the shoulder. He turned to the girl and could see signs of recent crying. Her reddened eyes held all the sadness he, too, felt. She spoke quietly again and he realized that she was asking him if he'd like something to eat. He shook his head.

He told her he had to go out for a little while, to the chemists. He held out the prescription the doctor had given him, almost like a child with a note to the teacher, a validation of his absence.

He put on his coat slowly. His movements were heavy and lifeless. Lifting his hat he spoke intently to Agnes, reassuring her he would be back as quickly as possible and that she must check is wife's condition regularly until he returned. The girl nodded her acquiescence. Bowers opened the door and pulled his coat tighter about his neck as the frigid wind gusted around him. He stepped outside and the door slammed closed.

Agnes stood in the desolate hallway. Only the ponderous tick of the grandfather clock set against the far wall broke the silence. This was her home, had been for two years, yet at that moment she wished she were somewhere, anywhere else. With Bower's instructions in mind she walked to the bottom of the stairs intending to go up and check on her mistress. As she placed one foot on the tread a nameless dread suddenly filled her.

She stared upwards. At the top of the stairs the landing ran both ways. She could see the door of the master bedroom where Lilian lay. Agnes loved Mrs Bowers, thought her wonderful, yet she could not take that second step. She could not make her way up those stairs, *she could not go into that bedroom!*

Atavistic fear fought a duel with duty and common sense. Agnes knew there was no reason on God's earth why she should not go up those stairs. Yet...

She mentally chided herself. Come on, Agnes, get hold of yourself, girl. Acting like you're daft! The maid took another tentative step up before suddenly turning and running from the hallway and down into the warmth and companionship of the kitchen.

Police constable John Johnson cursed as his foot crunched through the film of ice plunging him ankle deep into freezing water. Another string of expletives filled the air as the bone-chilling liquid rose over the top of his boot and down into his sock.

The profanities were ground out quietly through teeth clenched tight with frustration and rage. That's all he needed at the start of his shift. He lifted his foot out of the deep puddle, which had been hidden by a coating of snow, and shook his leg as if to shake it dry. He knew the gesture was futile. The damage was done. His sock was sodden with the dirty slush.

He sighed and knew all he could do was carry on walking his beat. His face wrinkled with annoyance as every second step was accompanied by an uncomfortable squelch. His misery was compounded by the snow which had relented for a few hours but now began to skim down again on the bitter wind.

As he made his way along the Limehouse Basin, a route which provided a link between the Thames and the Grand Union Canal, he wondered whether his decision to join the Metropolitan Police a few months earlier had been such a good idea.

Johnson was a tall, strapping man with a fair complexion. So many people had told him that with his height and build he should join the police. After a while the idea of being in uniform appealed. He imagined himself the object of general admiration. They said girls liked a man in uniform and if truth be told that was perhaps his main motive for joining the force. He had no doubt he cut a fine figure in the dark blue of the Met. However the walking in the snow with a boot full of ice, on a winter's evening, was not what he envisioned.

He crossed the road and made his towards the river. The waterfront was the furthermost edge of his beat. From there he would turn and make his way back into the heart of district.

The streets were almost empty, only the occasional scurrying denizen could be seen in the distance. The constable knew that the night would be quiet. The criminals didn't like the wind and snow any more than the respectable folk.

Suddenly he stopped and listened. Carried on the breeze was the faintest of cries. He waited for a repeat. When none came he thought it might have been the call of a seagull, although he had never heard the birds active at night before. He was about to move off again when he heard the cry again. It was human and it was of someone in deep distress.

The policeman moved quickly in the general direction of where he thought the sound might have come from. The area he was in was a labyrinth of wharves. Dark buildings merged into one another. Johnson stopped and listened intently. No other sound but the wind and a far-flung ship's horn broke the silence. After another few moments he began to relax. False alarm.

His heart-rate began to settle down into its normal rhyme and he turned to resume his regular beat when he heard it, a faint moan. It seemed to come from one of the narrow entrances to a wharf nearby.

The policeman moved forward, listening intently. Then it came again, a moan which subsided in a little despairing sigh.

The truncheon was the only protection afforded police officers but he grasped it tightly as he moved silently into the opening. He peered down the entrance. At first he could see nothing but then against the snow there were shapes, dark shapes. It seemed as if there was someone on the ground a second figure bending over them.

'What's going on here?' His voice bounced and echoed between the brickwork of the narrow confines. There was no reaction from the two figures. He called again. 'I'm a police officer. What's happening here?' It was if he didn't exist.

Angered by the temerity in ignoring a policeman he stepped nearer the two figures. As he did so he took out the tubular whistle which was part and parcel of an officer's equipment.

He called again. 'Did you hear me, mate? I'm a police officer and I want to know what you're up to.'

Nearer he could see that the figure leaning over whoever was on the ground was a woman. The end of the long cloak lay splayed out across the snow. Luxurious black hair streamed down over the hood.

John Johnson was a reasonably brave man, but as he approached the two figures a sudden sense of terror gripped him and it was only by a supreme act of will he continued.

He reached out and touched the shoulder of the crouching figure.

His last image on earth was of a white face of terrifying beauty and a mouth open and bloody.

Then he fell back in the snow and the vampire took him

An unfocused, unknowable want racked her body. Lilian tossed and turned in a delirium. Reality and unreality merged and parted. The material world ebbed and flowed through her half-open eyes.

She could see that she was in her own bedroom but then crimson billows flooded her mind. Images of grinning terrors and naked bodies locked in frenzied lust danced across her vision. Amid it all was the figure of Mina, naked, desirable. Calling to her. Calling to her…

Lilian sat up. Though she felt dreadfully weak, her mind was clear. She knew only one thing. She had to go to Mina.

The light from the lamp was turned low but there was enough illumination for her to find her clothes. Every movement was exhausting. Her body, drained of blood, could not generate enough energy to her muscles, so the simplest movements became Herculean tasks.

Painstakingly she at last managed to dress. Her boots proved to be the most difficult. Every time she leant forward to put them on she would become light-headed and nauseous. Twice she almost fell face first onto the floor as she tried to fit her feet into the boots. At last by a dint of perseverance and treating the process as a series of slow separate, careful stages she managed to don the footwear.

Cautiously she opened the bedroom door and looked out. The landing was empty. Stepping onto the thick pile of the Axminster carpet she pulled her coat around her shoulders and made her way silently to the top of the stairs.

She looked along to the hallway. There were no signs of the household. She began to make her way downstairs. Her movements were stiff and uncertain. It was the gait of an old woman. At one point she had to stop as a wave of vertigo made her feel as if she was going to pitch forward. Clutching tightly onto the banister she waited until the dizziness subsided and then she resumed her slow descent.

It seemed an eternity before she reached the bottom and she stood there for a few moments gathering her strength. Her biggest fear was that her husband or any of the household would appear and bar the way.

From the direction below stairs she could hear the faint buzz of voices and a burst of laughter. Steadying herself Lilian Bowers let go of the banister and crept over to the front door.

As she reached for the handle the chime of the grandfather clock broke the silence, startling her. Her heart, beating furiously in an attempt to compensate for her bloodless state, fluttered even more rapidly and she felt faint. She closed her eyes for a few seconds and when she felt a little better turned the door handle.

She smiled. In a little while she would be with Mina.

Bowers had a nightmare in trying to find a chemist to fill the prescription. The local pharmacy on Kensington High Street was closed and he'd tramped all the way along Marylebone Road as far as Tottenham Court Road before he found a shop still open. His anxiety to get back as soon as possible was compounded by the fact that conditions had brought traffic to a standstill. No taxis or buses were moving so walking was his only alternative.

An errand which should have taken him ten minutes had demanded an hour and a half and by the time he reached home he was in an angry mood. On entering the house he went straight up stairs. He was anxious Lilian should have the prescribed medicines as soon as possible.

He tapped the door gently and waited. When there was no reply he turned the handle and peeked into the room.

He saw the bed was empty. But it was only when he saw the wardrobe wide open and signs of her clothes scattered across the floor that fear struck him to the core of his being.

Chapter 21

The journey had been an endless and excruciating ordeal of jolting and jogging. As the horse-drawn cab rattled over cobbles and pot-holes every judder sent pain lancing through Lilian's wasted body.

She lay back against the leather seat, barely able to keep from crying out as the cab made its way through the snow-bound streets of the capital. A gap in the drawn blind showed her a city of silence. Barely another vehicle on the road. The white blanket deadened sound, turning London mute.

On the box the driver lowered his head against the flailing gusts and cursed himself for taking the fare. Almost every other cab in the metropolis was at a standstill. He, too, was about to leave the rank and head back to the stable when the woman approached, a beautiful woman who was the colour of death. She had asked him to make the journey to Limehouse. The driver was struck by the sheer sexual allure she exuded as she looked up at him from the pavement. Despite his reluctance to refuse a creature of such seductive beauty he had no intention of fighting his way through several miles of stricken roads.

It was only when she offered him the ring he changed his mind. She took it from the finger of her right hand. Even in the half-light he could see it was a thing of rare beauty. The diamond cluster sent rainbows glittering and dancing from its centre.

The combination of the imploring look from the beautiful woman, coupled with the magnificence of the ring, changed his mind. He told her to get in. In a low, wasted voice she gave an address in Limehouse.

Now, after a struggle of nearly two hours they were nearing the end of the odyssey. The driver was unfamiliar with this part of east London and he called down to a passer-by who pointed towards the road he was looking for.

The entrance to Church Row had two iron posts in the middle preventing vehicles going down the narrow thoroughfare. It was here the cab stopped. The melancholy horse lowered his head against the driving snow and stood stock still as the driver climbed down. He made a cursory attempt to wipe the sheeting of whiteness from his coat and face before opening the door.

For a moment he thought the woman was asleep, or worse. She lay still. Her face was ashen and there was no sense of life about her. It was only when he called to her three times did her eyes open slowly. She seemed to take a few seconds to gather herself. The driver repeated they were nearly at her destination. A wane smile flicked briefly and she thanked him in a weak voice.

He held out his hand and she grasped it gratefully. She barely seemed to have the strength to rise from the seat. As she stepped down the driver looked at her again. She was so obviously distressed; so obviously very ill. He looked along the solitary length of Church Row. On one side there were tidy houses with gardens while the other was a terrace of non-descript dwellings. Perhaps because of the lack of life on the street, or the straightness of the row which made the end converge in a point at some distant infinity, the place seemed vaguely menacing.

The driver, who was a typical hard-bitten cabbie, generally caring for nothing except the fare being paid, felt a twinge of unease that he was leaving woman so obviously ill alone in this desolation.

He told her that the cab couldn't go any further but that she could reach her destination by walking to the end of the thoroughfare. She thanked him. Her voice, though faded, was cultured and melodic. She began to make her way slowly down the row. He watched her struggle through the snow, her balance precarious. He held his breath as at one point he thought she was going to fall. But she managed to right herself in with a slow, measured effort. It was then he called to her. Asked her if she'd like him to walk her down. She seemed oblivious to his question. She tottered onwards. He called again but when she failed to respond he shrugged and climbed back on his cab. As he turned the horse he looked back up the row. He could see her in the distance. For some reason he thought of a funeral.

Bowers stood outside the police station. He leant against the wall. His mind raced and whirled. He was overcome by utter despair. Gone! She was gone! He relived the horror of finding Lilian had disappeared. The mad, shouting run through the house. The screaming at the servants. The frantic search of every room, every cupboard, every pantry.

He had ranted and raved at Agnes, who was in hysterics. He had managed to get her to calm down enough give her side of the story. At first she had tried to say she had looked in on her mistress but after Bowers questioned her fiercely, browbeat her on detail, she admitted that she had not paid a visit to the room after he left. He found her mumbled reasons for not doing so, she was 'afraid' only sent him into a greater fury. He dismissed her on the spot and gave her ten minutes to leave the house.

A frantic hour passed while he rang every friend and relation they had. This time there was no social pretense for asking if she was there. He told all that she had been ill and had disappeared. All had promised to ring him if she turned up.

The police were his next step. His visit to the station had infuriated him. He had expected the entire machinery of law enforcement to swing into action to find Lilian. Instead what he got was a bureaucratic desk sergeant who painstakingly and meticulously wrote down the facts. George Bowers came near to hauling the man across the desk. His wife was missing! His wife was missing!!

Missing spouses, it seemed were a daily occurrence in London and the desk sergeant made it plain that a city-wide hunt was not going to be a priority. As far as he was concerned the matter was in hand. It was only by a combination of persistence and mentioning a few highly-placed friends Bowers had managed to secure an interview with a Detective Inspector.

The plain-clothes officer was sympathetic but after elucidating that he had no evidence that his wife had been removed by force he, too, slipped into procedural mode. A lecture on how many people went missing every day was lost on Bowers. He shouted angrily that he wasn't interested in how many *other* people went missing he wanted them to find his wife.

The detective told him if she hadn't returned in a few days they would of course circulate her description to all hospitals in the area. At one point the officer had even subtly but unmistakably hinted at a lover being involved. The dangerous look in Bowers eyes told him to back off that particular line of enquiry.

George Bowers was now adrift in a sea of despair. He looked blankly around. People moved back and forth, all with their own dreams and hopes and fears, all oblivious to the utter desolation of the smartly-dressed man who stood dazedly outside the police station. Finally stirring from his stupor Bowers moved stiffly away from the entrance. He had no idea what to do next.

She awoke in the darkness. A stygian blackness that pressed on her like a mask. Lilian called out. She called out for George. Only her own voice echoed back mockingly. She tried to sit up but she was so weak. It was as if her limbs had turned to water. Again she tried to sit up before falling back, a sob of frustration escaping into the dark.

So weak. So helpless. All energy gone. Fear gnawed at her soul. Where was she? How had she got here? She closed her eyes to think. The gesture was unnecessary as the darkness was all embracing, but the human reflex remained.

She tried to recall what had happened. She was in bed and George…The images swam and merged. There was a journey, and snow. Fragments, strange and disjointed appeared and reappeared in her mind's eye. Houses and people and a strange place. She opened her eyes again hoping somehow this was all a dream and she'd be back in her own bed.

She felt faintly sick and turned her head to the side. The backs of her hands felt the rough texture of stone. She moved them carefully, feeling the expanse fan out as far as her outstretched arms. A floor, she was on a stone floor.

The feeling of nausea passed and she raised her head and listened carefully, hoping to hear some noise, some auditory clue to where she was. The only sound which broke the silence was her own laboured breathing.

A house! The image blazed across her mind. She had stood in front a great house. In the snow. She could picture the whiteness caught in the cuticles of the windows. A heavy door. How had she got there? Again fragmented pictures of a long journey. And something sparkled! Something she held. She thought she could see herself falling down in front of the house. Then the memories skipped away before she could tie them down, before she could impose order.

Lilian steeled herself to make the ultimate effort to move. Taking a deep breath she levered herself into a sitting position, her arms trembling at the effort. Painfully she slowly turned onto her hands and knees. The attempt had made her feel dreadful. Every limb screamed and her head started to pound with a deep-seated throb. After taking a few seconds to gather herself she tottered to her feet and stood there swaying uncertainly till the thudding in her brain subsided.

The completeness of the dark was so disorientating. She had no idea whether she was a large room or a small one. Then she remembered the echo when she'd called out. How long the echo was would surely indicate the size of the chamber.

She called out, not a word but just a sound. By the resonance she was sure the room was relatively small. The stonework on the floor would certainly suggest she was in something like a cellar.

Shuffling forward, with her arms outstretched, she began to search for a door. Her fingers jarred against rugged stonework and she carefully traced along its length. Her plan was to follow the lines of the room until she came to a door.

It was then she heard the tinkle of mocking laughter.

A thrill of terror shook Lilian Bowers. She turned desperately trying to gauge where the sound had come from. A sob escaped her lips and her voice broke as she called out, 'Who's there? Please, who's there?' Her question was answered by laughter again. It was then she felt cold hands grasp her by the shoulder from behind. A voice, sweeter than music whispered her name. Lips played at her neck. All the need in Lilian Bowers came to the fore. The psychic power of Mina overwhelmed her senses once again. She gave herself to the hungry mouth. A terrifying passion was born and she whimpered with lust as there in the inky blackness Mina's hands, claw-like, closed around her breasts and the vampire's canines penetrated her soft flesh.

The erotic charge of the revenant's bite took her to a place of sublime sexual excitement. The feel of that relentless mouth on her neck, draining her of vitality, but raising her to supreme orgasm was worth her very soul.

The feeding seemed to go on for an eternity, the soft sucking sounds were the only things to break that dark silence. The sublime sexual pleasure began to give way to a falling, a loss of being. Lilian felt her heart literally grow cold. Her senses receded. Hearing became faint, touch numbed until she could no longer feel the lips on her neck or the fangs in her flesh. Desolation filled the void once inhabited by her humanity. Slipping away, slipping away.

She felt amorphous, her limbs no longer held her and she knew she would have fallen had not the vampire's hands on her breasts held her in an iron grip. She knew she was drifting towards death. Her mind, no longer able to even create interior pictures, was cloaked in blackness. Darkness. Darkness. Everywhere.

It was then Mina stopped feeding. Lilian's heart fluttered its last feeble beats. The vampire held her up with one arm while with the other she slit her own wrist with a delicate slash of her fangs. The cold, thick blood oozed from the wound. Hardly had the cut been made than the accelerated metabolism of the *Nosferatu* began to heal it. Mina placed the cut against the mouth of the dying mortal.

Lilian was barely aware of the action. Death was only a few heartbeats away. The revenant's blood spilled over her lips, running down her chin. A few drops trickled slowly into her mouth.

Weakly she tried to spit it out but the vile bitter liquid ran to the back of her throat and she swallowed…

Chapter 22

Conan Doyle looked with sympathy at the broken man before him. The novelist cleared his throat. 'A whisky, I think, Mr Bowers.' His soft Scottish accent held nothing but kindness. Bowers sat unmoving until the glass was placed in his hand. 'Drink it down, man, ye'll feel better. It's not called 'The Water of Life' for nothing.'

The study was comfortable. Books lined the walls and a pen and ink drawing of Doyle's most famous creation, Sherlock Holmes, adorned the desk. The author waited until George took a healthy swig and then asked him to continue. Bowers shook his head apologetically.

'Look, I'm sorry Sir Arthur, coming to your door like this but I just don't…just don't…' The younger man's voice trailed away as he broke down. He vainly tried to wipe away the tears which began to trickle down his face.

Conan Doyle, with his burly appearance and large moustache, looked for all the world like a benign walrus. However despite his seemingly placid looks he was a shrewd and vigorous man who was not only extremely intelligent, but also infinitely resourceful. It was now he kindly but firmly encouraged Bowers to go on with his story. When at last Bowers reached the end, and told of the disappearance of his wife, the writer got to his feet and walked around the room.

Finally he broke the silence.

'It's certainly a strange case, Mr Bowers. And ye say the police have been no help?'

'They've circulated the hospitals. Put her picture up in the station.'

'And nothing? No possible sightings of her?'

George Bowers shook his head. Conan Doyle walked around the room again. Finally he sat behind his desk. 'The problem is, Mr Bowers, that if ye write stories about a detective, folk think ye *are* a detective. I get dozens of people writing to me, asking me to solve cases. But I'm only a writer, I'm *not* Sherlock Holmes.'

Doyle could see the man in front of him diminish as he spoke the words. All who came to him wanted him to have the deductive powers of his fictional creation.

He leant forward. 'But that doesn't mean there's nothing you can do, Mr Bowers.'

Bowers looked at the huge eye on the door, with its attendant motto WE NEVER SLEEP. Conan Doyle's suggestion that he go to the Pinkerton Private Detective Agency was not one which would have occurred to George. Raised in the belief that the British police force were the best in the world, and that only the properly constituted authorities should handle these matters, he now realized that to instigate his own investigation was the only way left.

He pushed the door open and stepped inside. The office was a hive of activity. Men moved backwards and forwards between the numerous desks. Papers were hand over. Pictures of criminals adorned the walls. Strangely enough Bowers found the energy of the room encouraging, at least it was a change from the lacklustre atmosphere he encountered every time he went to the police station.

As he reached the front desk a thin, rather daunting woman approached.

'May I help you, sir?' The warmth in her voice belied her severe look. Bowers took a breath. ' My name is Bowers, George Bowers. I'd…I'd like help in finding my wife. She's…she's disappeared.'

The woman acted as if what he's said was the most natural thing in the world.

'Of course, sir. I'll see the manager and arrange to have one of our detectives take your details.'

She walked across the room. Bowers was relieved. He hadn't known what to expect but he was pleasantly surprised by the matter of fact way the woman had handled his request. No rolling of the eyes, no heavy sighs of exasperation, all the reactions he'd come to know at the police station.

He saw the woman speak to a small, compact man and they both looked in his direction. George presumed the man was the office manager. He had the fierce, abrupt look of a man who manages.

The woman then went over to a desk where a middle-aged man sat. In front of him was a cup of tea. The secretary nodded in Bowers direction and the man at the desk took a quick sip of tea and then made his way across the room. Bowers could see that he had a slight limp.

He reached the front desk and put his hand out.

'Mr Bowers? My name is Harry Davis.'

Chapter 23

CUTTING FROM 'THE EAST LONDON ADVERTISER'

POLICEMAN AND CHILD IN DOUBLE 'WILD ANIMAL' KILLING

The bodies of a policeman and a ten year old child were found in Limehouse Basin in the early hours of Friday morning. Both victims showed signs of savage wounds to the throat. It is thought that the deaths may be the work of a wild animal, possibly brought to this country by a sailor…

     Davis was relieved that the snow had at last showed signs of abating. The flurries were lighter and for the first time in weeks there was the hint of a rise in temperature. He was grateful for small mercies. Tramping through the streets of London in a blizzard was not conducive to a man of his age, especially a man with a bad ankle.

     He stopped for a moment as he waited for the oncoming traffic to clear. He'd just finished the last of his visits to friends and family of Mrs Bowers. Her husband had given Harry a comprehensive list and he had worked his way through them meticulously. The distraught husband had assured him that he had contacted them all already and none of them knew her whereabouts.

     He had told Bowers he just wanted to double check in case anything had been overlooked, but his real motive was to ask the questions a husband wouldn't ask.

     At each house Harry had gently probed the character of Lilian Bowers, what type of woman she was. He was also able to ask the more brutal questions. Did she have a lover? Was she in some sort of financial trouble?

     These enquiries usually brought about angry or indignant looks but they had to be asked. Now he was certain there were none of the usual skeletons in the Bowers cupboard.

     A gap in the traffic allowed him to scurry across the road. In hopping over a puddle of slush by the side of the kerb he landed on his left ankle sending a bolt of pain up his leg. Christ! He kept forgetting! As he walked on red hot needles played around the damaged joint. He gritted his teeth and kept walking.

He turned his mind once again to his next move in the Bowers case. He had spoken to all the servants, including the girl dismissed by the angry husband. It was obvious none of them knew anything. What he did know was that Mrs Bowers had disappeared once before and had come back in a distressed state, unable to say where she'd been. It seemed logical that a second disappearance was linked to the same destination. Davis also knew that on both nights the weather had been vicious so unless the place was very near it was unlikely she had walked there.

Bowers had described her condition the first time she returned, so Davis was sure she could not have suffered that amount of distress if she had only travelled a relatively short distance. The detective believed it ruled out a nearby destination. He concluded she must have travelled a fair way and that would have meant transport.

He knew what to do next.

The change was terrible. She twisted and turned as her soul began to die. Her body became a thing of terrifying power. Muscles became invincible. Demonic energy burned its way through her being, cauterizing all that made her mortal.

Images of blood flowed like torrents through her mind washing away every emotion leaving her instead with a chilling singularity.

Blood first. Blood last. Blood always.

The super-heightened sexual urges characteristic of those in thrall to the vampire pounded her being.

Orgasm after orgasm followed as she reveled in thoughts of naked bodies on hers, she on theirs, doing things of hellish depravity.

Then came the great pain. She arched as a force gigantic seemed to reach inside her and tear away the centre of her being.

Tearing. Tearing. Tearing.

And then it stopped. There was a great lull. Her soul was lost and all that was left within her was a dark void.

She was a vampire.

'Thank God!' Bowers closed his eyes and whispered the words as he replaced the telephone. Davis had done what the police could not or would not do. On the phone he had just explained to George that he had made enquiries at every cab stand within a half mile radius of the house. At the third he'd struck lucky and found the driver who had driven Lilian Bowers the night she disappeared.

He looked down at the notes he had carefully taken as Davis spoke. An address in Limehouse? Why the hell would Lilian go to Limehouse? He then checked the instructions the detective had given him for meeting that evening. They were to rendezvous in a pub called Charlie Brown's, deep in the heart of the docks. Davis had assured him that he would have no trouble finding the place. Everybody in east London knew Charlie Brown's.

Bower's first instinct had been to rush down to the address himself but Davis had been very insistent that they go together. He had told George that it was a dangerous area, especially for those who didn't know it. He also added that two of them would be able to bring his wife home more easily than one. He left unsaid what that might mean. Davis was in court for the afternoon, giving evidence but he said he'd join the anxious husband as soon as he could.

Very reluctantly Bowers agreed to wait. He went to his room and drew a box from the bottom of his shoe cupboard. He opened it and took out a pistol. He then lifted up a handful of bullets and began to feed them one by one into the chamber.

What was dark was now light. She could see in the blackness. The super-sensitive eyes of the revenant scanned the wine cellar. She was indifferent to the trappings of humanity. Already the hunger was upon her.

The being that was once Lilian Bowers still had her appearance but the transition had also given her a new supernatural beauty. Her lips were fuller and redder, her eyes compelling. Her body had grown more voluptuous, breasts heavier, hips rounder. Her hair, too, was thicker and more abundant, the copper colour more burnished.

She moved towards the door which she could now see clearly. The world through her eyes was now almost sepia. All the finer senses were lost to the vampire and colour was only seen in the faintest of tints.

The door swung open at her touch. Lilian stepped into the room in which she had once spoken of her dead child. Jenny's memory was now indifferent to her, a mere shadow from another existence.

Standing in the centre of the room was Mina, her sister. Mina smiled, showing the full extent of the lengthened canines. She turned towards the settee. Lying there was a young man, perhaps in his late teens. He was unconscious. His face was deadly pale. Fair hair fell across his forehead and partially covered one eye.

Lilian crossed the room and stood over the still figure. She could see the fine blue veins just beneath the skin on his neck. She could hear his heart beat.

She knelt and began to feed.

Chapter 24

Bowers stared at the shrunken head. It stared back at him amid the most fantastical and bizarre setting he had ever experienced. Charlie Brown's pub was packed with sailors and dockers. The place was thick with tobacco smoke and the din of voices. Accents and languages from every part of the globe peppered the air.

The bar was stiflingly close. Bowers tried to ease himself some elbow room, but the place was jammed to the gunwales. A beefy, loud-voiced stevedore nudged him aside as he made his way through carrying several pints of beer in his massive hands.

George mumbled a faint apology and tried to find some space. Charlie Brown, the pub landlord, watched the scene impassively from behind the bar.. Bowers noted the sturdy build and broken nose and thought he looked just the type of man who could keep a place like this in order.

He was pushed aside again as a couple of sailors crushed past, shouting to shipmates at the other end of the bar. The action caused Bowers to spill beer down his coat. He wiped away the mess as best he could. He had actually taken little more than a sip of the strong London 'Bitter.' The taste, with its underlying tang of hops, was not to his liking. He had only bought it because he thought it was the right thing to order in a place like this. Bowers didn't want to be seen as standing out. He didn't realize his caution was unnecessary. Charlie Brown's pub was a gathering point of all nations and all types. A toff having a drink was unremarkable.

Having found a little space he again studied the shrunken head and the other curiosities which surrounded it. Lining the walls were spears and stuffed animals and carved elephants, a solemn Buddha and a hundred other items from the far ends of the globe.

George Bowers checked his watch. Davis was late. It had taken all George's self-control to wait for the detective. Several times during that long day he had resolved to go to the Limehouse address and seek his wife, now the delay was proving intolerable.

At the far end of the bar a small altercation was taking place. Voices were raised but Bowers saw Charlie Brown move in that direction and call out. He could not hear what was said but it had the desired effect. The ructions ceased.

George checked his watch again, for the third time in as many minutes. Suddenly he made his mind up. He would go alone. Lilian was his wife and he didn't need anyone holding his hand when looking for her. Besides, he told himself, every moment might count. Placing his glass on the bar he shouldered his way out of the pub, determined to find his missing spouse..

Davis cursed the traffic, cursed the legal system, cursed his swollen ankle. All three had caused him to be late. The trial, which should been dealt with quickly, had been held up by some legal obfuscation. Lawyers had gathered in conclave, like a murder of crows, to debate some fine point of law. This had held the whole thing up for the best part of the afternoon.

On finally leaving court the thawing snow had not helped the flow of traffic and it had taken the omnibus an eternity to reach Limehouse. Hurrying along had caused his ankle to swell painfully. It was with relief he turned into Garford Street and saw the cupola dome of Charlie Brown's.

As he stepped up to the entrance he noticed a couple of forlorn street women huddled under the shelter of the Blackwall Railway Bridge. Davis stopped in shock for a moment. Just for an instant he thought one of them was Mary, his estranged wife.

He looked again and saw that the resemblance was superficial. Nevertheless the shock had caused his heart to skip a beat for a few seconds. Pushing the door of the pub open he stepped inside.

The size and decaying splendour of the house surprised Bowers. To find such an elegant habitation rising amid the mean streets was not what he expected. George moved towards the main gates, which were a magnificent rusting fantasy of wrought-iron swirls and curves.

Peering through the metalwork he had to lean to one side to get a clear view of the house, due to the overgrown trees each side of the short path. He saw a glimmer of light on the ground floor of the otherwise darkened building.

Glancing around he took note of the dilapidated houses and run-down warehouses surrounding this great house by the river. He couldn't think of why Lilian should visit such a place!

He checked the address on the piece of paper before crushing it up into a ball and throwing it by the side of the stone pillars. He then pushed on the iron gates, half expecting in their rusting state they would resist. They swung open so easily that he stumbled forward onto the path. He regained his balance and walked up to the main door. As he approached the melting snow yielded and he heard the crunch of gravel.

At the main door he lifted the brass knocker and rapped smartly. The door of solid oak seemed to absorb most of the sound. He waited a few moments and then banged again with as much force as he could muster.

He waited. An icicle hanging from the ornate door lintel dripped steadily onto the metal shoe-scrapper set in the entrance. Bowers moved to the side and tried to peer in the window but the heavy drapes only allowed a sliver of light to escape from inside.

The cold was beginning to gnaw at his toes and he shivered as the wind whipped across the face of the house.

He was about to try the knocker again when the door swung slowly open. There, silhouetted against the glow, was a woman. Her face was lost in the shadow created by the backlighting but he swallowed as the opaque material of her dress showed the outlines of voluptuous figure. Bowers was held in the moment. He stared entranced.

'May I help you?' Her voice came out of the gloom. It was mellifluous and low.

Bower's felt his voice come from a long way off. 'My name is Bowers. I believe my wife came to this address, three days ago. She's missing.' The last remark tailed away. He felt…diminished in the presence of this woman.

Without a word she stepped aside and ushered him into the house. George Bowers took his hat off and stepped over the threshold. He found himself in a room of immense luxury to which he was oblivious. He was rapt by the presence of the beautiful woman he now recognized.

'You're Mrs Murray, I saw you once at…'

The blow was indifferent, a slight wave of the hand which sent Bowers spinning across the room. Shock and surprise mingled with the stunning effects of the slap. His head sang and blood poured from his broken nose. The man looked up at the smiling, beauteous figure who watched him with a terrible enigmatic smile on her face. He tried to speak but his addled senses were not up to the task and he sank into unconsciousness.

He swam to the surface from a deep black lake. Slowly his senses recovered from the concussive injury. His eyes flicked open and a blurred world appeared. The light sent jabs of pain stabbing into his brain. He closed his eyes again while his scrambled thoughts sought to reassert a pattern of logic.

Bowers slowly opened his eyes again and saw that he lay on a rough floor which he gradually began to realize was made up of flagstones. The circumstances of him being there suddenly became clear. The woman. Mrs Murray. He had been looking for…She hit him!

The shock of the realization brought Bowers out of the groggy state. She'd hit him! Why? Why? He sat up and instantly a blinding pain shot through his face. He yelped and gingerly touched his nose. He felt the dried blood and by the swelling and the difficulty he had in breathing through it he guessed it must be broken.

He got to his feet slowly and took stock of his surroundings. By the light of a dull yellow electric bulb he could see it was a wine cellar. The white-washed walls were festooned with dust and the cobwebs of many years. The cellar itself had several racks which rose almost to ceiling height, one behind the other, creating narrow passages between. Bowers saw there was a heavy door at one end of the room and without thinking he staggered towards it.

The handle was encrusted with rust. He turned it several times but the door was obviously locked. What the hell was happening? The surrealism of his situation made him incapable of taking it seriously. This could not be true!

He tried the door handle several times more and then shouted loudly to be let out. He called Mrs Murray's name. His voice bounced and echoed around the low-ceilinged room. He stopped. His head throbbed.

His mouth felt dry and he knew that before he could contemplate any further action he needed a drink. The first row of wine racks were empty so he made his way around to the second aisle. He stopped. His heart almost leapt from his chest.

Standing before him was Lilian!

Harry Davis put down his glass and prepared to fight his way through the crowd. There was no sign of Bowers. He'd been in Charlie Brown's more than an hour and was tired. The smoke in the bar stung his eyes and his ankle felt as if tiny devils were driving little white hot pitch-forks deep into the joint every time he tried to move.

He could only imagine Bowers had the same trouble as him travelling through the city. He considered calling his home but the chances of finding a telephone in this district were negligible. He then considered going to the address he'd been given by the cabbie, but the thought of traipsing through the snow at that time of night without his client in tow was not enticing.

Davis decided to go home. He'd call at Bowers house in the morning and they could take things from there. He gave a nod to Charlie Brown, who was an old acquaintance from his days on the force.

As he buttoned his coat he caught sight of the shrunken head. He shivered. Who the hell would want that bloody thing hanging in front of them while they had a pint?

George stared at his wife. 'Lilian?' It was his wife, but she was…different. Her hair fell to her shoulders in heavy cupreous coils. Her face was pale but imbued with a stunning beauty. Lips, lips red as rubies. His eyes were drawn to her dress. He recognized it but now it was off her shoulders, the buttons undone so that her breasts spilled out.

'Lilian?'

'George.' She reached her arms out to him. He moved forward slowly.

'Lilian how did you…Where have you…? His questions were lost on the air as she kept her arms stretched out to him.

'Come to me, George. Help me, George.'

Bowers moved to his wife. She smiled. He found the ruby mouth tantalizing. The teeth so white. He wanted to ask her…He wanted to ask her a question…But looking into her eyes thoughts drifted. There was something he must do but instead he looked deep into the depthless eyes.

She placed her hands on his shoulders and at her touch he felt an incredible jolt of sexual pleasure run through his body. His cock began to harden. He wanted that red mouth so much, so much.

He seemed to hear her voice in his head. Soft, soothing words. His sexual excitement increased as she leaned forward and put her mouth to his. Sweet, so sweet. The vampire who was once Lilian Bowers gently ran her tongue across his lips, licking and nibbling. Bowers was mesmerized by the sheer sexual aura surrounding the woman.

Her kisses moved down his cheek. She whispered strange unintelligible words which heightened his excitement. Her hand slid down to his erection. She rubbed his cock slowly and sensuously through his trousers. His muffled moans of carnality seemed to please her and she laughed, a chilling, mocking laugh.

George Bowers was so in thrall to the seductive power of the vampire he didn't hear the door of the cellar open.

He closed his eyes as Lilian kissed the sensitive skin of his neck. Her teeth played across the jugular vein. She laughed again and her laugh was echoed by Mina, who now stood behind their victim.

Death was approaching George Bowers, but at that moment he was lost in the throes of the greatest pleasure he had ever known.

Lilian's mouth was on one side of his neck, while Mina, behind him, gloated over the rich blood pumping through the other side.

In tandem the vampire sisters sank their fangs into the helpless man. Bowers stiffened in shock as the ecstasy of the unholy seduction turned to agony. He was held tight between them as his vital fluid was slowly drained.

His life began to slip away The last conscious image in his mind was of a shrunken head with dark blood spilling from between its sewn lips.

Chapter 25

The police had been to see him. Bowers had not returned home that night so the servants had contacted the local station. The investigating officers had found an entry in his diary about meeting Harry. Davis had explained to them the whole story, the vanishing wife, the meeting Bowers had missed.

The police went to the address Harry had given them. They seemed to think no one was living there. Harry had told them to double check his investigations and confirm with the cabbie that the missing wife had been taken to that particular address. Although they paid lip service to his comments he got the impression they were concentrating all their energies into the spate of deaths that had taken place in the east end in the past few weeks. The fact that one of the victims was a policeman gave an added impetus to the hunt.

The detective who had spoken to Davis had known him when he was on the force so there was little of the animosity the police generally showed when dealing with private detectives. Still a jibe about 'leaving it to the professionals,' while said in a jocular fashion, left Harry in no doubt that they considered his part in the investigation over.

Davis reported to his manager the state of play. He said he'd like to continue with the case. The manager, who had the constant belligerence of many small men, told Harry that they were a private company set up to make a profit and that a disappearing client was not a good bet when the bill was to be settled. With that he instructed the detective to take on another case.

The day was long and tedious. Harry had spent most of his time trying to locate stolen jewellery. The mistress of the house believed one of the maids had stolen rather expensive earrings, but didn't have enough proof to accuse the girl openly. Neither did she want the scandal of an official police investigation.

The woman was obnoxious, with the kind of snooty snobbishness that saw servants as less than human. Her haughtiness annoyed Davis intensely and it was with unalloyed pleasure that he was able to return that afternoon with word that her earrings had been found.

A trawl of the pawnshops in the area had uncovered the stolen items. The description given of the man who pawned the earrings fitted the woman's son perfectly. This spoiled, supercilious youth had stood behind his mother while she spoke to Harry and had made snide remarks about the innate dishonesty of the lower classes.

The woman was alone when Davis called with the stolen goods. Her face, as he described the thief in such specific detail that there could be no mistake as to his identity, took on stony expression. Davis, mischievously asked her if the description fitted anyone she knew. Her denial came through clenched teeth. Harry twisted the knife further, asking if she'd like him to bring the pawnbroker to the house, see if he recognized anyone in the household who might have taken the earrings.

The woman sat rigidly, frostily declining his offer and saying that as the items had been recovered she felt that was the end of the matter. As he left the atmosphere in the room was colder than the snowy scene outside.

The slow thaw continued. Davis splashed his way through Pennyfields, the area in which almost all of the Chinese immigrants brought over to work for the Blue Funnel Line lived. Limehouse was broken into little enclaves of the east, each district housing different ethnic Chinese groups. Pennyfields, where he walked was mainly for the Shanghai Chinese while those from Canton would more likely to be found in Gill House and Limehouse Causeway.

As he walked he gazed around at the restaurants, laundries and grocery stores, all surmounted with Chinese signs. He enjoyed the exotic feel of the area. It was hard to believe that only a few streets away the ordinary daily life of London went by. Here was a world unto itself.

He passed the ubiquitous groups of sailors who thronged the streets day and night. Four Lascar seamen laughed and jostled each other as they made their way towards the docks.

From the first impression of the house he could see why the police had eliminated it as a possible clue as to the whereabouts of Mrs Bowers. It stood bleak and desolate. The river mist eddied around the edges of the overgrown garden like a living, writhing thing.

From somewhere in the night a distant bell chimed ten o'clock. Davis shivered in the damp chill atmosphere and stepped through the front gate. Making his way up the path he rapped smartly at the door. When no sign of life appeared he rapped again.

After a few moments he walked round the side of the house. The garden was a tangle of weeds and overgrown bushes. A sad-looking Rowan tree dipped its branches over what was obviously once an ornamental pond. Davis picked his way through the sodden undergrowth until he reached the back of the house. He could go no further as the back garden had grown right up to the wall and formed an impenetrable barrier right along the full length.

He began to make his way around to the front of the house when he noticed a small window almost at ground level, probably, he thought, for a kitchen or cellar. He bent low and tried to peer in. Behind the filthy pane was only blackness. He straightened up and decided whatever had happened to Mrs Bowers she wasn't in this house.

A couple of drunk dockers who were passing called out cheerily to him as he reached the front door. He nodded in what he hoped was a comradely manner. As he turned to go he saw a ball of white by one of the Corinthian pillars which stood each side of the entrance.

He bent down and picked up what he found to be a piece of scrunched up paper. Carefully he unfurled it and by angling it towards whatever meagre light came from the street he saw it was headed notepaper-*Bowers headed notepaper!*

So now he knew why Bowers had not been at the pub. He'd come here! Davis looked again at the dark old house.

Harry Davis had a copper's instinct still. Something was wrong here, very wrong. He hammered on the door knocker loudly and continuously for a couple of minutes. When this produced no results he decided he'd go the police tomorrow. With the piece of writing paper as evidence that Bowers had been there he could make a good case for demanding they gain entry to the house, one way or another.

He put the evidence carefully in his wallet and decided to have one last look around before he left. He took the same route to the back of the house, trying this time to force a way through the bushes. He only succeeded in tearing his coat as he stumbled into a bramble bush. Admitting defeat he made his way back. On impulse he bent again to the low window. He wiped the glass in a vain attempt to see in.

He jumped back in horror as a white face, with bloody mouth swept past in the darkness!

He ran. He ran until he felt his heart would burst and every breath was burning and painful. He ran even though his injured ankle screamed. He ran until he dropped and then he lay on the ground and sobbed like a child.

Chapter 26

The altar-boy swung the censer backwards and forwards.

Clouds of incense filled the house of worship with a deep scent that reached back to biblical times.

As the priest intoned, the congregation repeated Latin responses learned by rote.

Father Jack Seward was coming to the end of the Benediction service. He turned from the altar to face the kneeling faithful. It was then he saw him, hunched over front pew. Their eyes met and Seward had never seen a soul so much torment.

'Mina? Mina? Are you sure?' Seward's incredulity was to be heard in every syllable.

'Sure? Of course I'm fucking sure, Jack! You think I'd be in this state if I wasn't fucking sure?' Davis' voice rose in anger. It was the first sign of animation since Seward had brought him into the little vestry behind the altar.

Jack looked at his friend. Haggard, dirty. He'd obviously had a terrifying shock. The doctor in him took over. Davis held out an unresisting wrist while Seward checked his pulse. It was racing slightly, but not in a way that was injurious.

Seward opened a small cupboard then took out a bottle of whisky and two glasses. He poured them both a generous drink. As Davis raised the glass to his lips the priest could see how badly his hand shook.

They both sat in silence for a few moments, each trying to come to terms with the vampire's return. They had seen Mina enveloped in a ball of flame in the train tunnel and now she was back.

Seward coaxed Davis back through the story once again. When he had finished Seward drank the rest of his whisky in one gulp. When he spoke his voice was resigned.

'We could go to the police.'

'You went to the police, last time, Jack. I *was* the police! I didn't believe till it was too late. You think it'll be any different now?

'Maybe with you being an ex-detective they might…' The sentence died on the air. Seward knew Harry was right. To go to the police with tales of vampires would at best bring derision and at worse at trip to an Asylum. Besides, bringing up an old case which involved the death of Sergeant McNeil and the staking of Seward's wife, Ellen, after she had been transformed into one of the undead, might have serious repercussions.

Both men knew what had to be done and who would have to do it, but neither of them wanted to articulate it if first. To face the horror, to face the loss of their immortal souls struck a deep primal chord of fear.

'You can wash up if you like, Harry. Have a hot bath and something to eat.' He patted Davis on the shoulder. Davis's smile was tired. 'Thanks, but I'll get home, tidy up. Get some rest. We'll need it.'

Harry got to his feet. Drew his hands across his face several times trying to wipe away the bleariness. The men exchanged a silent and solemn handshake. It was an unspoken blood oath.

As he turned to go, the priest spoke.

'We should find Jonathan.'

Davis nodded. As the door closed Jack poured himself another stiff whisky. He noted that his hand, too, was shaking.

They lay side by side. Sisters in blood. Both were beautiful and terrifying. Cherry mouths were dappled with gore. A few feet away lay the body of George Bowers. The drained corpse, eyes open in a final stare of horror, glowed with the translucence of death.

The vampire woman lay in smiling wait for the night.

Chapter 27

Davis had spent the day trying to trace Jonathan Harker. The last information on his whereabouts was almost a year out of date. A seedy solicitor's office at the Elephant and Castle in south London was the only starting point he had.

Harker had not worked there for several months. The senior partner in the firm had let him go more in sorrow than in anger. He told Davis Jonathan was an exceptional practitioner. He would loved to have had him as a solicitor, full-time, except that he was unstable and unreliable. One day he would be full of manic energy, showing brilliance and doing the work of two men, then there would be a hiatus that might last a day or a week. He would sink into a deep state of lethargy and lose all interest in the world around him.

The man told Harry he'd heard Jonathan was doing some pro rata work for a barrister at Lincoln's Inn Fields. The detective had made his way north of the river and there found out that Jonathan had done some work but again had proved unreliable.

By luck, one of the clerks had struck up a casual acquaintance with Harker and gave Davis the address of his lodgings, a tawdry rooming house in the slums behind St Pancras railway station.

He knocked on the door of the lodgings. Somewhere in the interior he could hear a woman's voice screeching angrily and then the crying of a child. Two young men walked towards him, eyeing him suspiciously as they approached. One of them whispered something to the other and they both veered off, taking a passageway some yards along. Davis smiled. He obviously still had the mien of a policeman.

He raised his fist to knock again when the door opened and an enormous woman stood before him. She was dressed in a shapeless shift of some sort and her sagging breasts hung low on her bulging belly. Tangled hair hung over suspicious, shifty eyes. Dear Christ, Jonathan, how have you come to this?

He asked her if Jonathan Harker lived there. The woman grunted something non-committal and began to close the door. Davis stopped it with his hand. A look of anger crossed the woman's face. Harry then did something illegal and told her he was a police officer and she was obstructing him in the course of his duty. The woman shrugged. She told him Harker didn't live there anymore but she knew where he was. Davis waited. A malicious smile crossed her face as she told him where he could find Jonathan before slamming the door shut.

The shock of what he'd just heard stunned him and he stood at the door for several moments before turning and walking slowly away. *Jonathan Harker was in a madhouse!*

Chapter 28

The building which loomed ahead of them was the supreme example of how the Victorians catered for lunacy on an industrial scale.

Seward shot his companion a foreboding glance as they made their way to the entrance. In his days as a doctor Jack had spent many weeks and months in just such institutions. It was only with the distance of time he saw it through a layman's eyes. It looked a place to fear.

Colney Hatch asylum sprawled across the landscape. It was about two thousand feet long, with a row of ornamental arches in the entrance and a matching style of windows on the first floor. The attempt at giving the design an Italianate feel was foiled by the somber municipal brick of its frontage. Large towers at each end, which acted as ventilation ducts, book-ended the building. A chapel sat in the squat central body of the asylum, a sign that when science failed only an appeal to a higher power was left.

Davis was amazed to see that the institution sat in a verdant plot of land, perhaps twenty acres in size. He'd half expected the place to be surrounded by the gothic trappings from the ghost stories he'd read as a child. Gargoyles and a dark lake at least.

They stepped inside and Davis let Jack take the lead. In his street clothes Seward looked like the doctor he'd been when Harry first met him. The starched collar, the tie and the sober brown suit spoke of a professional man. This was important as they needed his status as a physician to gain access to Harker.

Seward had been stunned by the news that Jonathan was in Colney Hatch, Lunatic Asylum. Harker was one of the most intelligent and level-headed men he had ever known, and to think of that splendid mind overthrown was devastating.

Both men agreed that even if Jonathan Harker was not going to be in a state to help them find and destroy Mina they would still bring him out of a house of madness. The bonds forged by the three men as they risked everything for each other twenty years before were unbreakable.

Seward told the attendant who he was and asked to see the Superintendent. As they waited he fiddled uncomfortably with the civilian collar. It had been so long since he'd worn anything but his priest's garb. He muttered a little act of contrition as he remembered the lies he had told the bishop for a leave of absence. He had toyed with the idea of telling the church authorities his real purpose and asking for their support but he knew the Catholic Church would never allow one of their priests to be involved in such a thing.

His internal prayer was interrupted by the arrival of the doctor in charge. He was an upright man, with a rather profuse grey beard. He was rolling his sleeves down as if interrupted in the middle of treating a patient.

His obvious annoyance was softened when Seward introduced himself and his companion. The doctor had read one or two medical papers Seward had written on the treatment of madness many years before, observations he had made while running a private asylum at Purfleet. It was there Dracula had used one of Seward's patients, Renfield, to spread the contagion of vampirism.

Davis smiled to himself as he saw Seward draw the superintendent aside and speak to him quietly and gravely. It was the way with doctors. Anyone not in the medical profession was not considered worthy or capable of sharing their esoteric knowledge.

He saw them nod wisely, doctor to doctor, and then the superintendent smiled. Seward shook him by the hand and the man walked quickly back up the corridor.

'So, what's happening, Jack?'

'I told him we were here on behalf of Jonathan's family who want him to receive private treatment.'

'And he agreed?'

Seward gave a slight shrug of the shoulders. 'This place holds about three thousand patients. You think he's worried if there's one less?'

The chubby attendant was loquacious. He spoke incessantly as he led them along the miles of endless corridors. The passageway they were on, which seemed to stretch into eternity, was, he told them proudly, the longest in Britain.

He kept up the stream of chatter even when the most disturbed patients were wheeled past, or carried struggling in strait-jackets. Davis felt his heart go out to the poor wretches who dribbled and screamed and cried their way along the miles of tiled passageways. The whole atmosphere reeked of urine and carbolic soap.

No matter how distressing the sights their guide chattered breezily on about the asylum's farm buildings and workshops. Jack and Harry took it in turn to make impressed responses.

With a hint of pride in his voice he told them they even had their own cemetery. Despite the grimness of the situation Seward and Davis could not help exchanging surreptitious smiles and then straightening their faces like guilty schoolboys when the attendant stopped suddenly, turned round and told them they had arrived.

He unlocked the heavy door and held it open. Seward and Davis walked into the sparse room. The walls were a drab green. The floor covered in a dull brown linoleum. A simple cot bed lay along one side of the chamber. A table and chair was set in front of the window. Slumped in the chair, his head leant to one side, was Jonathan Harker.

'Don't speak, don't do nothing. We've had to force feed him a few times lately. Don't seem to want to do anything.' The attendant held his hand towards Harker as he spoke, like a showman presenting something to amaze and astound.

They were stunned at the changes in Jonathan. His hair, which had turned grey overnight after his ordeal in Castle Dracula, was now almost completely white. It fell in lank strands across a face that was lined and colourless. The three friends were approximately the same age, but now Harker looked at least fifteen years older. 'Jesus,' Davis muttered quietly.

Seward walked over to Jonathan. He spoke gently. 'Jonathan. It's me, Jack. And Harry's here.' Davis stood beside him and squeezed Harker's hand. 'How are you, mate?'

Jonathan didn't respond in any way. There was no sign he was aware of their presence. Jack tried again. 'We've had a job finding you. What have you been doing?' Again there was no response. The doctor turned to the attendant.

'Is he on any opiates?'

'Nah, doctor said he don't need anything. Just sits there. No trouble or nothing. Just sits there.'

'Can you get me a wheelchair please?'

The attendant left without a word. Davis leant over and looked at Harker.

'What's the matter with him, Jack?'

'Nothing physical as far as I can see.'

'He doesn't seem to hear us.'

'I think he can. He just doesn't care enough to answer.'

'Doesn't care?'

'He's not on any medication so the state is self-governing. In the old days they'd have called this 'Acute Melancholia.'

'Acute Melancholia?'

'Yes, it's a state of mind that occurs when someone becomes so sad that they lose the will to live. They shut down all communications with the real world. Lose appetite. Have no interest in anything or anyone.

I'm afraid Jonathan is willing himself to die.'

The paraffin fumes from the little engine drifted into his face causing Constable Knowles to turn away in disgust. He was feeling queasy as a result of a ferocious drinking session the night before and the smell was enough to make him gag.

At the wheel of the craft Constable Benson was unaware of his colleague's delicate state. He scanned each bank of the river as the boat chugged its way against the tide, making for North Woolwich. The day was cold but the temperature was much higher than it had been for the last few weeks. The edges of the shore still showed a pelmet of snow but the thaw was noticeable.

The two officers were looking out at the Thames in all its industrial glory. Packed with ships. Goods from every corner of the globe, wharves and warehouses crammed with the wealth of empire.

It was the recognition that the riches created by the river, and its attraction for the criminal element, that had brought about the policing of the Thames. From the eighteenth century onwards a struggle had been going on to thwart smugglers, thieves, looters and a dozen other types of miscreants drawn by the lure of easy riches.

The hardest criminals to police were the dock-rats who hung around the quays, waiting to pilfer anything left unguarded for an instant.

Knowles looked across to the North shore. They were passing Barking Creek Mouth. He was grateful for the sight. They were nearing Woolwich where he could have the cup of strong tea with several sugars his hangover cried out for.

He turned to Benson and signalled that maybe he could 'short shore' so that they could get to Woolwich a bit quicker. Short shoring was strictly illegal. All river traffic had to stay port to port. It was dangerous to cross to the inside shore but faster.

Benson raised his eyebrows to indicate it wasn't a good idea. It was then they saw the bundle. At first it seemed like rags. The river was full of the flotsam and jetsam, but there was something about the way it floated which suggested it had more substance. Both officers were experienced in the retrieval of bodies from the river. Every years dozens of poor wretches were pulled out. Some dead by accident; some by suicide; some by homicide.

Knowles moved along the boat and grabbed the gaff, a long pole with a hook on the end. The craft swung towards the bundle in the water. Benson reduced the engine speed to a mere chunter and watched as his mate leant forward and tried to catch the object. The bundle bobbed away as the end of the gaff knocked against it. Knowles tried again and this time succeeded in taking hold. He drew it towards him. They could both see it was a body, face down in the murky water.

Benson cut the engine as Knowles pulled the body against the side of the boat. The two policemen leant over taking a grip of the hips and shoulders pulled the corpse on board. The dead man lay face down on the deck. Even the muck of the polluted river couldn't disguise the quality of his clothes.

Benson grasped the corpse by the shoulder and turned it face up. Both were appalled at what the saw. For Knowles the view was more than his already maladjusted system could endure and he lost what was left of last night's beer over the side.

Chapter 29

He hadn't spoken a word since they had arrived home. For more than two hours in Davis's little living room they had tried to break through the wall of silence. No matter what they said, no matter what they asked, Harker showed no response. The being who sat before them was little more than an empty shell.

On Seward's advice, they had agreed beforehand not to mention Mina until they had established some sort of initial rapport with Jonathan. The priest felt that in his delicate mental state such news might unhinge him permanently.

They talked of many things: Work, the news, potted histories of what they had been doing, always asking Harker questions. Nothing garnered a response. Finally, in exasperation, Davis looked him in the eyes and said 'Mina's back, Jonathan. Mina is back and we need you. We need you to help us.'

Seward pulled him away angrily.

'What the hell do you think you're doing, man. You want to destroy his mind altogether?'

'And it's not destroyed already, Jack? Jesus Christ, look at him! He's an automaton.' Davis turned again to Harker. 'Jonathan, she's back. *Mina is back.*'

They sat opposite each other in the kitchen. Each man was lost in his own thoughts. They had left Harker in the living room. Their friend had not responded to Davis's outburst. Now they were faced with the problem of what to do for the best. It was obvious that the Jonathan Harker they knew was gone forever. It was now up to them alone to face Mina.

Davis offered to let Jonathan live with him, but Seward said the idea was impractical. Jonathan needed constant care. He told Harry that he could not be left alone while he went to work.

It was then decided that Seward would find him a place in a home run by the Catholic Church. The home was normally for priests who had mental illness, or had fallen into senility, but he thought he had enough influence to get Jonathan in. Davis felt guilty but could think of no real alternative. When Jack told him that the nurses were nuns who would treat Jonathan with kindness, he agreed.

They had just begun to discuss their strategy of how to deal with the re-emergence of Mina when the door to the kitchen opened. Jonathan Harker stood there. His appearance was still gaunt and wasted, but both men noticed there was at least a spark of animation in his eyes that, up till now, had been dead.

He moved further into the kitchen. When he at last spoke his voice was cracked and low.

'I'm hungry. Could I have some fried eggs, please?'

As he made his way towards the Bowers House, Davis thought of the miracle of Harker's emergence from the dark night of the soul. Harry was a man of no particular religious beliefs, although the existence of vampires had forced him to concede there was a supernatural. However, he could only ascribe Jonathan's partial recovery to a miracle.

He was still fragile and somewhat disorientated, but he was at least *compos mentis* again. They hadn't wanted to tire or distress him with too many questions, so after he had eaten ravenously, Seward gave him a sleeping draft that would allow him a good twelve or fourteen hours straight rest. Perhaps then his recovery would be more advanced.

That morning, Davis had managed to convince his office manager that he needed to spend a little more time on the Bowers case, saying he wanted to track down someone who would take responsibility for paying Pinkerton's the money owed.

He rapped at the front door. As he waited, he wanted more than anything else to find that George Bowers was back home. He liked the man, and finding the notepaper at the door of the house by the river had given him a premonition of something terrible happening to his client. So shocking had been his discovery that Mina Harker still existed that it had driven him to more urgent considerations.

Now it was time to see how the land lay. If Bowers was safe he wondered what he should say. It was almost certain that his wife had become a victim of the vampire. If she was, he hoped that death had been her fate. At least her soul would rest in peace. However, if she had been given a baptism of blood and become one of the undead it would mean she was another unclean spirit to be freed by the wooden stake and decapitation.

Harry knew all those years ago how incredulous he had been when told that the killings in the east end was the work of vampires. He could see that Bowers, if alive, would think him mad. Still, one step at a time.

The door opened and a weepy eyed maid stood there. He cleared his throat.

'Is Mr Bowers in, please?' No sooner had he spoken the words than tears flowed down the girl's face.

'Sir, oh, sir…'

The morgue! How he hated and loathed the morgue! Harry had visited the charnel houses countless times in his work as a police officer, but he could never shake off his disgust at the smell of death.

He walked up the line of shrouded corpses, each with bare feet sticking out below the regulation blanket. Labels tied around their toes with coarse string completed the final undignified journey from life into corruption.

The detective, the same one who had been investigating Bower's absence, led the way to the end of the row. The policeman had been glad when Davis had called at the station on learning of George Bowers death. None of the servants could face identifying the corpse, and although there was ample proof in his wallet of who he was, the detective needed someone to confirm this.

'Got to say he aint pretty. You ready?' Harry nodded, and the detective drew back the blanket.

An involuntary intake of breath signaled the horror Davis felt at the sight before him. George Bowers was naked under the blanket. His fair hair was plastered flat against his forehead by the dried mud of the river. What made him a thing terrible to behold was the waxen, luminous whiteness of his skin. So pale was the body that it almost glowed with a phosphorescent aura. It was only then Davis noticed the wounds to each side of the neck. The mark of the vampire! The twin bites told him that Lilian Bowers had joined the ranks of the undead.

'Looks like somebody stabbed him in the neck. Few times.' The detective's voice was objective, the tone of one for whom death had become commonplace. 'Sail-makers needles I should say. Poor bastard. First his wife…That's Bowers, right?' Harry nodded and the shroud was pulled across. The detective asked him a few cursory questions but without any real enthusiasm. A death from the river. Not much hope of solving it.

They stepped outside, and Harry gratefully drew in a lungful of fresh air. He then asked the detective if the wife had been traced. He knew the fate of Lilian Bowers, but such questions would be expected. The policeman shrugged. Missing wife, another man. The answer in most cases. Davis wondered what this cynical detective would say if he suddenly blurted out she was a vampire and had helped drain her husband's blood. He knew it would mean a second visit to Colney Hatch, only this time in a strait jacket.

The two men exchanged some desultory conversation about the job and mutual acquaintances on the force then went their separate ways.

As Davis made his way back home, he couldn't shake the image of George Bowers from his mind. The bite marks and the bloodless flesh were horrible to behold, but what was worse was the look of utter ecstasy on his face at the moment of death.

Chapter 30

CUTTING FROM 'THE TIMES'

MAIDEN VOYAGE OF THE TITANIC

The White Star shipping line have announced that the Titanic, sailing from Southampton to New York on its maiden voyage, will leave on April 10th 1912. Departure time will be at noon…

CUTTING FROM THE 'EAST LONDON ADVERTISER'

THAMES TRAGEDY

The body of a man, thought to be a Mr George Bowers, of Kensington, was pulled from the Thames on Tuesday. The dead man had recently been in low spirits following the disappearance of his wife…

     Harker was still very frail, but at least they could see the man they had once known re-emerge slowly. The food, followed by a long sleep of almost eighteen hours, seemed to restore some vitality. Now the three friends sat once again in Davis's living room. This time Harker was listening intently to the details of Mina's return.

     Seward could see the effect the story was having on Jonathan. The wife he loved was returning as a vampire for the third time. Harker had helped free her by destroying Dracula, only to have the taint of the undead reassert itself. His decline could be measured from the time he thought he had seen Mina destroyed in the explosion. After that, his life seemed empty and pointless. A downward spiral ending in a madhouse seemed to complete the circle.

     Now she was back, and the horror was about to be relived again. Harker was afraid. They were all afraid because they knew the dangers into which they would plunge. Finding a being so powerful, a being of limitless strength with the power to dominate wills, was a truly terrifying prospect. They also knew that their cause was just, that humanity must always face the vampire, otherwise the powers of darkness would walk across the face of the earth.

Harker let the others do most of the talking, only interrupting to quietly ask the occasional question. Seward was pleased to note that the questions were shrewd and pertinent, the type of things that the Jonathan of old would ask.

Finally, the narrative ground to a halt. A few peripheral points were made, but each of them knew they were only skating around what no one wanted to talk about. *How they would hunt down and destroy the vampires!*

It was as if the universe rolled beneath their feet. The revenants, bloated with feeding, strolled through the city streets. They were aware of their effortless superiority over the mortals who hurried to and fro around them.

Mina reveled in her power. Vampire! Stronger than the strongest. Crueler than the cruelest. If only the humans knew what beings stood among them they would run and hide in the deepest places they could find.

Lilian was aware of the looks, the lust in the glance of every man and woman who passed. The irony. The vampire, who is sexless, has the power to sexually arouse. They remorselessly used this power to explore human frailty, all the more to learn how to exploit it more fully.

The undead felt the vitality of life cascading through the city. Each and every one who passed added a heartbeat to the throbbing tattoo which thrummed in the brains of the *nosferatu*. It took all their control not launch into the crowds tearing and biting, just to feel the splash of hot blood in the way some animals go on killing, even when not hungry, just for the pleasure of the frenzy.

At an unacknowledged level, deep in the brain of the vampire, is a mourning for the loss of the soul. They attack humans not just to feed but because their victims have what they crave most of all.

The cunning born of self-preservation had been the reason Mina had widened their hunting ground. She knew that so many killings in one area would bring intense investigation. She wasn't afraid of the human authorities. They would never ascribe the deaths to anything but the work of a natural predator, but she knew from experience that, eventually, those with the old knowledge might become suspicious. They might come with the means of her destruction.

At Ludgate, they reached the dome of St Paul's Cathedral, the iconic structure built by Christopher Wren. Mina stood at the base of the church. The edifice, hewn mainly from blocks of Portland Stone, rose into the night sky. This was a place the *nosferatu* could never enter.

With a sudden spring, she leapt several feet, and her fingers found grip in the minute joins between the massive bricks. She began to climb the sheer face of the cathedral, Lilian following in an effortless glide. The vampires rose high over the city until they reached the great dome. Here they stood side by side on the leads, staring down at a city that was now their realm.

More than a hundred feet below, London went about its business unaware of its bringers of death.

The church was deserted. The sound of his shoes clicked on the terrazzo floor, sending echoes bouncing off the walls. The eyes of the crucified saviour seemed to gaze at him reproachfully as he made his way down the aisle. On reaching the altar rails, he genuflected and made the sign of the cross before stepping forward and opening the tabernacle which held the communion hosts.

Seward could have gone to the chapel house and taken some of the communion wafers, but he wanted to avoid being seen. Besides, he felt the hosts in the tabernacle were sanctified in God's house and therefore somehow more holy.

He drew half a dozen wafers from the chalice used for giving holy communion and placed them carefully in a clean, white linen handkerchief, whispering an act of contrition to God for any sin he might be committing.

He closed the tabernacle and made his way to the altar rails. As he did so, he heard a door at the back of the church open then swing closed. He hurried to the side aisle as footsteps sounded.

Hidden behind one of the marble-clad pillars, he could see the chapel housekeeper make her way down the aisle. She, like him, genuflected in front of the altar before moving off and into the vestry beyond.

Seward moved quietly up the side aisle. *Jesus Falls for the Second Time. Jesus is Crowned with Thorns.* The stations of the cross stared out sightlessly

He reached the back of the church and took from his pocket three small bottles, the type used to hold cough mixture. They had been taken from Harry's medicine cabinet that afternoon and rinsed clean.

One by one, he held the little bottles in the holy water font. When they had all been filled he placed them in his coat pocket and then left the church.

In the night air, he put his hand to the communion wafers in his pocket and felt safer.

In the morgue, George Bowers lay silent and still. A few miles away, the vampire whom he had loved, and who had once loved him, lay silent also, his blood staining her dress.

Chapter 31

They waited until the bright day was well established. The snow was all but gone, and London was bathed in sunlight. Those studying the three men closely might have noted their collective air of melancholy.

They had taken an omnibus to Limehouse and then made their way on foot to the house by the river. Seward and Davis carried bags which held the paraphernalia for destroying vampires: garlic flowers, holy water, the communion hosts and pointed wooden stakes. In Davis's bag was also a heavy mallet, with which they intended to pound the stakes through the hearts of the *nosferatu*.

In daylight, the house seemed passive. The grim façade now appeared no more than the shabbiness of neglect. The wild, tortured shapes of the garden were now no more than overgrown weeds. Davis knew the effect night had on the imagination. When he'd fled in terror from the house after catching a glimpse of Mina, he'd felt as if he were in hell. Now the place looked merely mundane.

Jack looked towards Harker, trying to judge whether in his fragile state this ,nd what they were about to do, might be too much for him. It was a relief to see that apart from signs of his recent trauma he seemed calm and collected.

On the way to the house, Davis had told them that they must be bold and walk straight in, no hanging around or looking furtive. Uncertain behaviour would draw suspicion. From his time on the force he knew that the boldest and most brazen of criminals invariably went unnoticed by the public.

Bracing their shoulders, they strode through the gate without hesitation. Three respectably dressed men appearing to go about their lawful business.

Once at the front door, Davis noted the heavy oak and classic Brahma lock. Nothing short of a cannonball would let them through. After a short, hurried consultation, they decided to split up and make their way around the house.

Seward and Harker moved left while Davis followed his path of the night before. As he retraced his steps, the traps and pitfalls of the previous journey were reduced to mere tangled weeds and fallen branches. He reached the spot where he had peered through the low-level window. Even in daylight, he had to brace himself before bending down and gazing through the glass.

Dirt and verdure from the garden covered the pane. It was only possible to make out the faintest of shapes. He wiped at the glass but with little effect. Davis then tried to open the window, although it was far too narrow to allow access.

The edges were encrusted with the grime of perhaps a hundred years, making the window impossible to shift. He grunted and heaved at the sash for several minutes before giving up. Frustrated, he considered smashing the pane but then decided that was a last resort. Besides, the gain might be negligible. He brushed the dead leaves and grass from his knees and jacket. As he moved towards the back of the house, he suddenly realized that despite the brightness of the day *no birds were singing*.

At the other side of the house, Harker and Seward made better progress. Here, the garden was in less of a ruin, and they were able to find their way more easily. The wall was blank, with no windows, but at the end, just before they reached the back garden, they found a door. It was obviously the entrance for servants and tradesmen. There was no handle. Harker optimistically pushed the door. It was locked solid. Seward pointed to the small brass plate surrounding the keyhole.

At this point Davis joined them. They considered going to the back of the house, but the detective assured them that access was impossible. It was a dense tangle of shrubs and brambles that would take them several hours to hack their way through, even if they had the tools to do so.

Harry then looked at the door. He shoved his shoulder against it, tentatively trying to see if age had weakened the hinges. It felt immovable. The other two looked slightly discouraged, but he merely smiled and took a locksmith's pick from his inside pocket. Davis was no expert, but his years on the force had taught him the basics of the burglar's art.

He crouched down and began to probe gently at the lock. He was grateful that unlike the front door, which had a Brahma lock, perhaps the finest lock in the world and practically impossible to pick, this one was run of the mill.

He probed gently, trying to feel the levels. It was frustrating work. It could only be done with patience and a sensitive touch. Twice he thought he'd thrown the levers, only for the pick to slip off. He muttered a curse under his breath and looked apologetically at Seward who merely smiled.

He wiped the sweat from his face and tried again. The sounds of Limehouse coming to life could be heard from afar. Shouts and laughs, the rattle of wheels on cobbles and the cry of vendors drifted towards them.

Davis gave a little 'yessss!' of triumph as the levers clicked up and the lock sprung open. He stood up and gently pushed the door with three fingers. It swung open with a faint creak. The three men exchanged glances and then stepped inside.

Extract from Metropolitan Police Report. Case File D901879

...severe lacerations on each side of the neck. In the absence of evidence to the contrary it seems as if the deceased, George Alfred Bowers, inflicted these wounds on himself while the balance of his mind was disturbed, after being deserted by his wife. (The coroner suggests these wounds might have been caused by a long needle or perhaps an ice pick)

With no water in the lungs and evidence of massive blood loss, it is reasonable to assume that Mr Bowers, having stabbed himself in the neck several times at a location near to the river, staggered to the water's edge and tumbled in...

They looked around in awe at the splendour of the house's interior, taking in the priceless object d'art and the richness of the soft furnishings. When they had entered through the derelict kitchen, covered with the dust of ages, they had no idea such opulence lay above.

They stood in the centre of the living room. Seward moved across to the large bookcase and ran his fingers over a shelf of priceless volumes. The books rose in rows to the ceiling. Meanwhile, Davis prowled about looking for something that would confirm the presence of the vampires. He thought of what would happen if the police were to catch them in the act of burglary. What would be their defence? Vampires, m'lord. We broke in to kill vampires.

Despite the opulence of the room there was a musty unpleasant odour which caused Harker to wrinkle his nose in disgust.

Finding the vampires resting place and destroying them was imperative, and they decided to split up and search the house. Davis was uncomfortable about dividing their forces, but Seward reassured him that in the daylight hours there was little danger.

Harker and Davis volunteered to start the search at the top of the house. Seward took the kitchen and cellars. It was only when his two friends had climbed the stairs and he was left alone that Jack Seward realize how frightened he really was. He crossed himself and said a 'Hail Mary' before going back into the basement area.

Seward cautiously opened the door of what appeared to be the main bedroom. The place was desolate. Piles of household junk lay scattered around, all under a thick blanket of dust. The curtains, once of rich lace but now in rags, hung from the windows. It was obvious from the undisturbed carpeting of dust that no one had been in the room.

On the landing, he met up with Davis who told a similar tale of dereliction. They made their way downstairs and poked and prodded around. Harker opened the drawer of the *escritoire* by the front door and found several sheets of expensive notepaper and envelopes. There was also a gold fountain pen. He tried the pen, scrawling a line across the back of one of the envelopes. The ink hadn't dried, proof of recent occupation.

As he turned, he saw Davis with a piece of cloth in his hand. It was a ladies handkerchief with lace edgings. The detective held out one side so he could see the initials stitched on one corner.

LB.

After finding the handkerchief with Lilian Bowers' initials, the trio decided that this was conclusive proof that Mrs Bowers was now companion to Mina.

Another more intense search for their hiding place proved fruitless. They decided to lie in wait until the vampire women appeared and would try to catch them when they returned from their bloody feasting.

They had gone home and spent a restless afternoon there before returning to Limehouse just as the light was beginning to fade. The trio killed the final waiting hour in a pub called The Grapes, a small dingy place in Limehouse Reach.

Davis slammed the glass down on the table. 'Why don't we just burn the bloody place to the ground?'

Harker shook his head. 'And then what?'

'And then we send her to burn in hell!'

'Harry, you know what we're up against, man. Fire's no use. It has to be the stake.'

'I still think we can cremate her.'

'We thought that once before.'

The vivid image of Mina Harker, a stake in her chest being engulfed by white- hot flames, still haunted Davis. In his heart of hearts he knew what Harker said was true, he just didn't want to face the vampire again.

Having eaten little all day, they stopped at a coffee stall called 'Ye Olde Jimmy Thicks.' The wizened little man served them mugs of steaming tea and large slices of bread and butter, while keeping up a constant stream of chatter. The other denizens of the east end looked curiously at the trio of what they would call toffs gulping hungrily at the food.

Despite the rise in temperature, the air was chilly. They huddled under the doorway of a chandlers shop which gave an uninterrupted view of the house front from about two hundred yards away.

The night dragged on. Limbs began to ache and eyes began to sting from lack of sleep when suddenly, Seward hissed a word of warning. The faintest of movement could be seen on the pathway. For a moment, there was nothing, and Jack was beginning to think he'd imagined it. Then they saw them.

The two vampire sisters glided silently through the gate. Harker's heart raced, and he almost cried out in despair as he recognized Mina! All the love and fear and terror came back in a flood of emotion. The woman he'd loved and hunted. She was as young as when he'd first met her and more devastatingly beautiful than memory had ever painted! He might even have called out had

Seward not placed his hand on his shoulder at the critical moment and given it a warning squeeze.

The vampires stopped and looked around. Mina raised her head and seemed to be sensing something. The three watchers sank deeper into the shadows.

Mina's mien conveyed itself to Lilian, and she too seemed to be reading the air. The hyper senses of the *nosferatu* were able to pick out the most delicate vibrations. Mina stood there, her head held still, trying to read the air like some sleek, attentive animal. She then turned with a malevolent deliberateness and seemed to be looking straight into the shadows where they stood.

Each man held his breath. It seemed that nothing could hide from that remorseless gaze. Seward slid his hand cautiously into his pocket and felt the comforting outline of the communion hosts.

Just when it seemed they had been seen, Mina and Lilian turned away and slipped into the street leading to the river.

None of the trio moved for several moments. Davis let out a deep sigh, and the terrible tension of the last few minutes flooded out in relieved smiles.

Harker spoke, his voice choked with emotion. 'She looked younger. So beautiful. So beautiful.'

Seward patted him on the shoulder once more. 'Only beautiful on the outside, Jonathan. Only beautiful on the outside.'

The friends knew that they had watched the undead go out to hunt victims, but trying to stop them in the open would have been impossible. They had to find where they slept and trap them in an enclosed space. People would die tonight, but that was the price to be more certain of ending the horror.

They crossed the road and went round to the side of the house. Each man would have given anything not to go into that house, but each knew what had to be done. Slipping into the house by the side door, they prepared to wait in the darkness for the vampires return.

They watched in wonder as the flickering images on the screen jerked and bounced and lived. The bioscope was a wonder they had not yet fully comprehended. Movement from beams of light. There, in front of them, were streets and motor cars and omnibuses. The whole world on a white sheet.

Jim Dawson and Frank Olsen never tired of sitting in the muggy darkness watching the birth of Cinema. Both were eighteen. Jim, the elder by three months, was an apprentice cooper and spent his days making barrels. Frank worked in a sugar refinery tending the machines. Close friends from elementary school, they had discovered the movies and now spent almost all of their time, and most of their money, on the bioscope shows.

The last few bars of the accompanying piano faded away, and the gaslight was turned up. This was always the bit they hated, the return to reality.

With the rest of the audience, they shuffled out into East India Dock Road. Both the boys were hungry but the last of their cash had gone to paying for the cinema.

They began to make their way down the long avenue to their homes in Plaistow. They spoke excitedly about the film show, each eager to relive the pictures they had seen and speak about the programme ahead.

So engrossed were they in their conversation that they didn't hear her speak at first. It was only when she called again did they stop and look. The woman seemed to be in distress. She stood on the opposite corner and called across to them. Both boys stared at her. A vision. Under the lamplight, her burnished hair shimmered and glowed.

She called again. Her voice was sweet and enticing. They crossed over. Jack, unable to take his eyes off her, stammered out something about was there anything wrong, Miss.

She indicated with her hand that they follow her into the alley. The boys looked at each other. Frank's mother, strictly religious, had warned him many, many times about the sins of the flesh and the 'bad' women who led to corruption. He wasn't quite sure what she meant by corruption and how bad these women were. All he knew was that the sight of the woman walking ahead, her hips swaying gently, set his heart pounding.

A few yards down the passageway, they saw another vision, a woman with dark hair and scarlet mouth. She smiled and they were entranced. The second woman was smiling too. Such mouths. Such mouths to be kissed.

Without a word, the woman with the burnished hair took Frank by the hand and led him further into the alley. He went without a word. Jim stared at the creature before him. He felt a tightening in his groin, and his cock began to stiffen.

The wondrous woman seemed to sense his excitement and laughed softly. He had never heard a laugh so angelic. It was like the tinkling of the little music box his mother kept on the dresser.

She opened her arms. Like one in a dream, he moved towards her. Her eyes held his. He was only aware of her eyes and the unbearable need for her in his loins.

Her arms slipped around him. He closed his eyes as he felt her body push against his with divine friction as her hips moved against his erection. His blood sang in his veins as his excitement moved closer to climax.

The beautiful female laughed softly again as he pushed himself closer. Her lips brushed his cheek. She was kissing her way softly down his face. At the same time, she slipped her hand inside the waistband of his trousers. He felt cool, knowing fingers slip around his cock. He came in a frantic splurge, the orgasm racking his body.

At the same instant, she bit into his neck.

The wait seemed interminable. All three men crouched in the darkness waiting for the return of the vampires. Dawn wasn't too far away.

Seward slowly shifted his leg to a more comfortable position to ease a spasm of cramp. He was situated by the side of the *escritoire*, ready to cut off any escape by the front door. He shifted the crucifix from one hand to another and wiped the perspiration from the freed palm. In the lessening gloom, he could see all sorts of shapes forming and reforming as his fevered imagination conjured up terrors.

His conscience had troubled him when they had decided on this particular plan. To allow the undead to leave their lair and ambush them on their return was logical. It was the only way to contain them and prevent flight.

Jack Seward knew that this would mean allowing them to fall on more innocent victims. His companions had argued it was the lesser of two evils, better two more victims than countless others, but still he was wracked by guilt.

On the half-landing situated on the stairs, Davis huddled against the wall, trying to make sure he would not be seen as they came through the front door. He stretched his hand out and felt cautiously for the policeman's lamp each of the trio carried. He picked up the lamp, held the lens close to his coat and flicked the switch on for a half second. A jab of muffled light showed and then vanished. Good. The ultimate horror would be to left in the darkness with a couple of vampires.

He felt his heart beating fast and tried to take slow breaths. Harry, in his time as a police officer, had faced danger in many forms: a knife, a gun, a razor. Once even a scythe, but nothing compared to this. Nothing.

On the stairs leading to the kitchen and basement, Jonathan Harker wiped the sweat from his brow. He felt shaky and his limbs trembled. This was partly from fear and partly from the physical debility he had suffered over the past few years. He felt as though he was partly in a dream. Reality and unreality seemed to merge. So long had he been lost to the world that his mental equilibrium was still betwixt and between.

The picture of Mina haunted him. After all these years! Still young, still beautiful. He'd loved her so, and she'd loved him. When he had needed her after his escape from Dracula, she had come to him over land and sea. In turn, he had fought the arch vampire for her soul. Now he had to try once again to free her.

Harker was aware that in his condition he was the weak link in the chain. His illness, coupled with the fact that he still loved Mina, made him the most susceptible to the spell of the vampire. He knew that he might even have gone to her outside the house if Seward hadn't been there to steady him.

Tick Tock Tick Tock.

The beat of the grandfather clock was sonorous and irritating. Davis was tempted several times to rise and stop the pendulum. Only the knowledge that the deafening silence would betray them stopped him doing so.

Tick Tock Tick Tock.

Bloody thing! He had to fight down the growing annoyance. *I'd like to…*

The front door opened!

It swung wide, almost soundlessly. A weak shaft of light from coming day splashed across the carpet. The vampire sisters glided into the room. The rustle of their dresses were the only sounds.

Seward, hidden by the writing desk, could see their outlines for a few seconds, and then the door closed. They were alone with the revenants!

Each man felt a thrill of fear trickle along his spine. Each waited. Whatever route the vampires took they would face them, driving then back to the centre of the room, trapping them in a circle of crucifix and holy communion wafers. As dawn would break shortly, they would hold them in a cage of light.

Already through the heavy drapes, a muggy sort of grey dawn was beginning to form. The rustling of the dresses sounded again as the women moved silkily across the room. Seward peered intently, not daring to breathe. He thought that in the lessening dark he could make out their outlines.

At the other two points in the room, Davis and Harker clutched the crosses and hoped that they would not be in the route taken by the *nosferatu*.

Swwwsh!

The sound was of something being drawn across the carpet. Seward had the best view of the chamber, and to him, it appeared as if a whole of the opposite wall was moving. Then the edges of the book bindings glinted feebly in the growing soupy light, and he could see that it was the bookcase.

He could now see them a little more clearly. Even from a distance, their sensuality was overwhelming. Only the awareness of their true nature kept his mind focused.

Glory be to the father, the son and the holy ghost…

He repeated the little prayer over and over in his head. It calmed the fear and strengthened his resolve for the terrible task ahead. It was up to him. They had decided that they would all move on Seward's command.

The vampires had stepped behind the opened bookcase. So that's where they lay! No wonder we couldn't find it, Seward thought.

He was elated. With dawn upon them, they could wait until Mina and her companion slept and then end this horror. Seward

thanked God for this bounty and watched as the bookcase begin to close. The revenants were literally about to seal their own fate.
It was then Davis dropped the lamp!

Chapter 32

The chief engineer felt like a Liliputian as he walked the length of the engine room. Towering over him were twenty nine coal-fired boilers. Each boiler weighed almost a hundred tons and was fifteen foot high.

Giant bolts dotted the face plates of the gargantuan cylinders, holding in power that would drive the mighty ship through the Atlantic at 24 knots an hour. The largest moving man-made object in history. The engineer turned to his assistant and grinned.

'Don't forget to order the coal.'

Captain Edward Smith smiled at the reporter. The skipper of the Titanic folded his hands across his front. With his full-face and white beard, he looked very like the late King Edward V11, who had died two years before. The question of the safety of such a massive vessel was frequently asked, and one which he answered with complete confidence.

'I cannot conceive of any vital disaster happening to this vessel. Modern shipbuilding has gone beyond that.'

Chapter 33

With a terrifying swiftness the vampires were among them, bloody mouths wide. Fangs glinted in the murky light.

Seward saw Lilian sweep towards him. Dear God! So quick. He could see the bestial rage in her eyes. He managed to raise the crucifix in front of his face in time to check her attack. She hissed and spat, never taking her eyes off the little holy object.

'I believe in God, the father almighty…'

Seward called out the prayer loudly, keeping his arm straight out and carefully avoiding looking in the vampire's eyes.

Across the room Mina had been even swifter. In a movement, in which she seemed to pull the air past her, she reached Davis before he had a chance to raise the cross. He crashed backwards against the wall. Mina's fangs were only inches from his neck. He desperately tried to hold her off, but the limitless strength of the revenant drew her closer, her mouth searching for his flesh.

Davis let out a shriek of terror as he felt the earth-tainted breath on his cheek. In her fangs, he could see the remains of her last feeding, threads and speckles of blood. Her incisors brushed his cheek, and his strength was almost gone when Mina screamed. The cry rang through the room.

She turned. Harker stood there. In his hand he held a vial of holy water which he had thrown across her shoulder. With demonic fury, she prepared to launch herself. It was then he held the large crucifix in front of her face.

'And in his only begotten son, Jesus Christ, our Lord…'

Seward's prayer boomed across the room. The scene was from Dante's Inferno. The two hellish creatures were at bay, caught between the holy symbols held out by the men. The sounds coming from the vampire sisters were deep in the throat, the anger of animals.

By this time, Davis had recovered. He held some of the communion wafers in his hand. Without taking his eyes off of the *nosferatu*, he placed one on the stairs leading to the upper floor. Harker reached behind with one hand and did the same, sealing off the cellar. Taking his cue from the others Seward, while still watching the retreating Lilian, dropped a holy host by the door.

As he passed the edge of the window, Davis reached out and dragged at the drape. Weak dawn-light filtered sluggishly into the room. It was not yet bright enough to distress the undead but added further to their vulnerability. The sight of God's daylight falling on the creatures heartened the men.

Slowly they drove Mina and Lilian back towards the wine cellar. Even in their hellish fury, the vampires looked voluptuous. Pale, flawless skin and low cut dresses, which showed their magnificent breasts. Mina called to Harker.

'Jonathan. Help me, Jonathan. Help me.'

Her voice was plaintive, pleading.

'Mina?'

Harker spoke in wonderment. The voice he heard was that of the old Mina, the woman he loved.

'Don't let them do this, Jonathan. Help me. Help me be with you again.'

To his horror Seward saw that Harker was succumbing to the hypnotic, seductive power of the vampire.

'Jonathan, for the love of Christ!'

Mina reached for the mortal she had once loved. For a moment, it looked as if Harker would put down the crucifix. His arm faltered and almost lowered. Mina smiled a gloating, triumphant smile. It was then Jonathan pushed the cross almost into her face. She shrieked in frustrated rage, and slowly she and Lilian retreated towards the cellar door. The terrible loveliness of the women was only made more grotesque by the animal hissing and growling sounds they made.

'Born of the Virgin Mary, suffered under Pontius Pilate…'

Jack's voice grew stronger and filled the chamber. Mina and her companion, for the first time, looked vulnerable. The demonic rage was being replaced with an uncertainty. They looked about more frantically, still hissing and spitting but with the bewildered movements of trapped animals rather than supreme beings.

'From whence he shall come again to judge the living and the dead…'

The revenants were now backed against the open doorway. Another few steps and they would be driven into the cellar, where stakes would end their blood reign.

Lilian Bowers had been recently baptized into the undead. Her faculties were not as developed as Mina's. Only time would give her those powers. At this point, she was little more than an unthinking, trapped beast.

Mina Harker had accumulated cunning over her years as a revenant. She had escaped from those who had the old knowledge. Her eyes darted around the room. She saw a way out.

With a sudden lunge forward, she pushed the massive bookcase. The edifice, which would have taken a dozen men to move, toppled towards the mortals. They jumped aside as the books and shelves came crashing down.

Davis let out a scream of pain as the edge of the heavy structure struck his injured ankle. Seward and Harker were luckier, dodging the falling shelving.

The crash of the window frame caused them to turn in time to see the vampires smash their way through glass and wood and disappear into the coming dawn.

Chapter 34

The cellar was filled with the smell of corruption. Seward and Harker both stifled the gag reflex as the odour of stale earth and blood assailed them. The dim light revealed the wine racks. Harker nodded towards the space on the ground which had obviously been cleared as a sleeping place for the vampires.

Seward picked up an ingot of gold from the pile of money and jewels which lay scattered around. The bar of gold must have weighed ten pounds. He turned as Harker held out a pocket watch. It was a Hunter, the most prestigious of makes. He looked at the beautifully crafted timepiece and then flipped open the cover. He could see words engraved on the inside. He tilted the case towards the light so that he could read what was written.

'To George from Lilian. With all my Love'

In the upstairs rooms, Davis was systematically sanctifying the area so that Mina and Lilian could not return. At the windows he placed fragments of the communion wafers, and along the ledges he sprinkled holy water. When he had finished, he moved through the other rooms repeating the rituals.

The last place to be sanctified was a small chamber, little bigger than a pantry. It was situated on the landing at the end of a sharp right hand bend in the corridor. The door was stiff, and he had to push hard to force entry. The dull little room was unremarkable. An ancient chair, the stuffing spilling from a burst cover, was the only piece of furniture.

There was no window, and he was about to leave a communion host on the floor when he spotted what looked like a hatch in the wall. It did not look significant, but out of mere curiosity, he strode across and looked more closely. The square was almost imperceptible. The fit was perfect, and no edge was raised. Davis took out his penknife and slipped the blade into the gap. He started to work it backwards and forwards until he sensed there was a slight movement. He levered outwards, careful not to break the blade. His coaxing was beginning to work, and the hatch began to rise out from the wall.

It was slow work. A few times he almost gave up, wondering if it was worth the bother, but his policeman's instinct kept him at the task.

By now, one side of the hatch was almost free. He suspected the opposite edge was held by a hinge. He was able to get his fingers around the raised panel and started to pull. Nothing happened at first, but then he gave one extra tug and the door swung open.

He peered in and could see it led to the space under the eaves of the house. It was probably used as a storage hole. There was very limited headroom, and the cupboard only extended back a few feet. He gave a cursory glance and was about to close the door when he saw the box.

Seward knelt and prayed in the cellar. He called on God to cleanse it of evil. He and Harker had already repeated the ritual of holy water and communion hosts. Jack got to his feet and, with a final look around, stepped outside where Jonathan was putting the last of the valuables on the table.

The gold and jewellery shone and glittered in the daylight. They had drawn the curtains and flooded the room with weak sunshine. Harker picked up some coins, heavy and yellow. They came from different countries and different ages. He remembered the gold he'd seen at Castle Dracula when he was a prisoner there. Seward's voice disturbed his reverie.

'What do we do with this?'

'Give it back, I suppose.'

'To who?'

Harker shrugged. The riches were probably taken from many places at many times. It would be impossible to trace the owners. Even if they tried, how would they explain possession of them to the authorities? We took them from a vampire?

'We could leave them in the cellar,' Seward went on.

'We could, or we could do some good with them.'

'Some good?'

'Jack, you must know a dozen needy charities. We donate it to them. Spread them across several so that it doesn't look suspicious.'

'I don't know, Jonathan. The way they were obtained...'

'You're the priest.'

Seward shook his head. 'To hell with it. I'm not going to count angels dancing on the head of a pin. We'll use it to help some poor souls.'

Seward lifted the coverlet from the settee and set it on the floor. They began to pile the valuables onto it but stopped when they saw Davis come downstairs carrying a small tin box.

He placed it on the table. Harker looked at him quizzically. 'What's this, Harry?' Davis shook his head. 'Found it upstairs. It might be nothing. But look,' He prodded the heavy padlock with his finger. 'It's new.'

They all saw that the ordinary lock, of a type that could be found in any ironmongers, did not have a patina of age or rust. Seward spoke quietly, 'Open it, Harry.'

Davis looked around for a few seconds, and then his eyes alighted on the heavy gold ingot. He picked up the bar and began to hammer at the heavy padlock. It was sturdy, and it took about a dozen blows before it swung open.

He threw the broken lock aside and lifted the lid.

There were papers and many letters, some in heavy buff envelopes. Legal documents were wrapped with red ribbon. Heavy deeds. written on parchment with official seals, sat in bundles. Harker lifted papers at random and scanned them briefly, dropping them again as he took in the gist.

'This is Mina's lifeline to our world. Deeds, properties, banks, everything she needs. Jesus, with this we have a chance of finding her again.'

Chapter 35

CUTTING FROM THE 'EAST LONDON ADVERTISER'

MISSING MEN

Police are seeking information on two young men who were last seen leaving a bioscope in East India Dock Road. They have been named as....

(The bottom of page six)

They lay in the basement of a derelict sawmill by the river. The darkness was soothing. The air still full with the scent of wood and resin. Their flawless skins, marked by the rising sun, were blistered and burned. Within a few moments, the accelerated healing rate of the vampire metabolism would remove all damage.

Escape, blind escape, was all that filled their minds. Escape from the terrible sun. Photophobia, intense sensitivity to light, was a weakness the vampires carried.

They also feared those with the old knowledge, the mortals with crosses and garlic. The men who knew the power of holy water and the stake.

On leaving the house, they had ran blindly through the coming day finally taking shelter in the old mill.

Lilian's senses were scrambled. She had lost all power of thinking and would have run until consumed by the light. Only Mina's greater cunning kept them safe.

Now, as life went on above ground, Mina Harker lay on a bed of earth and wood shavings and thought about her near destruction. To think, those mortals were all still alive! To think that they had found her again!

Memories of when she had been mortal flooded her mind. These thoughts were merely images unattached to emotion. She knew that she had been married to Harker and knew that Seward was once a friend, but she was as indifferent to them emotionally as a scientist studying a microbe.

She merely ran the scenes as a means of coming to terms with recent events.

Her hubris could not fully accept the fact that these men, so weak, so vulnerable, so lacking in her powers, had almost brought about her destruction again.

She remembered Dracula's baffled rage as his plans, and ultimately his existence, were brought to an end by these mortals. He had lived for six centuries, had commanded armies, had the power over the night and all its creatures, had the strength of twenty, yet she had seen him perish in the snow.

If a revenant of such power could be destroyed…Her thoughts grew less clear as the dark sleep began to close down her mind. In a little while, she would be as one dead. No more thoughts until sunset.

As her consciousness slipped away, Mina's vampire brain began to form a plan which would keep them safe for eternity.

Harker was astonished at the foresight of Mina. The pile of documents were a fortress made of paper. Bank accounts led to other bank accounts. Business letters to lawyers, accountants, estate agents, each a model of such preciseness that no mistake was possible. From Limehouse, Mina had sent her tentacles all through London and three or four other major European cities.

He felt tired. The events of the last few days had drained his weakened system. Seward and Davis had been very solicitous of his well-being, but he knew that they too were weary.

Jonathan had suggested that they go back to their normal lives while he spent a day or two going through the papers taken from Limehouse. He knew that they offered their best chance of finding Mina again. He also knew that there would probably only be one more chance. After that, she could disappear to any place in Britain and simply wait till they died. She had eternity before her.

The vampire hunters were counting on the fact that she would assume her papers were safe. This was important. If she knew the papers were discovered then she would simply abandon everything.

He rose and went to the kitchen and made himself a cup of tea. As he waited for the kettle to boil, he read a sheaf of the letters he had picked out.

He mentally saluted Mina for her shrewdness. Clouds of steam floating around his head told him the kettle was boiling and he put the papers on the table. Somewhere here was the key to finding the vampires.

Chapter 36

The hunger was raging. They had lain in the temporary lair for two nights without feeding. Mina's equilibrium was seriously disturbed by their narrow escape. The nearness they had come to destruction had made her determined to take no chances.

Lilian had thrashed and moaned as the need for blood became agonizing. She was a young vampire and hadn't learned to control her impulses. Now she stood ready, her eyes gleaming with anticipation.

They were south of the river. Mina had wanted to hunt far from Limehouse. The odds of them being found by the vampire hunters were negligible, but the *noseferatu* survived for centuries by just such caution.

The rain drizzled down miserably. The streets were empty. Lilian ached. Her need for blood grew by the second. To tear. To rip. To drink. A red tide ran through her mind.

Just ahead lay Tower Bridge. It had been opened less than twenty years before but was already becoming synonymous with London's skyline. The bridge was a strange hybrid of late Victorian engineering brilliance and a gothic castle straight from a fairy tale. Twin towers housed the mighty suspension chains which supported the bascule, the hinged bridge which raised and lowered to allow ships to pass through.

Through the rain came a party of five men. By the look of them they were dock workers. Their voices were loud, and they pushed and jostled each other as they approached.

Mina heard the soft moan of the hunter deep in Lilian's throat. She, too, wanted the kill, but while she knew they could take the five men, she did not want to risk doing so on the street in full view. The shadows were the place for vampires to feed.

The men were on the other side of the street and now almost level with them. Mina was about to step back when Lilian attacked.

She crossed the road in a blur of movement. Before any of the group could even register her presence, her fangs had torn out the throat of the nearest man. Blood splashed across the pavement. Shock and bewilderment stunned the men for a few seconds. The dying man lay on the pavement, his slashed neck sending a fountain of arterial blood pumping high in the air.

Lilian had another man by the lapels. He screamed a high-pitched wail of terror as her canines sought his throat.

Mina's fingers clamped around the windpipe of a third man, squeezing him into unconsciousness and dropping him to the pavement. She felt a blow on the side of the head. A fourth man was holding a docker's hook. The needle point of the hook ripped down the side of her face. She snarled and turned to face him, dark blood seeping from the slash. He held the weapon up in a defensive posture, but his mind could not accept what he was seeing. The gesture was merely instinctive.

Mina buried her teeth in his neck and felt the hunger begin to subside as the hot blood filled her mouth. She drank deeply. By her side Lilian fed also.

Neither vampire paid heed to the remaining member of the group. He ran screaming up the centre of the road, his voice echoing in the night air.

He stopped as he saw a motor car, lights blazing, approach. Standing in the middle of the highway, he waved frenziedly. As it slowed down, he could see it was a large, dark van. On the front, in white lettering, it said 'POLICE'

The man, frantic with terror, could only point and gabble to the sergeant who jumped from the Black Maria. At first, the officer thought he was dealing with a drunk, but when he saw the splashes of blood on the man's clothes and face, he looked towards where he was indicating.

There were figures on the pavement. Bodies scattered around. Leaning over them were two women. The sergeant wasn't quite able to believe what he was seeing for a moment. He then started shouting for the constables in the back of the vehicle.

The driver leapt out and started blowing his whistle. From the van came four officers, leaving a collection of bewildered prostitutes and drunks in the back.

The sergeant led the officers towards the mayhem. He called loudly again and again.

'Police. Police. Stand there. Police.'

As they neared, the carnage became clearer. The pavement was a carpet of scarlet. The two women leaning over the victims seemed unaware of their approach.

The group of police officers were perhaps fifty yards away when the women looked towards them. The veteran sergeant had seen many dreadful things in his twenty five years in the force, but he had never seen anything so terrifying as the blood dripping from those open mouths.

The women stood up. They seemed calm and unperturbed. The police were no more than twenty yards away when they turned almost casually and began to walk towards Tower Bridge.

Their movement seemed effortless, yet the group following began to realize they were not closing the gap. Indeed the women, despite the gliding, unhurried movement, were drawing further away.

The sergeant bawled at the driver to fetch the van. He and the others kept up the chase although the fugitives were now moving further ahead with every stride.

The Black Maria pulled up and the officers piled in, some standing on the running board. The car roared to life and sped after the vampires.

Tower Bridge was now only about three hundred yards ahead. The sergeant urged the driver to put his foot down. The van surged forward, and the driver and sergeant exchanged grins as they saw they were catching up.

The effortless stride of the undead never altered. They moved towards the bridge, their feet seeming to barely touch the ground. They could hear the roar of the approaching van. Mina looked back and saw that they were being caught.

A quick glance to either side showed that there were no openings, no way off the road before they reached the bridge. They were now close enough to see the texture of the Cornish granite on the stone facings.

A movement in the river caught Mina's eye. A ship, a great high-masted vessel, was approaching and she saw the road in front beginning to rise.

The sergeant gave a yell of triumph as he realized their quarry was trapped. The bridge was opening.

The vampires didn't hesitate. As one, they leapt onto the rising section. The angle continued to become more and more acute. On the ground, the police van had screeched to a halt and the officers stood open-mouthed as the two figures climbed up the almost sheer face.

Mina and Lilian reached the apex of their climb. The gap between the two sections of bridge was now about forty feet. Below the tall ship began to glide through. Mina looked back. There on the ground, the mortals stood transfixed by the sight of the two women balanced on the top lip of the rising bridge section. It seemed only a matter of time before the angle became so steep that they would plunge back to earth.

The gap between the sections was forty feet across. The vampires could have effortlessly made the leap, but they were powerless to cross the sluggish Thames. The undead cannot traverse running water by their own power.

They stood at the apex of the terrible incline while the police officers stared up at the sight that would stay with them for the rest of their lives.

Finally, the tall ship passed through, and the great bridge began to close lower and lower. The angle of the sections became shallower as they drew together.

The blood-drenched figures were almost at ground level. The sergeant ordered the van driver to start the engine. The road was clear.

The Black Maria thundered forward, headlamps blazing, but it was too late. The revenants slipped over the edge of a guard rail and dropped onto the footpath which ran alongside the Thames. They were instantly swallowed up by the night.

The sergeant turned to the constables and shook his head. How would they explain this at the station?

Harker left the bank. He had a quiet smile of satisfaction on his face. All day he had followed the trail of documents concerning Mina's financial affairs. He had spoken to the various managers and told them there were probable legal actions being taken against Mrs Murray in connection with her financial affairs and that he was serving a writ freezing the accounts until the matter came to court.

The lawyer knew the writ was spurious and, if challenged, would collapse. However, he also knew that Mina would not fight the action. It would mean speaking to the authorities. It would mean appearing in court. The action he was taking would not seriously damage her, but it would make functioning just a little bit more difficult.

His next step was to find where in London she had another place to rest. Then they would end this once and for all.

Chapter 37

<u>Extract from Metropolitan Police Report. Case File D100986</u>

...only witness to the actual attack. He is in Barts Hospital under sedation. Medical opinion is that it will be some time before a more detailed statement can be taken.

Sergeant William Evans. Warrant no 57993, has given a statement which in parts corroborates that of the witness. Sergeant Evans' account is verified by the four other Metropolitan Police officers at the scene (These statements are in a separate addendum. See appendix 4)

The four deceased were victims of a frenzied attack resulting in death by biting. All witnesses say that the perpetrators of the crime were two women who escaped the scene, despite assiduous pursuit by the officers.

It seems obvious that this was the work of lunatics. There seems to have been an element of cannibalism in the attacks. We will certainly enquire at every Asylum around the capital as to whether patients with this tendency have either been released or have escaped lately.

It seems unlikely that this could be the work of English women. It is more in the character of those from countries where such murderous and primitive emotions are closer to the surface.

Couple this with the attested acrobatic ability of the killers and it would seem all theatres, music halls, circus's and fairgrounds in the Metropolitan area should be checked out for any foreign acrobats...

The Egyptian Avenue was lined with sepulchres. From an entrance guarded by obelisk columns, it led to gothic grandeur. Death made ornate.

Highgate Cemetery was perched on the high ground to the north of the city. Here, many of the pre-eminent dead were laid to rest. George Eliot, the novelist, Michael Faraday, the scientist, Karl Marx, the revolutionary, all slept amid its gloomy splendour.

Among the dead lay the undead. Lilian and Mina were flushed with feeding. Amid the rotting cadavers they were beautiful beyond belief. The rip in Mina's face had vanished, her skin flawless once more.

The vampires had sought safety far from where they had killed. Here, amid the theatrics of death, they felt most welcome.

Seward placed the paper in front of them. The fire crackled and sparked in the hearth as the damp coal Davis had just thrown on struggled to ignite. Seward looked at the list.

'So, what do we do next?'

Harker pointed to the name of a firm of solicitors which he'd written a question mark against.

'You know how she thinks. That house will not be the only one. She has somewhere else to go, somewhere which will have what she needs.'

Harry took a swig of whisky and tapped the paper.

'So how do we find the place? Because that's the only chance we have before she vanishes.'

'If she hasn't already' Seward said softly.

'Why should she?' the detective replied. 'She doesn't know we've found the box, I assume.'

'Why assume that?'

'Because, Jack, she can't get back into the house. She has no way of knowing we found her cache.'

'Don't underestimate her, Harry.'

'I don't, but I don't overestimate her either. She must have another place and she doesn't know we have a way to find it.'

Harker stuck the poker amid the reluctant coals, trying to stir a blaze into life. He turned to his friends. 'What if she has more than one lair?'

Seward shook his head. 'Very unlikely.'

'Why not?'

'Because she doesn't *need* to, Jonathan. She's on her native soil. Dracula needed lots of places to hide because his weak spot was that he had to rest on earth from Transylvania. Mina doesn't have that problem. If she has another lair in London it's purely for practical reasons. To keep money, documents, clothes, things like that. That's why this is our only chance. We've got to find out where they sleep and end this now.'

The clerk bent over the desk finishing up the last work of the day. It had been busy. He rubbed his eyes. The strain of staring at the written word for twelve hours had taken its toll. He took his fingers away from his face and almost fell back in astonishment. Two beautiful women stood before him.

Dark hair and copper hair, stunning beyond belief. He was unable to take his eyes from them. The woman with the dark hair spoke, and it was as if music played. Her voice floated over him, and he listened to the tone and not what the words meant.

She seemed amused by his flustered manner. She looked at the other woman, and they exchanged silvery laughs. The dark-haired woman spoke again. He nodded and began to take down her instructions, all the while imagining her naked.

Chapter 38

They discovered the other lair was south of the Thames. Harker had gone to the solicitors address he'd found among the papers. When he visited the offices, he appeared every inch the superb lawyer he once was.

Jonathan knew that he would have little chance, or at least there would be a long delay, in getting the address out of another solicitor, so he had a plan. Knowing the ways of the law, he turned up at the offices in Chancery Lane very early, just as the place was opening. He expected there was only a junior clerk on the premises. He told them he was a solicitor for another law firm, neglecting to mention they had just recently dismissed him. With an air of one who has a routine task to carry out, he told the callow young man his firm had arranged to collect the address. He said it was in connection with an urgent matter.

The young man, a boy really, was uncertain as to what he should do. He explained to Jonathan that he wasn't allowed to give out any information about clients. He told Jonathan the senior clerk would be in half an hour and he could just wait. At this, Harker grew high-handed and brow-beat the boy into looking through Mrs Murray's files. He took the address, hiding his elation under a stern expression.

It had taken him several hours to round up Seward and Davis. Jack had been attending parishioners who were ill while Davis was trailing yet another possible adulterer.

The domed entrance to Greenwich Foot Tunnel, for some reason, reminded Seward of the subterranean shafts in *The Time Machine* by H.G.Wells. He imagined the Morlocks, the underground creatures who ate human flesh, would have been at home here.

His impression was strengthened as they made their way down the spiral staircase, winding their way fifty feet below until they were under the river. He listened and half expected to hear the thud of heavy machinery like the Time Traveller had done in the novel.

Twin domed entrances faced each other across the Thames, one on the Isle of Dogs and the other in Greenwich. The foot tunnel had been opened ten years earlier to allow men in South London to work in the docks.

Of the trio, only Davis had ever walked through the tunnel before. Harker was struck by the narrowness. It felt claustrophobic, a long tube of white tiles. There was a dip in the middle, and once part of the way in, neither end could be seen. It also passed though Jonathan's mind that above their heads thousands of tons of water pressed down.

They trudged through, each man lost in his own thoughts. All carried the instruments of destruction. Pedestrians coming the other way shot suspicious glances at the somber group.

At last they emerged from the dip and Harker felt relieved to see the way out. The walk had been about five hundred yards long, but he felt as if he had been down there forever.

When they were above ground again, Jonathan gratefully drew in several deep breaths. Seward was amused to find he was grateful there were no Morlocks.

They made their way to Greenwich High Street, a bustling thoroughfare not a stone's throw from the Royal Observatory where the world took its measurement of Longitude.

The house was in a small mews not far from the park. In the bright daylight, it looked charming. A row of small cottage-style houses lined each side. At the end was a blank-faced building which might have been a stable at one time but was now freshly whitewashed and had a new heavy door in the middle. A small window with net curtains was the only other break in the solid front.

Davis checked the numbers as they made their way down the mews. The building at the end was the place they sought. They looked around, each of them very aware of how vulnerable they were in broad daylight. This respectable row of houses, in this respectable London suburb, was not the ideal place to burgle in the pursuit of vampires. Yet they had no choice. Daylight was their only time.

Harker stood on tiptoe and peered through the window. He could see nothing beyond the mesh of the curtains. Beyond was gloom.

Davis took a skeleton key from his pocket and, checking that they were unseen, began to tease the lock. Harker nudged him, and he stopped as a woman carrying a basket of potatoes passed the mews entrance.

They all stood still, aware of how suspicious they must look. Davis told them to forget who was watching. He reminded them boldness was the key. Act suspicious and it begets suspicion. He tackled the lock again. After a few moments, they heard the satisfying click of the levers being thrown.

They all exchanged smiles and stepped inside.

The place was filled with packing cases. Manifestos and carriers receipts were strewn across the boxes. Harker picked up a sheet and paper. It was a confirmation of goods being transported for a Mrs Murray. Eureka!

He showed the paper to the others and then pointed to a door off the room where they stood. They knew by the outside dimensions that there could only be one other room. If Mina and Lilian lay here then they were through that door!

The bags were opened in preparation for taking out the mallets and stakes. Each man put a set of rosary beads around his neck. Seward splashed holy water about them, giving them a blessing. Davis nodded, and they moved to the door.

There was no keyhole, only an old fashioned knob. Harker put his hand forward to grasp it. That was when the voice came from behind.

'Just hold it right there, mate.'

The boxes lay on the dock. Solid and massive. Dockers walked to and fro. Shipping clerks hurried backwards and forwards, carrying cargo manifestos. Sailors moved up and down the gangplank. Officers called down orders.

No one paid any attention to the heavy oak chests. They were merely cargo.

Finally, they were slung and lifted aboard the Blue Funnel vessel.

In the hold, a team of stevedores pushed and hauled the heavy crates into position amongst the other cargo.

Later that night, the ship set sail carrying the boxes to a new continent.

The police cells were dank and smelled of urine. They had been in custody for nearly three days. All three men were grubby and unshaven.

Their arrest had taken place on a Friday afternoon, and so they couldn't appear before the magistrates until Monday morning.

Seward pushed aside the chunk of bread. The coating of margarine was almost quarter of an inch thick, and he was suspicious of several unknown pieces of debris sunk into the pale, yellow layer.

Neither of his two companions had eaten much of the police station food over the week-end. They had sustained themselves mainly with cups of mahogany brown tea.

The arrests had been sickening. Just as they were about to perhaps find and destroy the vampires, the police arrived. It turned out that the solicitor in Chancery Lane, on learning that his clerk had given out the address, had phoned Harker's old firm. When he learned that Jonathan was no longer employed there, he'd called the police.

Seward could have groaned aloud with anguish when the officers insisted on taking them all away. Harker had tried to launch himself at the door where they believed the *nosferatu* slept, but two constables grabbed him and dragged him back protesting. The frustration was unbearable as they were asked mundane questions while only a few feet away, on the other side of a door, might lie evil incarnate.

Harker tried to bluff his way out. Seward tried to play both the doctor and priest card but to no avail. However, they nearly escaped the situation when one of the constables recognized Davis. The detective told him he was on a case. They could sense the atmosphere relax palpably. Then the bags were examined.

Taking out the heavy mallets and wooden stakes, the bottles of holy water and other paraphernalia, the mood changed again, and they found themselves under arrest in Greenwich police station.

As they finished their tea, they went over their tactics for extricating themselves from this dilemma. It would entail portraying Jonathan as a poor lunatic.

The plan was to inform the court that Jonathan had recently been released from Colney Hatch. Seward, as a doctor, would tell them Jonathan had delusions that he was being stalked by vampires.

He and Davis, an ex-police officer of exemplary record and a war hero to boot, had indulged his fantasy, hoping to wean him back to sanity gradually. They found out he was going to find the vampires, so they decided that they should go with him and pretended to believe his story. When he saw the place held no vampires, it might be his first step to recovery.

It was a story so ludicrous, they themselves couldn't help smiling, but it was the best that could be done in the circumstances.

To their amazement, it worked like a charm. Seward put on his most impressive physicians manner, Davis played the noble ex-policeman and Jonathan grinned like an idiot and spoke of the undead.

Not only did the magistrate believe them but he commended Jack and Harry on their concern for their poor friend.

With a warning about the law of trespass, they walked out free men. Their first instincts were to go straight round to the house in the mews and try again. It was decided, however, that discretion was the greater part of valour, and they would go home to wash and change before returning that afternoon. They felt reasonably confident that no-one would envisage them doing exactly the same thing again so soon. All knew that this was the last hurrah. If they did not find Mina and Lilian this time then the cause was lost.

Chapter 39

Molly Brown stood on the dock, looked at the great ship and was impressed. Not a great deal impressed her, but this sight surely did.

Although middle-aged, she still had the spark and vigour that had brought her from being the child of poor Irish immigrant parents to fabulous wealth. Along the way, she had done lots of back-breaking work and fought for a lot of good causes. Her husband had earned their fortune by a method of extracting gold from the bottom of mines.

She had been in Egypt when she learned that her grandson was ill, so she was returning to America in some style. Around her were the richest of the rich. Bruce Ismay, the managing director of the White Star Line, builders of the Titanic. Ismay had a haughty handsomeness which she didn't care for. She could see John Jacob Astor, reputed to be worth £30 million pounds. He was with his second and much younger wife. Nodding to Bruce was Benjamin Guggenheim, a son of the great financial dynasty. It was common knowledge that, although married, he was travelling on the Titanic with his mistress, Madame Aubert.

Men moved up and down the gangplanks of the majestic liner. Luxuries rivalling that of any in history were placed within the great steel walls. All was nearly ready. The Atlantic waited.

It was like a nightmarish form of déjà vu. They took the same walk under the Greenwich tunnel, passed the same endless white glazed tiling. There was also same feeling of relief when the exit appeared.

The trio had been to Davis's house and freshened up after their court appearance. Seward glanced across at Harker who looked pale and shaken. It was easy to forget how recent his recovery from mental illness had been. The solicitor had made a superhuman effort, but the strain of the past few days taxed his fragile inner resources. Seward was worried that he was about to break down.

Harker sensed he was being watched and turned to Seward. The priest gave him a reassuring smile. Jonathan nodded as if he knew what was going through his friend's mind. Jack was relieved to see that, although he looked shaky, his manner was still determined.

They were depending on the fact that the authorities would never consider it a possibility that they would return to the scene of the crime so quickly. As they approached the entrance to the mews, Davis emphasized again that they must walk in confidently. Absolutely no skulking!

The place was quiet on this dull April morning. There was no sign of life from the other houses, and they made their way down towards the end of the mews and the building which they hoped housed the vampires. Davis took the lead. His boots rang out a confident stride on the cobbles. Seward and Harker followed suit, although both felt instinctively they should be tip-toeing past the other windows. Seward had to fight down an almost overwhelming impulse to glance about furtively. However, they took their lead from Davis and moved on with business-like steps.

Davis reached the door first and glanced at the lock. His worry was that the solicitor who handled the property might have changed the fastening for something a bit more secure. With relief, he saw that all seemed the same. He took out the skeleton key. The others watched as he manipulated the lockpick. It seemed a surprisingly short time before they heard the click of the levers opening. Davis smiled and with a little theatrical flourish of his fingers pushed the door open.

The pale daylight revealed that someone had been there recently. The packing cases were gone. Papers and forms were strewn about the floor. The trio exchanged anxious looks. Davis jabbed a finger towards the other door, the one they had come so close to entering on their last visit. They each took a crucifix from the bags and, holding them firmly before them, moved quietly towards the closed door. Harker noted that they all kept silent and moved noiselessly, although there was no reason to do so. In the daylight the vampires would be helpless. Ripe for the stake. There was no danger of attack, but somehow, the sheer horror of what they were about to face made silence seem appropriate.

Seward put his hand on the door-knob. He looked at the other two. They were ready. Jack turned the handle, half expecting the door to be locked, but it swung open easily.

A waft of fetid air assailed them. An unclean smell. Instinctively, they all wrinkled their noses in disgust. Taking in shallow breaths through his mouth to avoid the stench, Seward stepped into the room.

Voices from afar. Strange. Echoing. Shouting. Moving. The rattle over cobbles. Thumps. Lifted. The hum of machinery. The sound of the sea. The cry of gulls. Then silence. Then waiting. Waiting for the darkness.

Chapter 40

The men looked around the small, non-descript room in bewilderment. It was empty. In the thick floor dust there were the outlines of oblong boxes.

Bitter despair covered them like a cloak. By the shapes on the floor, it was obvious that Mina and her companion had been there. Now they were gone! With a roar of frustration, Davis kicked out the shapes of the boxes imprinted in the thick dust. Seward stepped forward.

'Easy, Harry.'

'Easy? Easy? Christ, Jack, you know what this means. We've lost them. We've lost them. They could be anywhere in England right now. This was our chance, Jack, this was our chance!'

'Maybe not.'

Harker's voice sounded quietly from the doorway. They both turned to see the solicitor with a pile of papers in his hand.

'I think I know where they've gone.'

Davis stepped forward. 'Where, Jonathan?'

Harker lifted the papers towards them.

'They're sailing on the Titanic…today.'

Chapter 41

It stood like a colossus, a thing drawn from the days when the Gods sat on Olympus. More than forty six thousand tons, the Titanic was eight hundred and eighty two feet from bow to stern. The fabulous ship rose in tiers of steel plating to a height of one hundred and seventy five feet from the hull to the top of the four funnels.

As the passengers poured aboard the largest ever man-made moving object in history, the world stood in awe. Nine decks made up the social strata of this floating city. At the top was Deck A, a promenade deck where those who glittered and shone would stroll and play, far removed from the lower classes.

Turkish baths, a swimming pool, squash court, cafes, lounges, a post office, barber shop, gymnasium, electric elevators, the list of things conceived for comfort and style was endless.

A prosperous business man, taking a first class cabin, stood by the steward and gazed around at the magnificent décor. A line from a poem he had learned at school ran through his head.

In Xanadu did Kubla Khan
  A stately pleasure dome decree...

He smiled as he saw his wife gaze in unabashed wonder at the splendour around them. Life had been hard for them during the early part of their marriage. Even through the worst times, she had stood by him shoulder to shoulder. He felt his heart swell as he saw the happiness on her face. This voyage would pay her back a little for all that she had done.

He gave the steward a few coins. When they were left alone, they held hands like little children and looked around again in wide-eyed fascination. The man felt wonderful things lay ahead.

In a luxurious and silent suite, several large trunks lay undisturbed. They had been delivered the night before. Among the very explicit instructions were that the rooms occupants would come aboard just before sailing and were not to be disturbed under any circumstances. In the two largest boxes, Mina and Lilian slept. Earth from their native soil was packed in linen sacks around them.

In the ship's cargo bay, many other cases like this were packed among the hundreds of pieces of luggage. Hessian sacks full of earth lay jammed tightly together.

The vampires were carrying their contagion to the new world.

The train chuntered and chattered along the Hampshire countryside. Seward came along the narrow corridor, precariously balancing a tray of tea. The engine lurched over a set of points, and he muttered a curse as the liquid slopped over the tops of the cups. He offered a quick mental act of contrition to God for taking his name in vain and then stood at the door of the compartment until noticed by Davis. The detective drew back the sliding doors and took the tray from Seward, who muttered his thanks.

The noise of the door wakened Harker, who had been dozing by the window. He looked pale. Seward could see the strain was beginning to take its toll. He would have liked to have examined him properly but knew that Jonathan would never agree. Jack made a mental note to keep a very careful eye on the solicitor.

With the tea being passed around, accompanied by some rather tired looking biscuits, they talked about what lay ahead.

In the paperwork they had found a letter confirming two first class tickets on the Titanic. Unfortunately, the letter was partly torn and the names under which the tickets were booked had been lost.

As he sipped his tea, Harker spoke to the others about another set of papers which confirmed that a cargo of wooden crates, classified as industrial earth for botanic purposes, had been sent to New York the week before.

Harry furrowed his brow and tapped the papers held by Seward.

'But why the hell would she send a load of earth on ahead?'

'Because the vampire thinks like a cunning machine, Harry.'

'Yes, but surely she'd be carrying the earth with her. What's the point of sending some on ahead?'

'Double protection. Remember Dracula placed boxes of earth all around London. Well, that gave him a lot of different sanctuaries.'

He held out one of the pieces of paper. Harry turned his head so he could read it.

'You see, boxes of earth to about a dozen locations in and around New York. She's taking no chances.'

They were quiet for a few moments, each man lost in his own thoughts. For Harker and Seward, echoes of the chase across Europe in pursuit of Dracula came to mind. Davis stared out of the window as the green countryside began to make way to the outer suburbs of Southampton.

Seward broke the silence.

'Why do you think she's going to America?'

Harker shrugged. 'I don't know. Maybe Europe knows too much. Vampire lore is wide-spread. We almost ended their reign in the place at Limehouse. I'm sure over the years she's been exposed to vampire killers a few times. America is fresh, young, bursting with energy. New blood. A country with no history of her kind. Just think what she could do in a land that size, Jack. She could feed for centuries and not raise a hint of suspicion.'

Seward nodded. 'Yes, I see what you mean. She could have base camps from the Atlantic to the Pacific. Leave resting places right across America.'

The prospect of the vampires bringing an ancient European horror to another continent was overwhelming. No man spoke until the train rhythm altered, and it began to slow down as it neared Southampton station.

Chapter 42

The horns sounded, the cheers echoed and the lines were cast off. The gargantuan engines, driven by super-heated steam, pushed the massive pistons of the vessel. The Titanic slowly moved away from the dock.

On the bridge, Captain Edward Smith watched as the gap between the dockside slowly widened. Smith, with his dark naval style uniform, brass buttons and peaked cap, looked the epitome of what a sailor should be. Strong and square, with calm eyes.

He checked his watch. Twelve noon precisely. Captain Smith wanted no delay. This was the maiden voyage and everything had to be perfect. The eyes of the world were upon his ship. He was also aware that great things were expected of her in terms of time. With a top speed of twenty three to twenty four knots, there was no reason the Titanic shouldn't break the record for crossing the Atlantic.

Suddenly, one of the seaman on the bridge called out. To his horror, Smith could see a large ship drifting inexorably towards the Titanic. It was a liner. He could clearly see her name, *The New York*.

The smaller vessel had slipped her moorings and was heeling across. Collision seemed imminent. Smith and his officers barked orders, and time seemed to stand still as the leviathan answered the helm and slowly but surely managed to clear the rogue vessel. Tensions eased on the bridge, and smiles of relief replaced grim, worried expressions. It had been a close call.

They had barely left the dock and there was almost a disaster. Smith hoped that wasn't a portent. Pushing the thought from his mind, he returned to guiding the great ship seawards.

The man with the bushy grey beard and piercing eyes made his way along the promenade deck. William Stead was going to America at the specific request of President Taft himself. Stead was known throughout Europe as a reformer and political commentator. He was also a crusading journalist who had been imprisoned for his expose of child prostitution. A peace conference was taking place at Carnegie Hall, and he had been asked to be a principal speaker.

The ship was magnificent, yet Stead could not still his feelings on unease. A leading spiritualist, he had been constantly plagued in recent years by feelings of his own impending death. The sea and drowning was a subject that had haunted him, and he thought of the two stories he had written some years back, both concerning the sinking of great ships.

With an effort, he drove these thoughts from his mind and continued his stroll. Surely such a ship as this could never…

Visions, such terrible visions, stabbing and jolting through his head like an electric shock. He reeled across the deck, almost falling as his mind was flooded with pictures of blood and crimson mouths. Skin white as death. Eyes dark as hell.

Just as suddenly as they had come, the visions ceased. Stead held dazedly to a rail until he felt his legs would hold him. One or two passengers looked at him curiously. He gathered himself for a couple of moments and then somewhat unsteadily made his way towards his cabin. He didn't notice that he had stopped by the entrance to a large stateroom. He didn't know behind locked the doors Mina and Lilian waited for the night.

The dash to the docks was agonizing. The train had stopped maddeningly just outside the station and had sat there in a hiss of steam for almost fifteen minutes until the signals at last let them pass. They had raced to the taxi rank and by blatant queue jumping, much to the noisy protest of several fellow travellers, had managed to get a cab to the docks.

Every minor hold up, every delay, had brought them to the edge of despair. Although the distance was relatively short, their impassioned desire for haste had the driver's nerves at a pitch. The poor man was convinced that his frantic passengers were about to get behind the cab and push it to go faster.

At last, they reached dock where the Titanic was due to depart. Seward ran on ahead, the other two trailing behind. Davis was hampered by his weak ankle, and Harker was in state of exhaustion.

When they reached where Seward stood, all three men could only watch in despair as the great ship sailed out towards the open Atlantic.

Chapter 43

TELEGRAM: WHITE STAR LINE

"Wish to board the Titanic at Queenstown. Stop. Please reserve three second class passages. Stop. H. Davis European Branch Pinkerton Detective Agency. Stop."

The waiter, under the steely gaze of the *maitre d'*, gave a last polish to the plate with the crest of the White Star Line in the centre. The first class dining salon was opulent beyond belief. Tablecloths of dazzling white, chairs almost royal in their design, glasses of sparkling crystal, cutlery of the finest quality, all embossed with the company design.

Music played softly and elegantly in the background. The murmur of wealthy voices drifted through the air as the first class passengers dined in splendour. Plates heaped with lobster, plovers eggs, and caviar were served by almost impossibly servile waiters.

Molly Brown was eating heartily. She was not of these people, but she had too much money to be excluded. Around her sat the richest of the rich. The Astors, Guggenheim with his mistress, Ismay, and the Chairman of White Star.

In the gentle, refined contentment of the truly fortunate, two women of stunning beauty held the attention of those around them.

Mina and Lilian sat like enchanted beings from a fairy tale. Fellow diners, male and female alike, were caught and held in their gaze. The soothing effect of their voices was compelling. So beguiling were they that no one noticed that they only raised the wine glasses to their lips but did not drink, only moved their food around their plates but did not eat.

The harbour lay under the stare of the almost-finished cathedral. St Colman's was a neo-gothic masterpiece of spires and carvings. Begun more than forty years before, it was nearing completion. The men stared up at the towering edifice and then looked over the harbour to where the Titanic lay.

The land sweeping down to the sea was verdant. Lush emerald grass met the blue, dark water. Dotted around the hillside were white cottages, like so many dolls houses. Along the seafront, houses and shipping offices made up the bulk of the town.

The journey had been frantic. After missing the ship at Southampton, they learned there would be a brief stop at Cherbourg before picking up the final few passengers in Ireland. They knew they could never catch her in France before she departed, so they headed across the Irish Sea.

Queenstown sat on the edge of Cork Bay and was the starting point that had sent many millions of emigrants across the sea to seek better lives. It was here the Titanic lay anchored, ready to turn her mighty bow to the open ocean.

All the men looked tired. The day and night had been a blur of trains and carriages. Always at their heels was time's winged chariot. If they had failed to catch the ship before it left Ireland then the vampires would be free to found an unholy dynasty in the New World.

They took a brief respite before boarding. Harker was a spent force. His face was a ghastly shade of grey, and there was a slight tremble to his hands. Seward leaned over and spoke to him quietly while Davis was standing at little way off, eating a hunk of bread and cheese hurriedly grabbed on the run.

'You alright, Jonathan?'

Harker nodded. Seward could see the whites of his eyes had an unhealthy film across them. He took his friend's wrist and felt for his pulse. Harker made a mild protest but let him proceed. Fast, too fast. His heart was racing. Any more strain might kill him.

'Jonathan, I think maybe you should let Harry and me take it from here.'

Harker looked at him in surprise. 'What?'

'Your heart, it's racing. Dangerous. You've done more than enough. You kept us on the trail when we could have lost them. We know what to do. You stay here. Rest.'

Harker looked at his friend for a moment and then let his gaze drift out to the great ship by the harbour. There was a moment's silence, and when he spoke, his voice contained all the sadness in the world.

'I died the day Mina became a vampire, Jack. What you have in front of you is just another version of the undead.' He sighed deeply. Seward was unsure whether it was because he was having trouble breathing or because of his mood.

'There's nothing this world has to offer any more for me. You know what I've been doing. Marking time till I die. Well, now I have something to die for, Jack. Mina! I want to free her. I want her soul to go to heaven where it really belongs. And if I can help do that then I know I can let go of this life. I know that she'll be waiting for me.'

He shook his head. 'Stay behind? I don't think so, Jack.'

Seward placed his hand briefly on his friend's shoulder and then reached into his pocket and took out a little bottle of pills. He pulled out the cork and tapped a couple of tablets into his hand which he then handed to Jonathan. The solicitor took them without comment and swallowed them. They were a powerful drug. In normal circumstances, he would have been wary of giving them to a patient in Harker's condition.

But these weren't normal circumstances.

Some looked frightened. Some looked happy. Some looked sad. Some looked worried. More than a hundred souls gathered on the boat which would carry them out to Roches Point, the outer anchorage in Queenstown harbour. It was there the Titanic lay, waiting to carry them all to a new life.

Hopes and fears and dreams were crammed together in that mass of humanity. There was a multitude of reasons for leaving, but the one central theme was to start anew.

Amid the babble of accents and languages, Seward and his companions were notably withdrawn. The three men stood apart from fellow passengers. More than one traveller noticed the grimness which surrounded the trio.

The trip across the choppy harbour was brief, and soon they were clambering aboard. Waiting to receive them, one of the crew members wondered why, amid the piles of possessions brought aboard by the emigrants, these three men held only the smallest of hand luggage. Who would sail to America and need so little?

People called out. Junior officers waved their arms and tried to sort out the milling mass who came aboard. Davis spoke to a purser and produced the tickets which had been waiting for them at the office on the harbour. After a quick glance, he called for a steward to show them their berths.

Despite the urgency of their mission, all the men were distracted by the wonders of the Titanic. The sheer scale, the magnificence of the décor, the amazement that such a thing could be conceived and executed by the mind of man was overwhelming.

Their fellow travellers from the short journey across the harbour were led almost without exception towards the third class accommodations. Seward and his companions were guided by a cheerful Welsh steward along a bewildering labyrinth of corridors and through an eternity of doors and stairs. At last, they stood before a small stateroom.

'Here we are now, gents. Shelter Deck C. Know it must seem a bit confusing like, but you'll soon get used to it, see.'

The steward flung open the cabin door. Seward noted with amazement the style and finish. Having travelled by sea several times in his life, he could see that second class travel on the Titanic was as good as, if not better than, first class on many other ships.

At one side of the cabin was a double tier bunk and on the other a single bed. A small curtain could be drawn across to separate this bed from the rest of the cabin. It was obviously ideal for a family, a couple and a child. A substantial dressing bureau with wash-hand basin attached was set back against the bulkhead at the far end of the cabin.

The steward looked at their Spartan luggage and asked them, not without a certain sly humour, if they needed any help unpacking. Harker declined with thanks and pressing a few coins into his hand saw him off the premises.

Harry sat down on the bottom bunk and sighed with relief as the weight left his swollen ankle. It had been throbbing for the best part of the day. He reached down and rubbed gently. Even through the thick sock, he could feel the heat from the inflamed tissue.

Davis looked at the cabin approvingly. Nice, very nice. The best Pinkertons could afford. He felt a chill of anxiety at the thought of what he'd done. Without authority, he'd booked three passages on the Titanic in the name of the Agency! He'd signed a legal document stating that he was booking it on their behalf. Christ! He'd committed fraud!

He knew that was mere bagatelle when weighed against their mission. He smiled to himself as he imagined using that as a defence in court. The thing is, m'lord, I only did it to save the world from vampires.

Harker went to the other bed and lay back, closing his eyes. The pills had helped, and he felt better than he had a few hours ago. A headache, which had been snickering at the back of his head all day, began to recede. He felt Seward take his pulse, but he kept his eyes closed. He was tired but not finished, not yet.

Moving away from Jonathan, Seward went to the little wash basin and ran some water into his cupped hands before lowering his face into the deliciously cool liquid. He repeated this several times and then dried his face on a towel by the side.

'So, what do we do now?' Davis' question hung on the air. None of the other two answered. Then Seward spoke.

'I hadn't really thought that far in advance, Harry. Getting on the bloody boat first seemed the priority.

'Okay, now we're on the 'bloody boat.' Anybody got any suggestions?'

Jonathan opened his eyes and squinted across. 'We get something to eat. I'm starving.'

The great ship sailed across the ocean as if it were moving on a sheet of glass. No motion was discernable, and all over the ship, passengers of all classes marvelled at the stillness.

In the first class sections, elegance and riches abounded. They strolled along the decks or sat in the Saloon or the smoking room, with its inlays of mother of pearl. In the lounge, the orchestra played light operetta.

A bugle sounded to the elite, calling them to eat the finest.

In the second class sections, the petite bourgeoisie aped their betters and tucked into fish or chicken and felt themselves a cut above those travelling third class.

Deep in the bowels of the ship, those at the bottom of the social strata found their way to their modest cabins. Food here was modest too. Children huddled close to their parents and asked what life would be like in America. Mothers hushed crying infants to sleep. Fathers sat in the third class dining room and pretended they knew much more about the ship than they actually did.

From out in the dark Atlantic, the Titanic appeared to be something from a fairytale. Ablaze with light, the sounds of the many orchestras drifting out across the night air. On the bridge, the helmsman turned her nose towards the colder waters of the North.

And the bands played on…

Chapter 44

Arthur Cransfield took in great gulp of air. For ten hours he'd been in the engine-room. The roar of the great machines and the stifling heat had seemed to go on forever. Now he stood in the cool of the night air and gazed across the placid ocean. From inside, he could hear the music playing. He looked over the rail and watched the waves rushing against the side of the ship before falling back in whitecaps.

There was something hypnotic about the *whoosh* and *sloosh* of the waves breaking and falling and then being reborn. He was so intent on the motion that he didn't hear them come up behind him. It was only when he heard the softest of silvery laughs did he turn round.

They were so beautiful he couldn't breathe. Dark and Copper. Mouths of vermillion. Skin pale as morning mist. They were smiling. Arthur tried to say something. Tried to clear his throat, but nothing would come out. His heart pounded in his chest.

The woman with the dark hair moved nearer. He could feel the sexual allure coming off her almost in waves. His eyes were locked on hers. Her mouth opened, and she ran her tongue slowly and lasciviously over those crimson lips.

He felt a hand on his shoulder. The woman with the copper hair traced her hand playfully down his arm and onto his hand. He wanted her to leave it there. He felt himself harden. He wanted these women so much.

The dark woman was against him, smiling, teasing. Her hand slid down his trunk. His erection grew painful. Still, she held him in her gaze.

Now both women were running their fingers gently across his groin. As they did so, they shared secret smiles. They were laughing at him, but Arthur didn't care. He just wanted them to do what they were doing.

The woman with the copper hair cupped her hands around the bulge in his trousers and squeezed gently. He gave a little moan of ecstasy and thrust his hips forward, closing his eyes in anticipation.

Keeping her hand on his cock, she kissed the side of his face. He felt lips and coldness on his skin. He felt the other woman open his collar and begin to nibble his neck. He lay back against the rail, and they began to feed.

When he was drained, the vampire sisters pushed the lifeless figure over the side.

Arthur Cransfield's body made a tiny splash and then joined the ceaseless dashing and rushing of the waves.

William Stead woke from a blood-drenched sleep. He cried out in the darkness of his cabin and then fumbled desperately for the light switch. As illumination flooded the room, he sighed with relief and fell back on the pillow. His nightshirt was soaked with sweat, and his heart beat a rapid tempo. He took several deep breaths and tried to calm the jagged thoughts which tore through his brain.

Women. Dreadful, lovely women, with bosoms as white as snow and lips as red as blood and teeth glinting like razors. He'd seen them. Like the spirits of the dead he saw once when at a séance. He wasn't afraid of the dead. The dead would never harm the living, but these women struck him with dread to the depths of his mortal soul. Ever since he'd had that psychic experience as he walked the decks, his mind had been overthrown with feelings of doom and horror. Running through his dreams of the terrible women was the sound of a great tearing. Then there was screaming and crying and a flood, a wave of water and people sinking. Sinking under the waves with their eyes open. As they sank, their mouths opened and they screamed, and those screams came bursting to the surface and were so loud and terrifying that his ears bled.

Above it all, smiling terrible smiles, were the women with sinful mouths.

Dawn was approaching. The dark blanket of the Northern sky began to break with streaks of grey and silver. Aboard the Titanic, the passengers slept. The churning powers of the great seventy two thousand horse power engines drove the juggernaut forward.

In a first class suite, Mina Harker prepared for sleep. Lilian, her mouth smeared with blood, had already sunk into the silence of death vampires called rest. She lay in the coffin in the little side chamber.

They had arranged that their cabin must never be entered. Mina had told them her sister had a nervous condition and was sensitive to light. The White Star line had agreed that special locks be fitted and that only Mina and her sister would have the keys. With her unlimited money, the shipping company was only too happy to oblige a customer of such obvious wealth.

She looked out of the porthole and saw that day would soon be upon them. Mina drew the curtain closed, shutting out the growing light. In her cold, cunning vampire brain, she went through the stages which had brought them to this and would lead them to new feeding grounds in America.

She had dispatched boxes of their native earth to many locations around their landing point. This would give them alternative resting places if the situation demanded it. In the hold of the Titanic were also several crates of soil which would provide them with extra security.

The boxes in which they lay had a layer of dirt under the velvet lining. Mina felt her senses begin to slip. Blackness began to crowd her brain. Time for the dark sleep. Although supremely self-possessed, part of her mind told her that this journey was not one she would have chosen freely.

Fear, or as close to fear as a vampire feels, drove her to this new direction. The mortals with the old knowledge had found them, had almost destroyed them. Mina was a cold, thinking machine, and she knew that any chance of them being found again was very remote. But it was a possibility. Her pursuers had found her many years ago and had almost ended her existence. Only a few days ago, it had happened again.

She decided a new land, where blood ran fast and vigorous and strong, would give them a feeding ground for centuries. In a country so huge, their presence would pass unnoticed.

In a country that innocent, no-one would know the old ways. No-one would know how to stop them.

Mina lay down. She closed her eyes, and her thoughts melted into the void.

In the crews quarters, an engineering officer called in and asked if any them had seen Arthur Cransfield. He'd failed to report for his shift. A quick poll among his shipmates revealed that he hadn't been seen since his last stint in the engine room. This was puzzling. Cransfield was a steady man, not a drinker and not given to shirking. The engineer asked them to keep an eye out for him and went off to report his absence.

They had freshened up and eaten. All felt better. Seward was still slightly
worried about Harker. He could see his friend was making a supreme effort to appear fine, but there was a weariness behind his eyes which showed his health was deteriorating. In another situation, Jack would not have allowed Jonathan to keep going on the powerful pills, but he knew there was no alternative. Desperate remedies...

Over the simple meal in the second class dining-room, they had discussed their tactics. They knew the vampire women would hide in the daylight hours, and the daylight was the time they needed to find and destroy them. Now, as they strolled along the promenade deck, they tried to focus on how they could find the location of the *nosferatu*.

Seward stopped at the ship's rail and peered out across the ocean. Two young girls ran past, pointing excitedly to the seagulls trailing alongside the ship. A sedate couple, obviously their parents, called vainly after them about the dangers of falling.

Still looking out to sea, Jack set out the possible courses of action.

'So, gentlemen, we're on the ship. We know the vampires are somewhere, but how do we find them?'

Harker wiped the water from his eyes, induced by the constant sea breeze blowing into his face, and then spoke slowly.

'There's only one way, we hunt them by night and destroy them at dawn.'

Davis laughed shortly. 'Brilliant analysis, Sherlock. Why didn't I think of that?'

Harker smiled and then continued. 'Thank you, Doctor Watson. As far as I can see, there's two ways we find them. One, we search the boat at night, when they'll be active. Then we...'

Seward cut in sharply. 'Search the boat? God, Jonathan, have you any idea how big this ship is? And how many people are on board? Counting passengers and crew, it's got to be more than three thousand souls!'

'Yes, but we don't have to search every inch of the ship, Jack. We can cut it down to one section and one class of passenger. First class.'

'How can we possibly know that, man? They could have…'

'Could have what, Jack? Booked second or third class? Shared accommodation? No, money is no object, and seclusion is vital, so they'll be travelling first class.'

From somewhere ahead, they could hear an orchestra playing light opera. Seward could make out the faint strains of *Cavalleria Rusticanna.* Around him, people walked and talked and laughed, unaware of the malevolent evil among them, not realizing that the three grim-faced men were perhaps the only thing that stood between the world and the curse of the vampire.

Davis spoke. 'That makes sense, Jonathan. Now we have to get access to the first class facilities. That won't be bloody easy. They won't want people like us mixing with their 'betters.'

'We'll cross that bridge when we come to it, Harry. First things first, we establish their presence.'

'Then what?' Seward's tone suggested that he was still unconvinced.

'Then we do one of two things. Either we hope they haven't seen us…'

'I like that part of the plan a lot, Jonathan.' They all laughed at the earnestness of Davis's response.

'Then we can follow them, find out where their cabin is and wait till daylight and then…' Harker left the conclusion unsaid.

'And the second thing?'

'The second thing, Jack, is that we get a copy of the passenger list and try to unearth them using that.' Harker was aware of the grim, unintentional humour within his use of the word 'unearth.' Neither he nor his companions found it the least amusing. Not in the least.

Chapter 45

<u>Extract from Titanic Log. 12th April 1912</u>

...no sign of the crew member despite extensive searches. It can only be surmised that he fell overboard some time during the night. Another search will be attempted before informing the immediate family...

Captain Smith shook his head as the officer reported the result of second sweep of the ship. Bad luck. Bad luck. First they had almost collided with another vessel before they had even left Southampton, now this. A man disappears.

Smith turned to the young officer and told him to carry on with his duties. He turned up the collar of his heavy jacket. The air was getting chillier, but the ship was sailing fair and a record crossing was looking very possible.

The grandeur was intimidating. All around him, the genteel elegance spoke of riches and a breed of people alien to most of the civilized world. The wealthiest of the wealthy. Every gesture, every effortless movement, told they were the truly blessed.

Harker pulled at the stiff collar biting into his neck and tried to appear at ease. The dress suit had been obtained by one of the stewards. They had told him a story of lost luggage. The suit was for a man slightly smaller than Jonathan, and he was painfully aware that the trousers verged on ridiculously short. However, by lengthening his braces to their full extent, he managed to stay this side of comical.

Seward and Davis were outside, prowling Promenade Deck A. Here, the first class passengers took in the sea air or sat in the elegant stateroom. It had taken them all their ingenuity to secret themselves among the elite. The Titanic was designed to keep the classes apart, and only by a series of torturous circumventions and glib, brazen lies, did they manage to penetrate the sanctum of the great and the good.

As always, music played. To Harker, the music only underlined the fact that he was a character of a glamorous theatrical extravaganza. It was all there: lights, music, costumes, and actors who were at home in their parts.

The heat and brilliance of the illuminations had started another headache. He took out the little bottle of pills Seward had given him and slipped two into his hand. He frowned as he noticed there were only a few left.

He stopped a passing waiter and asked for a glass of water. As he waited, he marvelled once again at what a wondrous creation the Titanic was. Built mainly by men who would never be able to afford to sail in her, the ship was a tribute to the skills of a nation.

The waiter returned. Harker was startled by the way the man glided up to his side almost magically. He thanked the servitor and watched him glide away with that same effortless motion. Jonathan wondered if waiters took lessons in gliding across rooms effortlessly.

He swallowed the pills and was just about to place the glass on a small shelf when he saw them.

He felt a thrill of terror sweep over him. For a moment, he thought he would faint. Harker instinctively stepped back, taking partial cover behind an ornamental pillar.

Mina and Lilian glowed even in the midst of all that grandeur and beauty. It was as if an aura surrounded them. They seemed to shimmer. People stood slightly aside as if unable to believe such beauty existed.

Both wore long elegant gowns, cut low. The décolletage showed their heavy, ivory breasts to their full advantage. Even from that distance, the sensuous, cherry-ripe redness of their mouths showed wide and welcoming.

Surrounded by admirers, they nodded and smiled and captivated.

Harker felt his senses in turmoil. His heart beat furiously. Sweat broke out on his brow. A sickening feeling of fear gripped his insides.

As the *nosferatu* went through the dark pantomime of pretending to observe human conventions, he wondered what those beguiled by them would do if their true natures emerged. In his mind's eye he saw those smiling mouths open and tear the throats and drink. He saw those delicate arms throw men twenty feet across the room and those long fingers carry them up a sheer wall.

For a moment, Harker felt an irresistible impulse to run from the room. His fear grew in waves, and it was all he could do to stay behind the pillar. What kept him there was not courage, or the need to save humanity, but his love for Mina.

Even as one of the undead, he still loved her. Not for her beauty, but because of the woman she once was. She was, and would always be, the love of his life. It was for this he stayed. It was for this he would drive a stake through her heart.

In the telegraph room, wireless operator Jack Phillips rubbed his face wearily. From the start of his watch, he'd been dispatching Marconigrams almost without a break. Passengers had been sending out an endless stream of salutations since they had reached the open sea.

He looked at the pile of paper and sighed. It would take him hours to get through this lot. He idly speculated how much profit on the messages the White Star line would make. The price for ten words was twelve shillings and sixpence, or three dollars. The task of calculating how much all those hundreds of words would cost made him dizzy. Certainly the sheer volume kept them so busy there was little time for incoming messages. He took a sip of the lukewarm tea on the table beside him and returned to the sending dots and dashes out into the ether.

Harker recognized Benjamin Guggenheim. He had seen his pictures in the papers. A lovely woman was on his arm. Jonathan didn't know her, but something in their demeanor suggested they were not married. They lacked the comfortable familiarity of spouses.

Guggenheim and his companion were speaking to Mina and Lilian. Jonathan could see even from a distance how entranced the couple were by the presence of the two revenants. Finally Guggenheim, in turn, placed a courtly kiss on the hands of the two women and sauntered off, his companion slipping her arm possessively through his.

Harker was torn between going to find Seward and Davis and waiting to follow the vampire women. He cursed himself for his earlier indecision. If he'd gone when he first spotted them he could have spoken to his companions and formed a plan. He had no way of knowing how long Mina and Lilian would be in the room.

The decision was taken out of his hands as the revenants walked slowly towards the grand staircase. This was perhaps the single piece of décor which embodied the grandeur of the Titanic.

A thing of wondrous polished beauty, it rose with a gracious sweep to the level above. The rising treads divided in dual elegance to the left and right. Up the centre of the stairway separating the diverging sweeps was an ornamental barrier, intricately fashioned, with a classical figure at the bottom holding forth a lamp. Above the staircase was a glass dome which in daytime flooded the stairway with natural light.

Harker waited until Mina and her companion had almost reached the top of the stairs before he followed. He felt his heart pounding. He was deathly afraid. Jonathan knew of the supernaturally heightened senses of the vampire. They read the delicate atmospheric vibrations of any situation. He knew his only advantage was that they didn't know he and his companions were aboard. That, coupled with the mass of humanity which thronged the ship, might mask his presence.

He kept them in sight as they moved along the passageways. Harker noticed that everyone who passed stared at them. Men and women alike were caught in the aura of terrifying sensuality. He saw the vampires turn a corner and scuttled forward in time to catch a glimpse of them making their way towards Promenade Deck A, where Seward and Davis were prowling. He felt a jolt of fear. If the revenants came across his companions then all might be lost. They had to find their hiding place and stake them where they lay.

A slightly drunk man and woman tripped along the passage, giggling and pushing at each other. When the couple came level with Mina and Lilian he noticed that both went silent, and they moved past the vampires with sober expressions.

Here, the ship was quieter. The crowds had thinned out. He was uncomfortably aware that he was more exposed should they turn round. A ship's steward, balancing a silver tray of food as deftly as a juggler, swept past, wishing him a cheery goodnight.

His attention was distracted, and he almost missed the *nosfertau* go through one of the bulkhead doors. He hurried forward and saw a set of stairs leading to the lower decks. He hesitated. Surely, they would have cabins on the upper sections? He then remembered some of the first class staterooms were lower down.

He followed. The women went down another deck. He just caught a glimpse of their dresses as they descended several feet in front of him. When the trail led to yet a lower level, Harker had a premonition of danger. He listened. No sound. He risked a furtive peer over the stair rail. There was still no sign.

Then from behind him he heard the sweet, terrible laugh of the vampire

Chapter 46

The captain of the *SS Caronia* stood on the bridge and looked out over the Atlantic. The sea was calm and the air cool. All seemed well, but his seaman's instinct told him that such weather held ice.

The North Atlantic was feared for 'growlers', the huge drifting icebergs which bobbed around. Floating mountains which could smash a ship to matchwood.

There was no sign of trouble as yet, but the air was definitely cooling. He turned to the first officer and told him to warn the lookout to be extra sharp.

The ocean was as friendly as he'd ever seen it, but there was no sense in taking any chances

Chapter 47

A thrill of terror ran through Harker as he turned on the stairs to see the two vampire women only a few feet away. He felt unable to move as those beautiful, wanton faces stared into his. Mina, her mouth slightly open, her vermillion lips parted in a sardonic smile, laughed softly again.

'Jonathan. How old you look.' At this the two women laughed again, mockingly.

'How do you think I look, Jonathan?' She held out her arms as if displaying her body.

'Do you still want me, Jonathan? Would you like to take me, naked. Here? You can, Jonathan. You can have me. Both of us.'

As she spoke, her voice flowed over him, soothing, seductive, welcoming. He fought hard not to look at her. He knew he had to avoid her eyes.

'I expect your friends would like to join us. They will. They will.'

Harker saw them move slowly along the landing to the top of the stairs. He stood perhaps ten steps below that level. The man knew flight was useless. They would be upon him before he had descended two steps.

He desperately wished he had some sort of protection, but he hadn't expected contact. In his mind's eye he could see his bunk strewn with the objects of his salvation, the crucifix, the holy water. He was like an antelope about to go down before panthers.

He could hear the *swish swish swish* of silken dresses as they approached. They stood at the top of the stairs. He was unable to keep from looking into Mina's eyes. Slowly he raised his head and stared into those dark, irresistible orbs and felt his will beginning to drain away.

With growing horror, he realized that *this was what he wanted.*

He wanted those glistening mouths on his neck. He wanted those voluptuous bodies against his.

Death was only a few steps away when suddenly, a group of crew members noisily came clattering up the stairs. The mixed group, perhaps a dozen young men and women, were laughing and joking, calling loudly to each other. They were going on duty.

The delicate aura of seduction and submission created between vampire and victim was broken. Harker was freed from the longing to embrace the undead.

The vampire women stared balefully at the surge of humanity. They could with ease take Harker, even with all those present. They could kill all those present in the space of a few heartbeats.

Only the need for secrecy saved the unsuspecting mortals. To kill so many would lead to public scrutiny and a search of the ship. They were not afraid, but they did not wish to risk discovery, especially at sea where escape was impossible.

All these thoughts passed through Mina's mind as the crew members jostled past Harker. They were almost at the top of the steps and about to move around Mina and Lilian when Jonathan seized his chance and ran down the stairs, jumping the last few and landing solidly on the deck before racing off down the passageway.

The time between the group passing the *nosferatu* and Harker's run was only a few seconds. With the last of the mortals beyond them, the vampires took up the pursuit.

A young cabin steward bringing up the rear of the group glanced back. Not only for another glimpse of the beautiful women who stood so incongruously in that section of the ship, but also at the way they seemed to be moving down the stairs as if floating on air.

Harker tore along the passageways in a blind frenzy of fear. He didn't know where he was going. He passed through bulkheads, down a flight of stairs and past puzzled crew members who stopped to look back at the rather demented looking passenger.

Jonathan was tiring fast. His body, worn out with years of not eating or exercising properly, was not equipped for sustained flight. He didn't know if it was real or the result of his fevered imagination, but he could hear the *swish swish swish* of silk behind him, drawing nearer.

In his frantic run, he glanced around desperately for something he could use to create a makeshift crucifix. Some pieces of wood, a couple of lengths of piping. Anything would do, but there was nothing.

Swish swish swish. He almost sobbed aloud as the sounds seem to come from right behind him. Dear Jesus, guard my soul!

His strength was almost gone. His breathing burned in his chest. He came to a doorway which was partly ajar. Harker stumbled through it and found himself in what looked like a storage pantry. Cases of food and other kitchen goods lay around one section of the cabin. At the far end was another doorway.

Swish swish swish.

God help me! Help me! Harker slammed the door closed and slid a bolt across. He lay against the bulkhead and tried to take a few deep, searing breaths. He listened for a few seconds. Silence. He offered up a little prayer of thanks to the God he had neglected for so many years.

Collecting himself, he made his way across the cabin on legs that felt as if they would buckle under him at any moment.

The place smelled of fresh paint. It had obviously been just finished before the maiden voyage. He turned the handle and pulled. The door held fast. For a moment, a wave of panic gripped him until he looked up and saw a large draw-bolt had been slid across at the top. He sighed with relief. Harker reached up and tried to pull the bolt back. It was stuck!

He pulled again, but the thing wouldn't budge.

Swish swish swish.

This time it was real. He heard the rustling of silk stop outside the cabin door. To his dread, twin seductive voices drifted through the bulkhead.

'*Jona-thaaaan Oh, Jona-thaaaan.*'

Harker dragged furiously at the bolt. It would not move. He could see it was held in place by a thick layer of paint.

'*Jona-thaaaan. Jona-thaaaan.*'

The taunting, terrifying voices came again. He heard the rattle of the door handle opposite. It turned slowly, ominously. He heard a hiss of anger as the portal refused to open and he thanked his stars he'd put the bolt on.

Again, he tugged desperately at the paint-jammed fixture. His fingers, wet with sweat, slipped off. He muttered a curse of pain as one edge of his thumb skidded across the metal, shearing off a layer of skin and leaving a streak of blood over the newly painted surface.

'*Jonathan. Jonathan. Open the door, Jonathan. I love you, Jonathan.*'

Like Odysseus shutting his ears against the song of the Sirens, Harker put his fingers in his ears and fought against the voice which seemed to be deep in his brain.

He rocked back and forth, trying to drown out the sounds, praying aloud and calling on God to give him strength. Finally, the voices faded. The cabin was silent. Harker could only hear the beat of his own heart. Then he heard a groaning of metal. He looked towards the door which held out the undead and saw that the handle was in the open position, and that *the bolt was slowly bending.*

He watched in disbelief for a few seconds as the solid steel rod began to buckle inwards. The strength of the vampires was beyond belief.

Fighting down his rising panic, the man looked around desperately for something that would help him open the jammed bolt. A small tin of paint, it looked like red lead from the dried colouring down its side, stood beside a crate containing napkins. Harker picked up the tin and hefted it in his hand, testing the weight. It felt almost full. Another glance at the other door showed that the power exerted by the revenants was not only bending the shaft of the bolt, but also the horse-shoe shaped bracket into which it fitted. In another couple of moments, either part of the fitting would snap. He shuddered as he contemplated what would happen next.

Jonathan raised the paint tin and began to hammer the edge against the jammed fitting, trying to drive it out of the restraining socket.

He was tired, and his arm ached, but his hope grew when after two or three blows the shaft began to reluctantly move. Flakes of paint drifted down as he pounded away. He stopped for a second and looked across at the other door. It was opening. The twisted, bent metal was almost wrenched away. Dear God, don't let them get me! Don't let them get me!

He renewed his pounding. The bolt was loosening. The edge of the tin was bashed with the treatment he was affording it, and he stopped and turned the can around to an undamaged rim. There was only about an eighth of an inch left, and the bolt would be free. It was then the other door crashed open and the vampires stood before him. He turned to face them.

The first officer smiled pleasantly at Davis. William Murdoch's voice rose and fell with a pleasing Scottish lilt. He had an open, friendly face, and his eyes suggested he was a man with a sense of humour. Those eyes twinkled when he spoke now to Harry on the Promenade Deck.

'A pair of criminals, ye say, Mr Davis? And you'd like me to go through the First Class passengers list with ye, so you can trace them?'

Davis was aware of how flimsy and somewhat ridiculous his story sounded. Some way off Seward sat in a deck chair. When they could catch no trace of Mina and her companion, they decided to try a bolder approach. Davis would show his Pinkerton's credentials and try to bluff information out of the officer. They also thought he should do this alone as Seward's presence might only complicate matters.

Jack glanced across as the ship's officer took in what Davis was asking.

'The thing is, Mr Murdoch, she, *they* may be involved not only in fraud, but possibly murder.'

'Murder?' You're saying there's a pair of murderers running about the ship?'

'Only a suspicion. That's why it would be really helpful if I could have a word with the women. I mean, they might not even be the persons we're looking for.'

'And why is it not the Metropolitan Police on the ship, Mr Davis?'

Harry shrugged. 'It's a matter of jurisdiction, Mr Murdoch. The crimes took place in America. If we can get to the bottom of the matter here and now, we can alert the American authorities and have them waiting.'

Murdoch put his hands behind his back and paced up and down a couple of times.

'I'll tell you what I'll do, Mr Davis. You give me complete details and I'll take them to the Captain. If he decides action's needed, we'll alert the American authorities ourselves. How's that?'

The last thing Davis wanted was the full might of the authorities involved. It only needed someone to contact Pinkerton's, and he might find himself in the brig awaiting arrest in New York.

Harry nodded his head as if considering the offer. He then told the officer that he'd consult with his office and find out their wishes on the matter. He thanked Murdoch. The officer tipped the brim of his cap and wished him goodnight.

As he watched the retreating figure, Davis hoped Jonathan was having more luck in finding the vampires.

Chapter 48

They stood in a tableau of horror. The vampire sisters, gleaming albescent fangs on red lips, moved towards the man who stood rigid against the door. In his hand, Harker still held the paint tin. He clutched it tightly as if it would somehow prevent what was about to happen.

The thing that was once Lilian Bowers ran her tongue around her mouth. Harker could see the hellish hunger rise within her. In tandem, they moved towards him. Only two yards separated the revenants from their victim. Harker knew nothing on earth could save him. He closed his eyes and offered up a prayer to the almighty, asking him to take his soul.

At any second, he expected to feel the hideous mouths on his flesh, expected to smell the scent of death and corruption under their sickly sweet breaths.

He heard a hiss of rage and then low, animal growls of anger and frustration. Harker opened his eyes. The *nosferatu* had come no closer. They stood only a few feet away, fury and bafflement on their faces. Never had the animal nature of vampirism been so clear to him as when he heard those deep-throated snarls and growls.

Harker couldn't understand why they hadn't attacked. Mina stared down at the deck and he followed her glance. A trickle of water, no thicker than a pencil was running across the surface. He looked up and saw that a leaking pipe was spraying water against the bulkhead from where it ran down and across to the other side of the cabin. There, it followed the line of deck until it ran into the scuppers.

They cannot cross running water. *They cannot cross running water!*

Harker offered a prayer of thanks to heaven. These creatures of almost limitless power and strength stood helpless before a thin line of H_2O.

Harker turned unsteadily and hit the jammed bolt another couple of times. His hands were shaking so badly that the tin almost fell from his grasp. The deep-throated growls of Mina and Lilian rose to a new pitch as he wrenched open the door and stumbled out into the corridor. He looked back to see those creatures of terrible beauty staring at him with burning, hate-filled eyes.

He slammed the door closed. With relief, he saw that the corridor he stood in was a different section of the ship, and he was separated from the vampires by several feet of steel plating.

He was taking no chances. His legs threatened to fold under him at any moment, but he didn't stop running until he'd reached his own cabin and placed a holy crucifix about his neck.

Chapter 49

They began to slowly undress. They were doing something strictly forbidden, and that made it even more exciting. Marion Nestrom giggled. Emily Peterson turned and shushed her. Despite the attempt at admonition, Emily couldn't help returning the grin.

The Turkish baths on the Titanic were like something from the Arabian Nights. Huge wall panels of blue and green tiles made it feel is if they were in a palace. The eastern effect was heightened by the Arab style lamps placed around. Exotic Cairo curtains draped over the portholes made the place seem like a seraglio.

The two women had bribed their way into the baths. A visit that morning had made them sure that lying naked among elderly, overweight dowagers was not the way to enjoy the facilities.

Both women were thirty years old and were taking this trip with their husbands. After ten years of marriage and three children each, they felt like girls again. The Titanic was a wonderful playground, and they intended to enjoy it to the fullest. At the end of the voyage lay everyday life, and the young women were determined to fill every moment of this trip with experiences.

In the deserted changing rooms, they slipped off the rest of their clothes. Both had firm, strong bodies, despite childbirth. Marion couldn't help but notice again how her friend's figure was much more 'womanly' than her own. They had known each other since childhood, gone to school together and reached womanhood together. Emily had always been more developed physically. Marion remembered in their early teens that her friend had the body of a fully grown woman even then.

With large towels wrapped around them, they padded silently around the baths. The Turkish baths were a series of rooms: steam room, hot room, temperate room, shampooing room and cooling room. Adjoining was the swimming pool.

Emily pointed to the bizarre 'electric baths.' These were tubs with a cover over the top and electric light bulbs inside which were meant to heat the body and somehow do it good.

They headed for the steam room. The air was filled with the hot moist miasma. Almost immediately, the women felt perspiration begin to form on their faces and shoulders. Each breath took in the hot, damp air.

Visibility was almost non-existent. Clouds of steam swirled and writhed. It reminded Emily of the heavy London 'pea-soupers,' the fog which regularly choked the capital.

Marion sat on a small, low-lying bench and shut her eyes. Already, the steam was taking a toll of her energy. She felt languid and deliciously relaxed. A faint sound caused her to open her eyes for a few seconds. Emily had stood up and dropped her towel. She stood naked. Marion took in the large breasts, slim waist and rounded hips. Her gaze drifted briefly to the luxuriant dark triangle between her Emily's legs. It only made her more aware of her own small bosom and straight figure. There was a time when images of her friend's body had haunted her thoughts. She had imagined things which made her blush to recall. Even now, those dangerous feelings flickered into life as she looked at Emily.

Marion was raised a Victorian woman and these thoughts disgusted and disturbed her, but she still found it was only with great difficulty she was able to drive them from her mind.

Emily was lying face down on a bench, her long back and rounded bottom dappled with beads of sweat. Marion closed her eyes again and drifted off into light doze. She was in that state where sleep and wakefulness conjoin.

Suddenly, she was aware of another presence. There was no noise, nothing material to give her this knowledge, Marion just knew!

She opened her eyes and saw them. Two figures were coming through the mist. She could tell by their general shape they were women and fully dressed. Marion was sure they had been caught. She groaned inwardly at the fuss her husband would make. He was a man spectacularly devoid of imagination and would never comprehend why they would do this.

Two lovely women with faces as pale as snow. She noticed that, despite the heat, neither of them perspired. Emily was now aware of their presence. She raised herself on her elbows and half turned to observe the new arrivals.

'I'm sorry if we've broken the rules. We'll be happy to…'

Marion's voice drifted into nothingness as the darker of the two women approached her. She could now see what wonderful eyes the woman had. They were dark, depthless. The woman sat beside her and smiled. It was such a magnificent smile. Marion loved that smile and loved those dark eyes gazing deeply into hers.

Then those crimson lips were on hers and chilly fingers were touching and stroking her cheek. Marion opened her lips as an insistent tongue pushed into her mouth. The kiss was sweet, but something under the surface made her feel slightly repelled.

She felt the towel being tugged down and cold fingers played across her breasts. Marion reached out and pushed the searching hand harder against the hot skin. She felt the woman toy with her nipples and then slowly begin to kiss down her neck and chest until she had taken the erect nub in her mouth and began to suck gently.

Marion's body was overwhelmed by the rising waves of sexual pleasure. Her eyes opened partially, and she could see Emily, now lying her back, as the red haired woman kissed her way down her friend's body. She saw Emily writhe as the strange woman slid her tongue across her torso, licking her belly in long lascivious sweeps. Emily, helpless in the seductive grip of the vampire, groaned aloud as the *nosferatu* slowly drew her long supple tongue across her breasts. Lilian's mouth closed on the firm orb, and her victim let out a little groan of ecstasy and agony as the fangs pierced the delicate tissue.

Marion's own sexual excitement was rising to a climax. She let her head fall back as the vampire kissed her way to the open neck. The mortal woman whimpered with pleasure as the icy lips played over the burning, sensitive skin of her throat. She felt the nip of teeth and then a sting of pain. She opened her eyes for a few seconds. Emily lay helpless and submissive beneath the beautiful woman with the copper hair. She could see the open mouth fastened on her friend's breast. She could hear the animal sucking sounds as a trickle of blood ran out between mouth and flesh and created a little scarlet thread down Emily's side.

Chapter 50

<u>Extract of Interim Report on Deaths of Passengers. 12th April 1912 by Dr William F. N. O'Loughlin, Ship's Surgeon, Titanic.</u>

...during unauthorised use of the Turkish Baths. The females appeared to have been in good previous health, although both appeared to be in an anaemic state..

At this point, death may have been due to heart seizures brought on by excessive and unsupervised use of the steam room.

Small wounds to the neck of one of the deceased, and the left breast of the other, suggest perhaps that some sort of hypodermic instrument was in use. It is too early to draw any verifiable conclusions about these marks, but it is possible that the deceased had indulged in the use of cocaine. If this is the case, then such drug use coupled with the heat could have very clearly caused failure of the heart.

At the moment, this is merely conjecture and a definitive cause of death cannot be established until a post mortem is carried out on arrival in New York.

Signed

Dr William F. N. O'Loughlin

The news spread from stateroom to café, to dining room, to cabin, to gymnasium. On to first, then second, then third class passengers. There had been two deaths. *Two women, naked as the day they were born, found dead.*

Doctor William O'Loughlin held out the report to his assistant, Dr Simpson. Both men where Irish, one from Dublin, the other from Belfast. O'Loughlin waited until the younger man had finished and asked him if he had anything to add. Simpson shrugged and shook his head.

Both medical men knew it was a bad business. Two passengers dead, and a crew member missing, and the voyage just started. O'Loughlin had been a reluctant recruit to the Titanic. After more than forty years at sea, he was worn out. His eyes were sunk deep in his head. His strong face, decorated with a 'Kaiser' moustache, was somewhat colourless.

His younger assistant, Simpson, was almost half his age, with a shock of dark hair and a trimmer moustache curled stylishly at the ends.

Neither of the two medics had experienced anything like the scene in the Turkish Baths earlier that morning. The sight of the young women lying like ivory statues had been shocking, even to experienced doctors.

After examining the corpses on site, they had them brought to the hospital where they studied them in more detail. It ended with them no further forward. The report O'Loughlin was to give to the captain was no more than a holding operation, a piece of medical flummery to fix the situation until they reached New York.

The two men made their way up to the bridge. As they did so, Simpson ran the case through his mind again. He kept coming up with the same nagging questions. How likely was it that two young women would both have severe anaemia at the same time, and if they had been injecting themselves with any substances, where was the syringe?

Seward handed Jonathan another handful of pills. He was reluctant to do so, but it was obvious his friend could not continue without the help of the medication.

Jack had been to the ship's pharmacy, using his status as a doctor, to persuade them to dispense the tablets.

As Harker, with shaking hands, took the pills, Davis and Seward exchanged worried glances. They could see their friend could not go on for much longer. Davis gave Jonathan a glass of water to wash down the pills. His shaking was so pronounced that they both heard the tumbler rattle against his teeth as he drank.

On his return from the encounter with the vampires, Harker had collapsed, and it was only by a dint of patient questioning that they had managed to get the full story out of him. They now knew the undead were on board and were in the first class section.

Davis leant over and placed his hand on Harker's shoulder.

'You've done brilliantly, Jonathan.'

Harker smiled. His eyes showed a man using up the last dregs of his life-force.

'I didn't do that much, Harry. Got myself locked in a pantry with two vampires.'

'Yes, but now we know for certain where they are.'

'And they know for certain where we are.'

There was silence for a few seconds as each man realized the hunters were also the hunted. Finally, Seward spoke out.

'There's not all that much time left, just a few days. We've got to find them...before they find us…'

In the cargo hold of the great ship, amid the canyons of crates and packages, several long boxes lay in the darkness. The thrum of the great engines filled the space with a steady heartbeat.

Within two of the wooden tombs, Mina and Lilian slept. Their blood dappled mouths were drawn back in malevolent smiles that showed their extended canine teeth. After their encounter with Harker and the feeding on the two women in the Turkish baths, Mina knew that their presence on the ship was less safe.

In her calculating vampire brain, she considered what the consequences of the night might be. One of the mortals with the old knowledge had seen them. She seethed with a cold, rage-less fury as she thought of his escape. To think, she had to stand helpless when she longed to tear out his throat and drink the hot fountain of his life.

Lilian was less versed in the ways of the *nosferatu*, still not cunning enough to play the mental chess the vampire used to survive. Mina had decided that they must abandon the cabin where they slept and find refuge in the hold. She knew that the mortals might take days to track down their actual resting place above deck. They might never find them before the ship docked, but she knew the revenants were too vulnerable at sea to take any chances. By the time they had found the cabin and discovered they had gone, the ship would almost have landed. Even if it hadn't, Mina knew it would take days to search this hold.

Their resting places, lined with earth, were placed at different points throughout the dark interior.

The vampires slept and waited for America.

Chapter 51

William Stead was still plagued by visions of hell. The spiritualist was normally at peace with his psychic gifts. The dead brought comfort to the living. Now, behind his eyes were blood and terror. The night was filled with scarlet horrors and a great flood. Again and again, he dreamt of water and death and beautiful women with teeth like razors.

Stead put his hands together in prayer and spoke to the God he was convinced he would soon stand before.

Seward met the ship's doctors on the pretense of professional consultation. They stood on the boat deck. Seward, with Harker as his supposed medical problem, described his patient's condition. After a few desultory exchanges about possible treatment, Seward steered the conversation around to the rumours of a double death on board.

At first, O'Louglin was reluctant to discuss the incidents, but when Seward spoke about his own experience of forensic medicine, he agreed to let him examine the bodies out of professional courtesy.

The doctor's assistant drew back the cover. The bodies looked like versions of the Sleeping Beauty. Packed in ice, they lay like lovely angels. No marks or sign of disfigurement marred their perfection. Seward saw at once the waxen paleness endemic to the victims of vampirism.

Simpson, his dark hair falling over one eye as he leant forward to open the gown of one of the dead women, asked Seward what he made of the wounds on her neck. Jack felt the familiar thrill of fear when confronted with the mark of the vampire. He made a non-committal reply.

The young women lay in repose, her mouth carrying the slightest hint of a smile. Seward turned her head slightly to the side to get a better view of the two holes in her neck.

Turning to the other corpse, at O'Louglin's invitation, he turned down the neck of her robe until the punctures in her breast were exposed.

Simpson was keen to hear Seward's opinion on the cause of death. Jack had prepared a story which he hoped would help in the hunt for the vampire sisters without making him look like a madman.

He informed O'Loughlin and Simpson that there were two women mental patients who had escaped from Colney Hatch Asylum only a couple of weeks before. He told them that these women had the same blood compulsion outlined by Krafft-Ebing in his treatise, *Psychopathia Sexualis*.

The listening physicians looked at Harker with dubious expressions, but he ploughed on. He told them that these women thought they were vampires and acted as such, coming out at night and biting victims.

He then played his ace card and said that this looked very like the same pattern of killings. Seward shook his head.

'Gentlemen, you might very well have these women on board. I have experience of these types of patients. My advice is to make a list of any two women travelling together, most likely first class. One of the women does have access to considerable wealth. They should definitely not be approached at night, when the madness is at its most potent. If you would be so kind as to bring me a list, I think I can help you track these women down.'

O'Loughlin looked at Seward for a moment and then burst into a deep rich laugh.

'I'll tell you something, Doctor Seward, if I didn't know you were a medical man, I'd think you'd just escaped from Colney Hatch.'

His face hardened, and his voice took on an angry tone.

'Now, if you don't mind, sir, we have real patients with real illnesses. I'd be obliged if you'd keep your idiot opinions to yourself in future.'

Jack Phillips yawned and stretched his arms wide. He'd been hunched over the Morse key for several hours, and his whole body had stiffened up. Like Harold Bride, the other wireless operator on the Titanic, his watch had been spent sending out an almost never-ending stream of personal messages from the passengers.

The transmitter in front of him was a rotary spark design and the most powerful sending equipment available. From this room, the ship could beam a signal a minimum distance of two hundred and fifty miles and nearer four hundred in normal daytime conditions. At night, the telegraph could function up to two thousand miles. Even to an operator like Phillips, it seemed to border on the supernatural that this construction of wires and valves could reach across the world.

He lifted another piece of paper and prepared to transmit, when shadows fell across him. He turned to find two men standing there, smiling. One of the men, with a moustache and fresh open complexion, gave him a cheery good morning and stepped over to the desk with a piece of paper in his hand. Phillips noticed he had a pronounced limp. The other man, slim with a handsome, intelligent-looking face, stood by the door and grinned in a friendly manner.

'Wondered if you could send this to London for me?'

The man handed Phillips a piece of paper. It seemed to be to some agency called Pinkertons. The message was brief:

"Am still investigating.
Davis"

The operator looked at the laconic message and then calculated the cost. The man, whom he assumed was Davis, chatted cheerfully. He was extremely interested in the wireless equipment and asked all sorts of perceptive questions.

Phillips was delighted for the opportunity to wax lyrical about the transmitter and spent ten minutes explaining how it worked and the performance it was capable of.

Eventually, Davis thanked the operator and said he mustn't keep him from his work. With a cheery goodbye, the two men left. Phillips smiled. It was nice to meet passengers who respected his skill and didn't just see him as an electrical version of a postman.

Outside the wireless room, Seward smiled at Davis and produced a copy of the First Class passenger list with cabin numbers he had lifted while Harry pretended to find the wireless fascinating.

Extracts of Titanic First Class Passenger List
Mr George Achilles Harder
Mrs George Achilles Harder
Mr Henry Sleeper Harper
Mrs Henry Sleeper Harper…
Miss Daisy E. Minahan
Dr William Edward Minahan
Mrs William Edward Minahan…

They pored over the lists with growing despondency. It had never occurred to them that Mina might take the simple precaution of travelling under a different name. Harker had assumed that she would be registered as Mrs Murray, her maiden name, and the one she had used since returning to London.

Failing that, he had tried *Harker*. When this too failed, he felt even more desolate. Although he knew that Mina would never feel love again, the tiny comfort that they were still connected by name would have eased his pain a little.

He put down the list and went to the bedside table where he took out the bottle of tablets and poured four into his hand. Seward, for a moment, was about to urge caution but then realized the futility of the act. If they could not stop the vampires then nothing would really matter anyway.

As Harker sat on the bed taking the pills one by one and chasing them down with gulps of water, they tried to surmise what name Mina might use. The other obvious one was Lilian's surname, Bowers. This, too, proved fruitless. Suggestions got wilder. Variations on Dracula, Vlad Dracula. They tried Seward's name, Davis' name. Van Helsing's name. It was the connection of Van Helsing that gave Harker another possibility.

He thumbed through the list while the others watched anxiously. He drew his finger carefully down a page and then stopped. He looked up.

'We've got her.'

Chapter 52

Neil Marten made his way through the labyrinth of decks and passages, trying to find his way back to the third class cabin he shared with his brother. Even after a few of days on the Titanic, he was still bemused by the size and complexity of the ship.

He had just been to the ship's Post Office on Lower Deck G to send a card back to his mother. The brothers were leaving Ireland for a better life. They were tired of scraping a living from bleak, barren land on the coast. Neil was excited about America. He'd seen photographs, and once saw a moving picture show at the county fair. The film had shown New York, and he'd been astounded by the skyscrapers and miles of streets and the shops and the traffic and the bridges across the Hudson. It seemed like a place created by a race of giants.

Neil stopped. He was lost again. The third class accommodations were spread around a number of different decks. Coupled with the teeming mass of emigrants, English, Italian, French, Irish and a dozen other nationalities, the place was like a maze and the Tower of Babel combined. Marten saw a group of passengers approach, and he was about to ask them for directions when he heard them speaking what he thought was Italian. He smiled and passed on.

He stood at the end of the passageway and looked bemused. The long corridors ran off to his right and left. He had no idea which way to go next. Neil smiled as he thought of what his brother, Anthony, would say when he got back.

He took a chance and moved left and found himself at the entrance to the third class dining room. It was crowded. The waft of food drifted over him. Both he and his brother had been unable to believe the quality and quantity of the food they were given. Used to simple, repetitious fare at home, both men were putting away prodigious quantities at meal times.

Marten was relieved. He thought he could find his way back from this point. He carried on and took a right hand turn at the end of the passage. He was just going through a bulkhead door when he heard the sound of a woman crying. He stopped and listened. There is was again. He followed the sound which seemed to be coming from around the stairway.

The subtle vibration of the great ship ran up through the soles of his shoes as he stepped up to the space under the steps.

A woman was huddled over, crying. Her face was hidden. He leant forward a little.

'Excuse me, ma'am are you alright? Is there something I can do?'

The crying continued. He moved nearer. The depth of the woman's weeping was terrible to hear. He reached out and gently touched her shoulder.

'Is there anything I can…'

She looked up, and the last thing Neil Marten saw on earth was a face of demonic beauty. As her fangs sank deep into his throat, he was dimly aware of another presence. His neck was held in a clamp of iron, and he felt a second mouth on his skin.

Under the stairway his life's blood was drained. In the dining room a few yards away, the rattle of plates and clash of cutlery were ignored as the normal sounds of life at sea.

Chapter 53

They stood at the door of the first class suite. Passengers strolled backwards and forwards along the deck. Laughter, kisses, arguments, love, hate, sadness, all the things that made up the human condition moved back on forth.

The night was clear. The sea was calm.

Harker had finally traced them under the name of Westenra. He knew the undead had no sense of humour, but there was an element of dark laughter under Mina's choice of name.

Lucy Westenra had been her best friend and the first victim of Dracula when he arrived in England. She had also been the love of Jack Seward's life. They had driven a stake through her heart and cut off her head when she became a vampire.

It seemed to Harker that Mina needed to keep some sort of link with the arch-vampire, even after his destruction. When she had become one of the undead, she had haunted the places where her master once slept, and now she used Lucy's name. Perhaps even vampires needed a past to cling to.

The three men knew now where the revenants slept. This would be their last sleep.

In the morning they would end their unholy existence.

Chapter 54

<u>Message to Captain of the *Antillian* Sunday April 14th 7.30am. Picked up by the Titanic</u>
"Three large bergs five miles Southward of us…"

It wasn't an easy thing to do, break into a first class cabin in broad daylight in sight of several dozen people. They decided that, as in previous burglaries, boldness was best. Harker and Seward stood by Davis as he picked at the lock.

Voices raised in false jocularity were hard to maintain when in danger of being caught breaking and entering.

The trio had decided they would destroy the vampires where they lay and then, when night had fallen, try to get rid the remains by dumping them over the side. Just how they would achieve this wasn't clear to any of them, but they decided time would take care of that particular problem.

With a click, the door lock released. Each man wore a crucifix around his neck. Seward carried the bag with the stakes, mallet and garlic. In another small case, Harker had the surgical saw for removing the heads of the undead.

Pushing the door open, the men stepped into the cabin. At once the faint odour of corruption, associated with the vampires presence, assailed their nostrils.

The place was in semi-gloom, and Harry walked across and drew the curtains aside, letting daylight flood in. As he did so, Harker carefully locked the door behind them.

They looked around the sumptuous room. The carpets were deep and lush with breathtakingly splendid décor. Harker noted the large trunks piled around the place, lying partially open so that dresses of the finest quality could be seen carelessly strewn about.

They made their way cautiously to the sleeping quarters. Here, luxurious beds with their covers undisturbed dominated the chamber. Seward nodded towards two large cases. The others acknowledged his gesture, and Harry once again drew aside the curtains to let in the morning.

Despite the protection afforded by the paraphernalia they carried, and the presence of daylight, all the men felt deadly afraid. All had faced the *nosferatu* and knew the dangers they brought. Logic told them that the monsters were helpless now, but primal fear overrode common sense.

Harker held the crucifix, keeping it at a point fixed about a foot from the nearest case. He nodded to Davis that he was ready. The detective took a deep breath and pulled the lid aside with a swift gesture. A mixed feeling of despair, and perhaps relief, swept over the group as they saw the case was empty.

Chapter 55

Message to Titanic Sunday April 14th. 9.00am

"Captain Titanic- Westbound steamers report bergs, growlers and field ice in 42oN from 51oW, 12th April. Compliments-Barr

SS Caronia.

Phillips and Bride put the message aside. It would be delivered to the bridge as soon as they could get a break from the constant stream of civilian traffic.

Bride had already handed over the earlier warning to the *Antillian* they had picked up at 7.30 that morning. It had been passed on. Those higher up would know what to do.

The early evening air was growing colder. The Titanic sailed serenely on. The sea was flat, and the great ship was ploughing steadily onwards at a speed of more than twenty knots. Captain Smith was satisfied that a record breaking crossing was on the cards.

On the bridge, the officers moved to and fro. There had been some information about the presence of icebergs, but there was no sign of them. The sea seemed perfect.

The course was altered slightly to South/West, and the three thousand souls on the great liner prepared for dinner and another evening at sea.

Captain Smith dined with the first class passengers who hung on every word of the man who commanded a floating city.

Out at sea, great mountains of ice creaked and groaned and floated onwards.

Harker had almost wept with despair and frustration when they found the vampires had vanished. He cursed himself once again for underestimating the cunning of the revenants. He knew he should have expected something like this. They had seen him. They knew they were being hunted. Jonathan just didn't expect their response to be so immediate.

Davis was the one member of the group who kept focused.

'Alright, so they've gone.' The matter of fact way he said this made Seward smile, despite his despondency. Harry took a drink of tea and continued.

'The only other place they can be is the cargo hold.'

Harker broke in.

'Not necessarily, Harry. They could have booked another few cabins under different names. They could have hiding places all over the ship.'

'It's not likely, Jonathan. Firstly, they didn't have all that much time. The Titanic was almost fully booked when we forced them to run. Secondly, if they do have more earth boxes it's almost sure they'll be in the cargo hold.'

'So, what do you suggest?'

'It's getting dark. It would be crazy to go into the hold searching for those monsters now. We start in the morning.'

Seward stood up and walked over to the little wash basin. He began to rinse his hands and spoke in a somber voice.

'That means they'll be hunting tonight, again. If we do nothing some poor soul will die.'

Harry looked him squarely in the eye.

'You think I don't know that, Jack? You think that doesn't bother me? What would you have us do?'

'Pray for the soul of whoever dies tonight.'

Chapter 56

<u>Message from the *Mesaba* to the Titanic Sunday April 14th, 9.40pm</u>

"Saw much heavy pack ice and great numbers of large icebergs, also field ice…"

High in the crow's nest, Fred Fleet and Reginald Lee could hear the music drifting up from below. The air temperature had dropped dramatically. Both mariners had experienced ice on the ocean, and there was that feel to the atmosphere.

Sailors feared icebergs. Those monoliths could destroy the mightiest of vessels. Feared most of all were the 'growlers,' bergs of dark ice.

Fleet on the port side stared out across the flat, undulating water. There was no moon, and light from the ship sparkled across the ever moving surface of the sea.

On the starboard side, Reginald Lee shivered. What a bloody watch to pull. Below, there was warmth and music and good food, but he and his mate were perched high in the sky with nothing but each other and the ocean swell.

Both men felt tiredness around the eyes from peering into the darkness for extended periods. It was astounding that on the most advanced ship in the world there wasn't a pair of binoculars.

Down below, Captain Smith stood on the bridge. There was an air of calm contentment. The vessel was handling beautifully and speed was being maintained. It seemed as if the Titanic was a dream ship.

In the third class section, Anthony Marten searched desperately for his brother. Neil had been gone for more than two hours. Anthony knew his brother often got lost making his way around the ship, but he'd never been missing this long. He tried the dining room where some of the men would hang out, smoking and chatting. He then went to various people they'd struck up acquaintances with since the start of the voyage.

One of the men he spoke to recalled seeing him passing the dining area earlier. Anthony walked the passageways and called his brother's name hopefully. Anxiety was making way to the beginnings of panic.

He stopped and wondered if he should inform someone in authority. He was reluctant to take this course simply because he didn't want to start official action only for his wayward brother to turn up and make him look foolish.

Marten stood just inside the bulkhead door. He didn't know that his brother was near, very near. Only a few yards away, behind a partition by the stairway, lay the drained corpse of his sibling.

In the hold of the ship, Mina and Lilian lay sated. The hunger was filled and both women had an evil radiance. They did not sleep. Night was their time. Mina had been shaken by the presence of the hunters. She had enough respect to know they posed great danger. She would have liked to move among the humans, to hear their heartbeats, to smell the blood running through their veins, to feel their helplessness, but survival was all that mattered now.

They would hunt briefly and then return to this dark, safe place and wait. Only a few more nights at sea, and then they would land.

Land! The thought of the word made her smile.

The second class dining saloon buzzed with the muttering of many voices. Waiters weaved between the tables. While the room didn't stand in comparison
with the splendour of the first class arrangements, it was nevertheless impressive. What was second class on the Titanic was first class on most other vessels.

Seward pondered the menu: Fish, Chicken, Roast Turkey or Lamb? Davis had made his choice in a matter of seconds. Harker, looking ghastly, had tried to ask for a piece of toast only, but his companions had insisted he eat properly. He deferred to Seward in picking the main course.

Over the edge of the menu, Jack eyed Harker's condition. He was deteriorating rapidly. His skin was ashen and covered by a thin sheen of sweat. His mouth hung open slightly as if he had difficulty in breathing. The shaking in his hands had also been noticeable when he held the menu.

Jonathan desperately needed rest and treatment. The demands of the last couple of weeks were too much for his fragile health. Seward sighed. God willing, this will be settled soon, one way or another.

Sensing the waiter's growing impatience, he opted for the Lamb. He thought the iron in red meat would do Harker good.

As the waiter departed, Seward looked around. At every table he could see happy people joking and laughing. They were excited by the novelty of the voyage and looking forward to landing in a new country, innocent of the malignancy which lay below their feet. Seward envied them. Ignorance really was bliss.

The captain of the *California*, less than twenty miles from the Titanic, looked out at the ice field ahead. Dear God it was cold! He ordered that the wireless room send out a general warning to all ships in the vicinity.

In the crow's nest, Fred Fleet rubbed his eyes and peered intently into the blackness. When staring out at sea so long in those conditions, one's sight could play tricks. There seemed to be something taking shape, something dark.

He narrowed his eyes and tried to make whatever it was clearer. There was certainly something out there. It was some miles away, but it was getting bigger.

Fleet rang the alarm bell and then telephoned down to the bridge. He reported a 'dark mass' ahead. There was no real response, and it seemed as if there were no officers available.

The ship held her course while what Fred now recognized as a 'growler,' grew closer. Bride, the other lookout, was now aware of the danger. He and Fleet were baffled by the lack of response from below. There's a great bloody berg out there, for Christ's sake!

By now, they could see the size of the object. It was taller than the bloody ship!

Down below, the enormity of the danger was finally recognized. The berg grew massive. The officer's voice was hoarse and frantic. *Hard-a-port! Hard-a-port!*

Fleet and Bride could only watch as the Titanic made a last minute effort to avoid the berg. The ship was turning and turning but with an awful slow-motion movement which seemed to take forever. Nearer. Nearer. Nearer!

Chapter 57

Mina's eyes opened as a slight shudder ran through the hull of the ship. Her super-sensitive vampire senses caught the tearing and grating of steel long before it was recognized by the mortals above. Lilian, too, was possessed of these heightened powers The revenants looked at each other and knew their survival was in danger.

Most of the passengers were below decks. The slight shudder of the ship caused no alarm bells to ring.

Harker, who was reading, looked quizzically at Davis who shrugged. Harker was asleep. Jack was about to resume his reading when the great engines slowed down and stopped.

On the upper decks, passengers saw the huge berg loom over the ship. There was no panic. The collision had felt slight, no more than a grating and a mild bump. Chunks of opaque ice scattered about the decks. One man kicked a lump the size of an orange and sent it skittering down one of the stairways. Amid the laughter, a party of slightly drunk passengers gathered slivers of ice to put in their drinks.

Captain Smith ordered an immediate damage report. The impact seemed slight, and at this point there was no undue worry.

Below the water line on the starboard side, the great ship had been mortally wounded. A great tear, three hundred feet long, had been ripped in her side. The icy waters of the Atlantic began to flood in. On the decks above, teeming humanity carried on the business of life, unaware the vessel was dying.

Thomas Andrews was in his stateroom. Not yet forty, he was the man who built the Titanic. The managing director of Harland and Wolff, the Belfast yard which constructed the liner, he was also head of the draughting department. No man in the world knew the ship as he did.

Andrews had sailed on the maiden voyage as he did on other ships, to be on hand to iron out any early problems. He had been hunched over his desk, making notes, when the judder ran through the ship. He listened as the engines slowly died away.

The shipbuilder was gathering his coat to investigate, when a knock at the door signalled the entrance of a young officer. Andrews was already halfway out the door before the sailor could ask him to come to the bridge.

Seward and Davis strode along the corridor. Things seemed normal, apart from several passengers milling around looking mildly curious. A group of young men hurried past them, boisterously calling to each other as they raced to get on deck.

Harker was still lying down, his exhaustion getting the better of his curiosity.

Making their way on deck, Seward and Davis found people strolling around, some looking at the great berg off to the side of the ship while others played with the chunks of ice scattered around. Possibly an hour had elapsed since they had felt the collision. Music from the band added a strange gaiety to the becalmed ship.

Seward gazed out across the flat sea. A fragment of poetry came to mind.

'As idle as a painted ship
Upon a painted ocean'

Andrews, grim-faced, stood before Captain Smith and his officers.

'The rip in her side is about three hundred feet long. I'm afraid the damage is fatal.'

One of the second officers, unable to contain himself, burst out.

'The watertight compartments, sir. They're supposed to seal off damaged sections. Surely that's all that's needed.'

The shipbuilder shook his head.

'That's the theory, but the damage…the damage. Water is filling the compartments one by one, pouring over the top of one into the next. It's an unstoppable process. The ship will go down slowly by the head.'

The silence in the room was unbearable. Finally, Captain Smith spoke in a low voice. 'So what are you saying, exactly. Mr Andrews?'

'This vessel is dying, Captain. My advice is to abandon ship at once.'

Smith nodded his head as if in understanding, but the terrifying consequences of what he had just heard were almost too terrible to contemplate.

He knew that the Titanic had places on the lifeboats for about a thousand people.

There were more than three thousand souls aboard his sinking ship!

Chapter 58

Jack Phillips desperately tapped out distress signals to all shipping in the vicinity.

"CQD CQD CQD MGY"

This was the generally recognized distress code for shipping. MGY was the Titanic's own identification number.

Phillips felt his fingers sweat and slip off the Morse key. He wiped his hand and began again. This time, he added the new international code for ships in distress.

"CQD CQD SOS SOS SOS MGY"

The nearest ship to the stricken vessel was the SS *California*. It was close enough to mount a rescue. However, the wireless operator slept soundly in his bunk. He had signed off for the night.

Fifty eight miles away, the *Carpathia* picked up the signal, but it was too far. By the time she reached the scene, the Titanic would be at the bottom of the ocean.

Chapter 59

Mina and Lilian moved around the darkened cargo hold. Ears, which could hear beyond the range of any human, heard the crash of water running through the bottom of the ship. They heard the slosh and roar of the sea battering its way towards where they lay.

The smell of salt was strong in their nostrils. Like beings in an alien environment, these sights and sounds jumbled their senses and upset the delicate system of radar which gave the vampire their unique abilities.

Mina could feel the panic rising within her companion. Lilian was a young vampire and hadn't yet learned the cunning needed to survive.

She paced the claustrophobic lanes between the stacks of cargo. A wild rage was upon her. She hissed and snarled. Her long copper mane tumbled about her face, making her look like a creature from some dark, classical myth.

Mina's calculating brain tried to reason out the steps they should take. They needed two things, earth from their native soil, without which they could never rest, and something to transport them across running water.

The restless murmur of humanity sounded above her head. She sensed a growing unease. This feeling of being trapped was alien to Mina. She had fought many foes and escaped from many situations, but this was different. It would take all the ferocious survival instinct of the revenant.

Mina moved along the rows of cargo until she came to a number of oblong packing cases. These were the boxes of earth brought along to increase their safety margin while at sea. She slid her long fingers under the lid of the top box and lifted.

With a splintering and groaning of wood, the lid was ripped open. The heavy nails pulled out as easily as a knife from butter. Mina threw the bulky lid across the cargo hold where it landed with a crash some thirty feet away.

The deep, dark earth filled the crate to the brim. Maverick grains trickled over the edge and formed little hillocks on the steel deck. The vampires could smell the damp, comforting tang of the grave.

Mina looked around and saw several suitcases. The expensive leather and brass bindings spoke of quality. Dotted across the surface of the luggage were labels which told not only of the owner's travels, but the owner's wealth in affording such travels.

Vienna, Athens, Madrid, Paris. The labels were a miniature world tour. All this was lost on Mina as she snatched two of the smaller cases and, with a twist of her finger, broke open the locks.

The cases were filled with women's clothing. In one, fine silk underwear with labels that indicated their expense. The other case held a bride's trousseau. A veil of Valencienne lace, a thing of breathtaking beauty, was hurled aside. A full-length white dress made of silk floated through the darkness as Mina flicked it away.

She dug her fingers into the rich, loamy earth and began to shovel it into the empty case. Lilian did the same with the other valise. They worked without words, each vampire focused on the task of ensuring they survived.

As they excavated the dirt, all they could hear was the groaning of metal and the onward rush of the ocean coming closer.

The steward battered on the door. Harker's eyes flicked open. He had been in a semi-delirious sleep. Mina, as she once was, kept calling to him from a window, but no matter how fast he ran, he couldn't get any nearer. She kept calling and calling, but he couldn't reach her.

'Put your life-jacket on, sir and go on deck.'

Harker, still dopey from his sleep, looked at the steward quizzically.

'What?'

'Your life-jacket, sir. Put it on and go up top. Captain's orders.'

'Life-jack…?'

The steward was gone. Harker could hear him as he moved down the corridor shouting the same thing through every cabin door. Jonathan shook his head as if to clear the fuzziness and then looked along the passageway.

People were moving around in an aimless, bewildered manner. It was almost one o'clock in the morning, and most still looked dazed. Almost all of them wore life-jackets. He saw a man with two small children. He was holding them by the hands while his wife followed with a baby in her arms. There were tears in the woman's eyes, and Harker saw the man mutter words of reassurance as he guided his family towards the stairs.

Jonathan turned to look the other way and saw Seward and Davis coming towards him.

'What the hell's going on? Why are they telling everyone to go up on deck?'

'It looks as if we might be sinking, Jonathan.'

Harker looked at Davis as if he were mad.

'Sinking? Don't be bloody stupid, Harry, this ship can't sink.'

Seward put his hand on Jonathan's shoulder.

'Let's get the life-jackets.'

The children oohed and aaahed as the distress rockets climbed to a height of nearly a thousand feet before exploding in a spectacular welter of starbursts. The dark sky was dotted with dazzling colours of blue and red and white.

Officers hurried to a fro amid the people crowding the decks. Lifeboats were being launched, and the priority was the first class passengers.

Harold Bride sat beside Jack Phillips as he sent out a constant stream of calls for help. Bride saw that the senior operator was using the new SOS call sign.

The water flooded relentlessly through the stricken ship. One of the boiler rooms was under water. Those aboard began to notice the ship was beginning to dip slightly forward. The bow was going down, slowly but surely.

Chapter 60

Seward, Harker and Davis stood on the deck. Gradually, the realization was creeping up on all those on board that the unsinkable ship was going down.

In the third class sections, the passengers were neglected and left to their own devices as all resources were concentrated on helping the first class women and children leave the ship.

One of the junior officers stood nervously at the head of the stairway because there were fears that those below deck would storm the upper sections. He could feel the uncomfortable weight of a pistol in his jacket pocket. This was a weapon of last resort should anyone try to burst out. He had never fired a gun before and knew it was improbable he could fire on another human being. Still, orders were orders.

Mina and Lilian mixed with the milling crowds on the upper decks. They could feel and hear hundreds of hearts beating with a raised tempo, the tempo of fear.

The vampires felt their hunger grow as the tide of rich, red blood swarmed around them. They had to be restrained to survive. That was the all that mattered.

A first officer called above the babble of voices. He strained to be heard.

'Women and children first. Women and children first.'

The vampires moved towards the rail where a group of seamen were trying to free a lifeboat from the davits. What was noticeable in that seething mass of humanity surging about was a little circle of space around the two revenants. Even in the most terrifying moments of their lives, the humans sensed a greater evil.

They looked at Harker in amazement.

'We look for them *now*?' Seward's voice rose in disbelief. He couldn't believe what his friend had just said.

Harker spoke almost off-handedly. 'We're not getting off this ship alive, Jack. You know it and I know it.'

'How do you know it, Jonathan. How do you know that?'

'There's not enough lifeboats. I've read the specifications. They'll be lucky if there's room for a thousand people.'

Davis broke in. 'There's the chance of other ships coming.'

'Maybe, but look at the dip. She's going down fast. If someone is coming, we would have seen them by now.'

Davis looked around the deck and saw the chaos. Some of the lifeboats were going down half-full while others were overcrowded. He had one last hopeful stab.

'Maybe we can swim till they get here.'

Harker looked at Jack.

'You're a doctor, Jack, how long would anyone survive in that water?'

Seward shook his head.

'Let's go and see if we can end this now.'

Mina and Lilian could have forced their way to the front by sheer power, however that would mean drawing attention to themselves. Better to wait a few moments. The lifeboats were ahead and there was plenty of room.

The fear which gnawed at each of the revenants was that they find shelter before daylight. Tightly clutching the little cases of earth, they waited to leave the sinking ship.

Chapter 61

"CQD-SOS FROM MGY. WE ARE SINKING FAST PASSENGERS BEING PUT IN BOATS"
Marconi-gram from the Titanic

Guggenheim looked at himself in the mirror and was satisfied. His evening clothes were just so. He smiled at his manservant and then settled down to await his fate. At least he would go down like a gentleman.

The officer pointed his pistol at the group of passengers attempting to storm the boats. For a moment, he thought the panic-stricken crowd were going to rush him anyway. He called for them to be calm. His hand was shaking.

Thomas Andrews stood by the davits cajoling, encouraging and lifting frightened women and children into the lifeboats. Since the realization the ship was sinking, he had been working in a frenzy to make sure as many people escaped as possible. A young woman carrying baby moved forward. Gently, he helped her step into the boat. She smiled in gratitude. Andrews stepped back. It would be the last smile he ever saw.

Mina and Lilian were just a few feet away from the lifeboats. Only a few passengers stood between them and leaving the doomed vessel.

Suddenly, Lilian let out an unearthly howl as Harker pressed a crucifix to her face. There was a sizzling of flesh and the air filled with an acrid, unclean smell.

Those around Lilian recoiled in fear as the vampire's scream rang out across the ocean. All fell back a few steps. Lilian, the sign of the cross burned into her cheek, was truly awful to behold. Her eyes blazed with a baleful, hate-filled redness. Her lips were drawn back in a bestial snarl, showing her canines.

Harker moved across to her, driving her away from the rail. Mina fought back her instinct to leap on the man and pushed her way to the lifeboat. She was only a couple of feet away and about to step aboard, when Seward appeared from one side and threw a crucifix into the craft. She turned with demonic fury, only to be confronted by Davis, who held out a communion host before him.

The vampire staggered back before the holy wafer. Davis thrust it forward. She stumbled away, knocking several people aside as she fled before the symbol of righteousness.

An officer who had been standing nearby saw the commotion and called across, asking what was going on. Seward and Davis kept their eyes firmly fixed on the retreating revenant, who hissed and snarled in frustration as they drove her slowly back from the safety of the lifeboat.

Suddenly, she turned. With an effortless, gliding motion, she disappeared into the crowd.

A well-dressed man pushed his way to the front. The second officer was about to order him back when he saw it was Bruce Ismay, managing director of the White Star Line. The two men stared at each other for a few seconds, and then the officer stood aside and let Ismay step into the lifeboat.

As the craft began to lower, the White Star director looked back and saw the officer staring steadily at him. He had never seen a human being look at another with such contempt. Ismay lowered his eyes and fixed his gaze on the bottom of the boat.

The shock had scrambled her senses. Lilian staggered blindly through the bulkhead door and back into the main body of the ship. Her sense of time and place was gone. Escape! That was the only message which pounded through her chaotic brain. The men with the power to end her existence were behind her.

Harker followed the fleeing vampire. He saw her knock people aside as she made her way along the deck and through a doorway. His heart pounded in his chest, and he gasped as his weak body tried to cope with the unexpected demands, but he knew that Lilian was moving erratically and slowly. His attack had disoriented her, and she would take a while to regain her power. If he was going to end her existence, this was the time.

He reached the opening and stepped through just in time to see her hurtling down a flight of stairs. An elderly man, helping his infirm wife up the steps, was sent crashing back as she brushed him aside.

Harker's instinct was to stop and help, but he knew that would be fatal. Calling a hurried 'Sorry' as he rushed past, he reached the next landing as Lilian ran along a corridor.

Holding the crucifix firmly in his grasp, he followed. Her brilliant copper hair flew out in wild streams behind her.

He felt his stamina giving out. His legs felt weak and he had difficulty catching his breath. Only adrenalin and the will to destroy the *nosferatu* gave him the strength to go on. Lilian let out a great scream of rage. She had run into a dead end.

Harker felt a surge of triumph. Thank you, God, thank you.

Keeping his gaze fixed firmly on the vampire, but being careful to avoid looking directly into her eyes, he held the crucifix out before him while drawing from the long inside pocket of his coat a stake. He held the pointed wooden weapon like a small hand spear. Cautiously, he moved towards Lilian. He could see her red mouth twisted in a snarl of frustration. The ugly, cross-shaped burn marred the porcelain beauty of her face.

He was within three feet of her, the stake poised ready, the crucifix holding her in place. A deep, vicious growl low within her throat was the only sound heard.

Lilian's eyes darted beyond Harker. She called out.

'Help! Please sir, help me. He's trying to kill me. He's trying to kill me.'

Jonathan ignored the statement. It was, to his mind, just a ploy to put him off guard. He continued to move nearer. The stake was poised to strike. The vampire called again.

'Help me, please help me.'

It was then Harker heard the sound of a pistol being cocked somewhere behind him.

Chapter 62

Chaos reigned as the third class passengers reached the top decks to find that there were no lifeboats left. Those lucky enough to escape dotted the sea around the sinking ship. Cries of fear rent the air as people ran back and forth trying to find a means of getting off the Titanic. Men tried to comfort sobbing wives and daughters as they fastened life-jackets.

The ship was now going down bow first at an increasingly sharp angle. The whole front section was under water, and the first two funnels were almost submerged.

People were driven back towards the stern. The acute angle made it increasingly difficult and passengers moved as if climbing a steep hill. The ship's band played on, and the tune of 'Alexander's Ragtime Band' cut through the shouts and screams.

In the chaos, Mina Harker stood still. Her hyper senses scanned the ship for a means of escape. Her glance took in the empty davits. No lifeboats. The raised elevation of the ship had showed the drop to the ocean was perhaps ninety feet below. She considered the leap into one of the little craft drawing away from the stricken liner. People pulled at the oars frantically, trying to put enough distance between them and the Titanic before the undertow could pull them down as the ship sank.

Seward and Davis could see her in the distance. The increasing mass of humanity swept back and forth in a paroxysm of fear, making progress difficult. It was a double-edged sword. The crowds also made it easier to track Mina without her being aware.

Walter Stead helped the old woman into the last of the collapsible lifeboats. She held out her arms and cried bitterly to her husband. He was a frail, white-haired man but held himself with dignity. The old lady called to him again. Stead leant over and asked the officer in charge if the man could go with his wife. The officer nodded in agreement. He indicated to the old man that he get in the boat.

With a shake of his head he refused. His voice was quiet but firm.

'I think it's women and children first, sir, don't you?'

As the lifeboat began to lower towards the water, he blew his wife a kiss. Stead could see the tears stream down her face as she drifted out of sight. The old man looked at Stead. 'Fifty years this March, been married.'

He walked off and was lost in the confusion.

Chapter 63

Harker half turned towards the metallic click. He kept his eyes on Lilian, but out of the corner of his vision, he could see a young third officer standing there aiming the pistol. Water sloshed around his ankles.

Harker, with the stake still raised, called out in a calm voice.

'Officer, this woman is a murderer. She's murdered people on this ship.'

Lilian's voice was anguished, distressed.

'Sir, he's mad. He's mad! He's followed me from London. He wants to kill me.'

The gun wavered in the sailor's hand. He took a firmer grip.

'Move away from the lady and drop that weapon.'

Harker stood still. Water gurgled and sloshed further up the passageway. The officer called out again.

'Sir, I will not warn you again. Put down that weapon and stand away from the lady.'

Harker hesitated for a moment and then shook his head in resignation. A smile of malevolent triumph flickered across Lilian's face. It was then Jonathan spun and drove the stake deep into her chest.

A terrifying scream reverberated around the corridor. Lilian's face contorted with agony as she clawed feebly at the length of wood sticking out from her breast bone. Gouts of almost black blood poured from her mouth as she sank to the deck. The last dying echo of her cries were lost in the seawater as she slipped under the surface.

The sailor stood petrified, unable to comprehend what he had just witnessed for a moment. His face twisted with anger.

'You bastard! You murdering bastard!'

Harker turned to him, his arms outstretched in a gesture of supplication.

'No listen, she was...'

Boom!

The shot caught him on the left hand side, smashing his ribs. He slammed against the bulkhead. Clutching the wound, he looked at the sailor in surprise. His mouth opened as if to speak.

Boom!

The second shot took him square in the chest which exploded in a welter of blood and shattered bone. Harker slumped into the rising water, his body falling across the still figure of Lilian Bowers.

Chapter 64

The doomed ship was wracked by a series of massive explosions as the boilers burst. Lights flickered and died. The stern of the Titanic rose higher in the water. Soon, she would be almost perpendicular.

Passengers clung to rails and tried desperately to pull themselves away from the rising torrent. Desperate souls jumped at the lowest point into the freezing ocean.

Mina walked up the sloping deck effortlessly. Behind her, Seward and Davis scrambled and stumbled, dragging themselves painfully on.

Wails and screams of despair filled the air. A man came tumbling down the incline, hurtling into Seward and almost breaking his hold on the ship's rail. If Davis had not grabbed his wrist, he would have careered down into the oncoming flood.

Mina had almost reached the stern of the ship. Hundreds of people were clinging on, hoping for a way off the sinking liner. A man, losing hold, tried to grab at her. She slapped him away, the blow knocking him mercifully unconscious. The body hurtled down, gathering velocity as it neared the rising tide of death.

The vampire's senses raced and reeled as her desperation grew. Despite this, she still clung to the small case of earth. Without that, any plan became worthless.

She was again considering a leap from the stern into the nearest lifeboat, when she saw them. Seward and Davis, the hunters!

Her mouth formed a twisted snarl as she watched the men drag themselves yard by yard towards her. Mina could see the large crucifix around their necks. Seward carried a communion host in his hand, while Davis held a bottle of holy water. As they approached, the revenant saw the top of a wooden stake jut from inside Seward's coat.

She looked around, her beautiful face showing the signs of an animal trapped. The crowds were so dense that even she could not break through in time.

The reverend Thomas Byles was surrounded by a group of people whom he was leading in prayer. The priest saw the vampire and was about to call over a soul he saw in torment, when he looked into her eyes and instead made the sign of the cross for protection.

Never had the priest felt he needed his God more than when he saw the face of the undead.

They faced Mina. Seward holding on with one hand while he made the sign of the cross with the other. Mina, at bay, snarled and hissed, her beauty even more terrible.

'Mina, we can give you peace. Let us save you, Mina.' Seward shouted above the cries of the people and the roar of the collapsing vessel. Creaks and groans of tortured metal filled the air as the back of the mighty ship was gradually being broken.

'Please, Mina, let me send you to meet your God. These sins are not of your making. You didn't choose this. He will understand. He will forgive you.'

Mina looked at Seward. For a few seconds, the hate and rage died in her eyes and was replaced by a beseeching need.

Then it was gone. With a growl, she leapt forward. Davis instinctively hurled the bottle of holy water in her face. The glass shattered. The vampire reeled back, her howls rising even above the cacophony surrounding them.

Seward saw her wipe frantically at the water around her hair and eyes. Smoke rose from her blistered skin. As she tottered back, Mina bumped against the stern rail, and at the same time, the Titanic gave a great juddering motion.

Mina, clutching her face, over-corrected. For a second, it seemed as if her supernatural reflexes would keep her upright. She balanced on the fulcrum of the rail and then slowly toppled over. Even then, she still clung to the small suitcase.

The men painfully reached the point where she had fallen. All was darkness and chaos. The sea churned. The water was filled with dead and drowning souls. They could see nothing of the vampire.

'It's over, Jack. Now let's see if we can get off this damned ship.'

Seward hooked one arm around the rail to steady himself and held out his other hand to Davis.

'You take care, Harry. God bless and keep you.'

Without thinking, Davis shook her friend's hand. Then he gave a puzzled smile.

'What are you saying, Jack?'

Seward nodded towards where Thomas Byles was leading prayers.

'This is where I'm needed now, Harry. You understand?'

Davis opened his mouth to protest, but instead he squeezed Seward's hand tightly.

'See you…eventually, Jack.'

'In a better place, Harry. In a better place.'

Davis began to make his way back down the incline, hand over hand as he clutched the rail. He knew jumping from the stern was certain death. Going as near water level as possible was the only way off.

The slope was now at an acute angle, and he felt as is he was sliding down a wall. The rising sea was now only twenty yards away. A deck-chair, which had been jammed under a stairway, broke loose. As it hurtled past him, he managed to reach out and grab it.

The white foaming water rose to meet him. Clutching the deck-chair tightly, he slid into the icy sea.

Chapter 65

The three gigantic propellers of the Titanic rose high in the air. Like windmills of the Gods, they had driven the great ship forward. Now they announced her death.

Mina Harker clung with one hand to the starboard propeller. Only the almost limitless strength of the *nosferatu* could have allowed her to reach out as she fell and grab that smooth metal.

There was not an indentation or a groove on the turned and finished piece of engineering, yet by sheer power, the vampire's elegant fingers clamped onto it in a vice-like grip which left her dangling a hundred feet above the ocean.

Her lovely skin was scarred and marked with the holy water, yet even as she fought for survival, her amazing metabolism was already repairing the damage.

In her hand she still kept a grip on the suitcase full of earth. Mina could see the water dotted with life-boats and debris. She took in the distance of the nearest and tried to gauge whether the leap was possible.

It was at this point the Titanic gave a great shudder and began a slow slide to the bottom of the sea.

Chapter 66

He felt the chill eat through to his very innards. The cold battered him like a physical blow. Davis clung to the deck chair and kicked as hard as he could away from the ship. Around him in the water, people floundered and struggled. A young woman, wearing a life-jacket, called feebly across to him for help. He could see her lips a deep blue colour from the sub-zero temperature. She had obviously been in the water longer than him, and her words were forced out in a strange vibrato voice as her facial muscles shook uncontrollably.

The detective could already feel his hands and arms go numb. He couldn't feel the grip he had on the frame of the chair.

He began to kick again in the direction of the woman, but it felt as if he was in the type of dream where no matter how hard we run, we don't move.

He saw her buffeted by an eddy of waves and then she drifted away. He heard her cry out for her mother, and then she was lost in the welter of struggling bodies and floating debris.

Thrashing his legs as hard as he could, he slowly put distance between himself and the dying ship. He glanced backwards briefly. The sight was truly terrible. The Titanic was now almost vertical. Less than half her length rose out of the water. Even now, he could see poor souls stranded at the top of the stern.

He turned away and kicked frantically, trying to get away before she finally went under. Harry knew that the undertow would create a whirlpool which would drag to the bottom anything within its pull.

It seemed like hours had passed. His body was slowing down. Hyperthermia closed in, and he felt numb. His teeth chattered. He was aware that his legs were still moving, but they no longer felt like a part of him.

Several hundred yards away in open sea, he could make out some lifeboats. He knew that to have any chance of surviving, he would have to reach them, but he no longer had the strength to struggle.

A feeling of lassitude began to steal over him. He didn't want to fight anymore. He stopped kicking. Sleepy, so sleepy. The strange thing was he wasn't cold anymore. A deep warmth flooded his being, and he felt calm.

Through half closed eyes, he saw those on the lifeboats looking towards the ship. Some women screamed, others stood still, their faces registering stunned disbelief at what they were watching.

Almost lazily, Davis half turned. The mighty liner, high out of the water, seemed to shudder for a moment and then slid under the waves. This brought fresh cries of horror from the watchers.

Water seethed and bubbled and writhed around the spot where she had gone down. There was an eerie stillness. The ocean had swallowed her up as if she had never existed.

Those left alive stared now in silent horror, unable even now to take in the scale of what had just happened.

Davis saw, rather than felt, his fingers slipping off the deck-chair. His limbs were too numbed for the nerve endings to register anything.

He was drowning. He felt his mouth begin to fill with salt water. A reflex action kicked in, and he tried to cough. He was now partly submerged, and his ability to react was almost gone. More and more water poured into his mouth and began to fill his lungs. He spluttered and fought fitfully, but he was now under the surface and felt himself sink down, down, down. It felt placid. He gave himself up to a feeling of calm well-being. Down, down, down.

Then, something disturbed his serenity. He was dimly aware his hair was being pulled and felt himself being drawn upwards.

Suddenly he broke the surface. He coughed out sea-water. His eyes flickered open. He could see the side of a lifeboat. Raising his eyes, he saw a sailor, a man with brown beard, who held him by the hair. Anxious faces peered over the edge of the boat.

He felt hands around his shoulders lifting him. He sank into unconsciousness.

Chapter 67

Captain Rostron gazed in disbelief at the tide of misery which came aboard his ship, the *Carpathia*, in the growing soupy light of dawn. He had been at full steam ahead for several hours after receiving the Titanic's distress signal.

Rostron had coaxed every ounce of speed from his aging ship, even to the point of turning off his passengers heating so that all steam was diverted to the engines.

He and his officers were unable to comprehend the scale of the disaster. The *Titanic? Down?* From what they could see of the number of survivors, Arthur Rostron dared not conceive the total number of dead. It had to be fifteen hundred, at least.

He walked among the stunned people who lined the main saloon. Blankets, dry clothes and hot drinks had been provided. What was noticeable was the silence.

In a corner, Harry Davis pulled the heavy woolen jumper over his head and then took another deep gulp of scalding hot coffee. Davis felt chilled to the bone but alive. Alive! He thought of Jonathan and Jack and sent God a little request. Take care of them, Lord, for they did your work.

Molly Brown was exhausted. She had worked tirelessly in the lifeboat organizing the rowing, encouraging, and cajoling. It had worked. She had helped bring them to safety. She looked around and couldn't see the 'dark lady,' as she called the strange, beautiful woman they had taken from the top of an upturned lifeboat.

She had said little and had refused to part with the small suitcase she clutched closely. Molly assumed it contained valuables. As the night slipped away, the woman seemed to become restive and shivery. She even hid herself in the bottom of the boat. Molly had tried to help her, but she remained impervious to all attempts at communication. It was only when the rescue ship appeared with the dawn that she reacted, gazing intently as the *Carpathia* drew nearer, all the while looking anxiously to the skies.

In the engine room, the pistons rose and sank and drove the liner forward. Men shouted at each other to try and make their voices heard above the thud and roar.

The hatch was hidden behind a mass of ropes, flanges, pipes and other detritus gathered on the ship. The rusted cover led to the scuppers. It had not been opened for many years. The wing nuts, locked with paint, corrosion and age, seemed unmovable.

Behind the door, lying on a thin bed of earth, lay Mina Harker. The place she slept was dank and malodorous. Rivulets of condensation trickled down the steel bulkheads. The beautiful vampire slept, her crimson lips parted in the faintest of smiles.

Thirty feet above her head in the saloon, Harry Davis also slept soundly. For the first time in weeks, he was free of fear.

Chapter 68

EXTRACT FROM THE 'NEW YORK TIMES'
MAN FOUND DEAD IN PARK

The body of a man, with savage injuries to his neck, was found in Central Park in the early hours of Friday morning. Police at this stage believe it may be the work of a rabid dog, but investigations will…

The End

Printed in Poland
by Amazon Fulfillment
Poland Sp. z o.o., Wrocław